THE RHEA JENSEN SERIES

BOOK 5

THE RHEA JENSEN SERIES

BOOK 5

SHERALYN PRATT

WICKED SASSY
SALT LAKE CITY, UTAH

© 2013 Sheralyn Pratt

All rights reserved.

This is a work of fiction. The characters, names, incidents, places, and dialogue are products of the author's imagination, and are not to be construed as real.

No part of this book may be reproduced in any form whatsoever, whether by graphic, visual, electronic, film, microfilm, tape recording, or any other means, without prior written permission from the publisher, except in the case of brief passages embodied in reviews and articles.

ISBN: 978-0-9743331-5-1

Cover Art: Angela Olsen
Cover design © 2013 Sheralyn Pratt
Published by Wicked Sassy
Salt Lake City, Utah

Printed in the United States of America

10 9 8 7 6 5 4 3 2 1

It's no secret that I love my male fans, and it just so happens that one of them gave me the name for this book. So Tony, this one's for you. Thanks for reading, you sexy beast.

CHAPTER 1

As long as my body was engaging in some level of self preservation, I was fine. I had to keep telling myself that. Panic and survival responses are normal when a person is involved in the various stages of drowning. Succumbing to the body's response to oxygen deprivation is primal reaction in all species. We all fight for life. Ignoring these same drowning responses while remaining calm, alert, and alive is called static apnea.

The trick of it is calmly convincing your body that the status quo of breathing is no longer an option. If you succeed in doing that, the body adjusts in miraculous ways. The main thing you need to watch out for is the moment the body stops fighting to survive. When courting death, peace and serenity are the danger spots that serve as cues to turn your instincts back on full alert.

I certainly wouldn't have described my state of mind as anything close to serene, even though the need to flail my way to safety had passed a few minutes back. The diaphramic spasms to force my lungs to breathe were behind me. I'd graduated to the part where my arms and legs were starting to numb and cramp as my body reserved oxygen for essential functions only. I told myself the cramping was okay. As long as my body was sending warning signals, I was still safe.

And the fact that the cramps were moving to my chest? Well, it was hard not to take those cramps a little more seriously, but I stuck to my original premise. My body still wanted to live. I wasn't drowning.

As I was repeating this reassurance in my mind, three quick taps came on my shoulder indicating my time was up. Knowing Dahl would pull me up if I didn't immediately stand, I raised my head out of the water.

"Breathe. Deep breaths," Dahl said, his baritone voice both soothing and insistent. "Carbon out, oxygen in."

He didn't have to ask twice. Inhaling was reflex, resulting in a mega head rush.

"Good," he coached. "Just like that."

"I could have gone longer," I said on an exhale.

He nodded as if he agreed with the assessment. "That's good. But four minutes was today's goal. Goal achieved."

His militant manner was calming for some reason, and it surprised me that it had taken this long for me to see this side of him. Yes, I'd always known that he was former military, but the few times he'd had a chance to show off his skills in my presence, he hadn't exactly shined. Probably because they'd all involved instances with guns, and Dahl was like me in that regard: not trigger happy.

After a month of working with him on skills like static apnea and other water survival tactics, I was learning that Dahl was more spy than soldier. Drop him into the heart of enemy territory and tell him to get out unnoticed, and he was your guy. Drop him in the same place and tell him to shoot his way out? You may not ever see him again.

"Your heart rate got down to thirty-two," he said.

That was low—way low for most people—but since my resting heart rate was forty-six beats per minute, Dahl had chosen to live with numbers like that during our sessions.

"That time I actually felt things shutting down," I said. "Just like you said they would. It's like the body knows what order to power down in order to stay alive for the longest period of time."

"It does," he said simply. "Two more minutes of break, then we're doing our laps."

I nodded. The man was an unforgiving machine when it came to training, which of course I loved. Bringing my breath back to a normal state, I watched as Dahl pulled himself out of the water and moved in front of a swim lane.

The man was massive. Nearly a full foot taller than me and with a hundred more pounds of muscle. He looked bigger than I imagined most soldiers to be, but despite his size Dahl wasn't bulky or awkward. His large hands were quick, his feet were light, and his body as mobile as a snake's when he was in the zone. It was an aspect of him I'd only seen while training privately, and it was a skill I definitely wanted to learn.

After a minute of rest, I joined Dahl on the side of the pool, choosing the platform next to his. He didn't speak—a fact I should have liked, but the silence only drew attention to the fact that Ty, my usual chatty training partner, wasn't present. And he wasn't present because he wasn't invited. And he wasn't invited because our personal relationship was on a break.

That's what I'd called it.

Not a "break up." That sounded permanent, and I hadn't been able to take it that far—not when Ty was still fighting for our relationship. I just wanted us to take a break… a vacation of sorts to reassess things. Sometimes a person got so invested in the drama of one relationship that they forgot that dealing with that drama was a choice that they can unmake—that they could live a completely different life without all the stress they've become accustomed to.

Ty deserved the right to a little perspective to see if he wanted to unmake his relationship with me.

My life was a mess. *I* was a mess. And over the past several months I had somehow allowed my personal feelings to rope in one of the best guys I'd ever met into thinking he was obligated to help me fix it. And the worst part of it all? Some part of me, deep down, wanted him to fix it.

But my life was not Ty's fight. Asking him to help me fight my way out of the hole I'd dug for myself was beyond unfair, especially considering who I was faced off against: people who, unlike Dahl and me, had no problem pulling a trigger.

Put it this way, I don't practice drowning because I think it's fun. I practice because I think it's very plausible that someday soon someone might try to drown me.

And, really, who wants to date that girl?

"Pull your head out of la-la land," Dahl said from my right. "Head in the game, Rhea. In life, breaks don't exist."

He was right. Of course he was. And pushing my head back into training mode, I waited for Dahl's mark before launching back into the water for a mile swim.

The laps were great for decompressing. The rhythm and repetition eased my mind, and the exertion got blood back into my extremities. In truth, I wanted to move the finish line up to a quarter of a mile, but this was Dahl's regimen. I'd asked him for it, so I wasn't going to argue. If I passed out, he would pull me out of the water and we could stop. That was our deal.

By the halfway mark, my strokes slowed even as Dahl pushed on like a machine. I needed to be that machine. I needed to find a way to move my arms, keep my core tight, and kick my legs even though my muscles felt like burning rubber.

I floundered for about another quarter-mile before suddenly hitting my stride. It was similar with swimming as it was with running. One moment everything hurt, you couldn't breathe, and every instinct was telling you to stop, and the next you were in a new gear where everything was easy and you had unlimited fuel. I was still riding the high when I finished.

One mile, I thought, coming up with a smile. I'd done it and I felt like I could still keep going. I was about to say as much as I moved to get out of the pool, only to find my arms didn't quite have the oomph to push me up. Instead they turned to rubber beneath my weight and I barely missed clacking my jaw on the edge of the pool on my way down.

Hats off to Dahl, he had completely tapped me out.

"That's it," he said, already dried off and ready to hit the locker room. "You made it. Congrats. If Uncle Sam got a peek at your PFTs, he'd want you." He pointed his finger at me, reminiscent of the iconic war-time recruiting poster.

"Good to know," I said on an exhale.

"I need to get moving," he said. "But I'll wait until your spaghetti arms pull you out of there. Wouldn't want you to drown."

"Indeed," I said, swimming to the ladder on the side of the pool. Barely. All of a sudden it was like swimming in sand and when I got there, Dahl was standing above me, extending his hand. I took it, and he lifted me out like a rag doll.

"You could have pushed harder," he said when my feet were on the ground. "You didn't even try to beat me."

"Because at this point you're able to lap me six times."

"But you could still try."

Saying *I am* sounded petty and immature, so I kept my mouth shut.

"Because we both know that there's one person you could be training with right now who you always feel compelled to beat."

Ah, a Ty reference. We'd almost made it an entire morning without one. Silence was my reply again as I reached for my towel.

"Don't think you're being original here, Rhea. Soldiers do what you're doing here all the time. They shut down, push everyone close to their heart way, and pretend the best way to love those closest to them is to spare them pain." He looked past me, eyes dark, clearly thinking of another time. Another place. Another person. "Trust me, it doesn't work. Thinking about the enemy and letting their threats dictate your life is a downward spiral. Think about something else, Rhea. Think about *someone* else—anyone else. Love. Next time someone asks you for a favor, say yes and get out of your own head for a while. Learning to do that may just save your life in the long run."

He walked away. No brotherly side hug, no chucking of my chin. Not even a *go, team, go* slap to my backside. He just walked off, which was how Dahl rolled. No muss. No fuss. Just taking care of business and moving on.

My kind of guy—even if sometimes I didn't want to hear what he had to say.

Reaching into my bag I grabbed a protein bar and ate it in a few short bites. My diet was different these days. A lot more calories and a lot more fat to compensate for the increase in activity and the cold weather. The protein bar would get me through the showers, but then I would load up my stomach and move on to phase two.

Because like Dahl said, in real life you didn't get breaks.

CHAPTER 2

Three hours later I stood on the saddle of Mount Olympus above the Salt Lake Valley. The hike was great in the summer time, but a completely new experience in the winter. The lower portions of the trail were so well traveled that a person didn't usually need snow shoes, which meant I could essentially run the first half on the trail. The gain in altitude was great for both my lungs and my muscles. Strenuous, but not so strenuous that I needed to bring a partner or tell anyone where I was.

I didn't bother checking in with many people these days. The more I could separate myself from them, the less likely they were to feature in what I faced next month. Besides, they all had lives, jobs, and day-to-day things that grabbed their attention. I didn't have any of that anymore. Just a future date with an ex-boss that may or may not change my life forever. March seventeenth, St. Patrick's Day. I wasn't Irish, but it made sense that the guy who had picked the date was. He was probably just superstitious enough to believe the fates would smile on him on a day like that.

Time would only tell if it would, but in the meantime I was doing my best to make sure Irish luck held as little sway as possible. It was why I trained all day, every day at anything that caught my eye. True, I had no idea what might be asked of me, but it was best to be prepared. And when it came to training physically, there really wasn't a better place than Utah.

Falling back into deep powder at the base of the jagged peak, I hit the snow in a snow angel position and stared up into the sky. There wasn't even an inch of blue sky, just a wall of ominous clouds edged in a grey that promised snow. I watched them, feeling smaller and smaller as I felt the power of the wind gusts pushing the clouds into the mountain combined with the complete magnitude of what hovered above me in the air. At times like this it was hard to believe that the world just a mile below me was even real.

"Things make sense up here," I said to the clouds, but really to God. Praying was new to me, and I'd never really gotten into the formality of it. I talked to God the same way I spoke to my own father. "There are laws, and if you work within them you are safe. If you defy them, you're in danger. It's not like when it comes to people, and I don't know what to do."

Silence answered me. Even the wind stayed silent, which was fine. I didn't need an answer since I hadn't really asked a question. And with God, you had to ask to receive. It was the law of heaven. My issue was that I didn't know what to ask for besides a miracle.

For the moment, I simply let myself be lost in the moment, in the perfect order of everything around me.

In nature every creature inherently knew where they stood in the order of things. Pure instinct told them what to fear and what to hunt. Just as surely as an animal knew to make its home where the all-powerful sky couldn't flood it or the wind claim it, it knew the rules of finding prey without becoming prey. Breaking the rules meant being removed from the world of the living.

Such was nature.

Human nature was an entirely different beast. Or at least relationships were.

There were no safe places—not when it came to the human heart. I'd thought I'd known that. I thought that Ben had taught me the pitfalls of the gauntlet called love over the years. I'd loved that guy since I was a kid—or I'd thought I had. But loving one person did not prepare you for the next time your heart would fall.

Ty had taught me that.

Man, I missed Ty. Being without him was like walking around with a cold rock in my chest that I just couldn't warm up, no matter what I did. With Ben, there had been no cold rock when we broke up, but a whole lot of anger and pain. Losing Ben had made me angry, while breaking things off with Ty made everything seem pointless and lonely.

It was a different beast to fight entirely.

"He's perfect," I whispered to the sky. Because I could. Because no one could hear me. And because saying the words the world felt right again for a brief moment.

I'd done the right thing breaking up with Ty, though. I couldn't confuse how perfect he was for me for me being perfect for him. Maybe if I hadn't accidentally sold my soul to a secret organization a few years back it might be a different story, but the truth was I could get Ty killed if I stuck around him.

And I did not want to get Ty killed.

Breaking up with him would have been a whole lot easier if our relationship were more like Kay and Dahl's—hot and cold, on again and then off again. Friends, then friends with Mormon-sized benefits, then off again—then on again, and back to being just friends before graduating back to the benefits before everything hit the fan again.

It was enough to make a spectator dizzy.

By my count Kay and Dahl changed their relationship status approximately every four hours of time they spent together, which meant it was never safe to assume that Kay had not recently pushed Dahl one step too far, or that Dahl had not just asked Kay to take ten steps back. They were always in flux.

Not so with Ty and me. We were more like two synced computers working on the same version of the same operating system. I knew how he worked, he knew how I worked, and we both worked together. Arguments were nearly always tactical, and had nothing to do with core differences in values.

We were a unit.

How do you look at someone like that a month before you're supposed to get married and say, "It's off"? No fights to blame, no negative qualities to site. Just the fact that you know people who might shoot him if it helps their end game. It's what I'd done two weeks ago, though. And it sucked.

But on the solitude of the mountain top, I doubted my decision. It was now less than two weeks away from the day that would have been my wedding day, and the closer the day got, the more I questioned whether I had done the right thing. The whole world was a dangerous place, after all, but deer didn't avoid having young because there were predators around. Fish still swam and birds still flew, despite what might happen around the next corner.

Nature didn't wait for life to begin. It just lived in the moment—*for* the moment. Humans weren't so good at that. *I* wasn't so good at that. Not anymore. It was one of the many reasons I'd come to rely on God for a little extra help.

"I would pray if I knew what to say, or even what question to ask," I said to the sky as the cold from the snow slowly crept through my layers of clothing. "But I guess in order to know what question to ask, I need to make a choice of wanting something. And right now I'm too afraid to want anything at all since it feels like I'm putting anything I touch in danger."

This time the wind answered me in a haunting howl.

"Live in the moment, or plan for the future?" I asked. "Do animals have it right? Is Ty right? That if we just stick together we'll figure things out together? That everything will be fine in the end?"

A gust of wind blew snow crystals across my face. If that was my answer, I wasn't quite sure what it meant.

"Or am I right? That if things are going to work with us, I need to get my affairs in order first and come back to the relationship when I'm a free agent?"

The wind screamed a little louder and this time I heard its primal message loud and clear in answer to a question I hadn't asked, but probably should have.

You should get off this mountain. Now.

I sat up, looking to the horizon below. I don't know how long I had been laying there in the snow, but it had been long enough for clouds to envelope the area around me. Storms moved quickly in the mountains. Luckily, these days, so did I.

"Got it," I said, and immediately started down.

CHAPTER 3

Silver 2004 Subaru Impreza sedan. I didn't need to look at the plate. I knew the car, although I couldn't really say the same about the owner. Her name. That's about all I knew. Her job. Oh, and she'd also known Ty for over a decade. Since high school, but they'd never dated. Just been close. Friends.

Uh-huh. I knew that little dance better than most.

Add that to the fact that Mindy had been a rather ongoing presence at Ty's place for the few weeks since we'd been on our break, and either Kay was coaching Ty on how to drive me insane or the two of them were…

I scowled, singling out my house key as I walked from my car to my front door, purposefully not looking at the Subaru.

It wasn't my business. It wasn't. Sure, I could spy. I could do a background check on Mindy to satisfy myself that she wasn't worthy, but I'd promised myself I wouldn't. I couldn't. All was *not* fair in love and war. Not when the other party was playing 100% by your rules.

I'd told Ty not to call. He wasn't calling. I'd told him not to text. My inbox was empty. I'd told him not to come over, and you could hear the freaking crickets in China over the silence at my front door.

Ty was doing every stupid thing I'd asked of him. The least I could do was not spy on him in his own house or dig up a rap sheet on one of his oldest friends.

Stabbing my key into the deadbolt, I unlocked my front door. It was dinner time and I was cranky. After leaving the mountain I went to my personal gym and then finished the day at the library. Reading. Learning. Researching. What exactly I needed to learn I didn't know. Counting down to my fateful day with The Fours was like studying for a final when you didn't know what the subject was.

In the end it was all a crap shoot anyway, so what was the point in studying? Especially when the enemy was watching you study and had already spent eight years cataloging your strengths and weaknesses based on extensive field testing. There was no skill I was going to develop in the next four weeks that was going give me the upper hand. Whatever was going to happen was going to happen. I knew that.

I just didn't know how to wait for it. And the wait was absolutely killing me.

On top of it all, I was in the middle of my first Utah winter. No beach, and definitely no sun. I thought I'd gotten used to the complete absence of water and the pound of the surf during the summer and fall. I thought I had Utah dialed in. But then the sun disappeared and the Salt Lake valley filled with smog that cleared every time there was snow fall, only to build up again. It was like living in a bowl of cheerless exhaust on a cloudy day, and a too-bright world of shining snow on the sunny days.

Some thought it was pretty. Maybe it was. I just still wasn't over how eerily quiet things got when snow insulated the world—especially when it snowed at night. A world covered in snow absorbed sound in a unique way that soothed me in nature but left me a little bit jumpy when I was surrounded by people. I knew why animals were silent, but people? Who knew what was going on there? And since the absence of any ambient sound left me restless, I'd started the habit of keeping a TV or radio on at all times at home.

But even with the TV on, I still heard the slush of Kay's tires as she parked in front of my house. Several seconds later I heard her move up my front steps and through the front door. Other than the TV and the sounds in my kitchen, she was the only other sound around.

"So cold!" she said, shutting the door behind her and hanging up her purse before removing her boots.

"Tell me about it," I said, turning the stir fry on the stove down to low and turning to face her.

"You know what I'd rather tell you about?" she said, slipping into some house shoes. "How absolutely crazy this state is that you dragged me to. This place is fully tweaked."

Based on Kay's glow, it had been a good news day. Unfortunately I'd had CSPAN on, not the local news, so I didn't have a head start on what she was talking about. "What happened this time?"

"A murder," she said, joining me in the kitchen. She'd gone home to change before heading over and wore jeans and a Lululemon jacket over a white top. As usual, she looked like a magazine ad. "It's not official yet, but I think Salt Lake has itself a vigilante. At least that's what I'm pitching it as." She gestured to the pan. "Smells great."

"Should be ready in five. What's your log line?"

Without hesitation, Kay went to the cupboard and started setting the table. "Suspected killer shot in his own home after legal system fails to prosecute."

It needed some fleshing out, but it was enough to get a raised eyebrow out of me.

Kay grinned. "I know, right? This state is a big story freak farm, and this story plays so well into other national stories. I hope police don't catch the guy too soon. They tend to perk up and get on the ball when vigilantes hit the scene."

Neither of us commented on the fact that she knew that out of personal experience. The police could get a little, well, touchy when you did their job for them. It was best just to lead them to the right place at the right time and give the appearance you were nothing more than a spectator.

"Have I heard of this case?"

"Probably not," she said, laying out napkins. "The housewife murder and the trial went down in Pleasant Grove before you got here. Last December Amanda Carson's teenage son comes home from basketball practice and finds her shot in the kitchen. He calls 9-1-1 and there's a full investigation. First thoughts of who did it go to the husband, of course, but turns out his alibi is air tight and there's not a stitch of evidence that he hired anyone to do the dirty work for him. There is, however, a former coworker of Amanda's who had a history of being very obsessed with her. He doesn't have an alibi for the time of death, but there also isn't any evidence tying him to the crime. So the police slap that ambiguous label of 'person of interest' on him and the investigation seemingly stalls."

"But they think he's their guy?"

She gave a quick nod, moving on to the forks. "If you trust the chatter of the officers on the scene today. They totally thought this guy got his due."

"And why do they think a vigilante did it?" I asked, checking the vegetables and then moving them off the heat.

She picked up the plates and brought them over to the stove. "I haven't seen the crime scene, but apparently there are some links between it and the one from a year ago."

"Like what?"

She shrugged, handing me a plate. "Don't know yet, but I can read a cop's body language. They were quick-footed, tense, and tight lipped at the scene. They think it's tied to the other murder, for sure. Either the same killer, or a vigilante enacting some kind of homegrown justice. Option two is obviously the stronger angle, because why would it be the same killer?"

"Wouldn't make sense," I agreed. "You don't kill your scapegoat in a way that points a finger straight back at yourself for two murders."

"Exactly!" she said, adding a small amount of rice before moving to the vegetables. "So I'm thinking that they're looking pretty closely at door number two—a vigilante. Which is bittersweet in a case like this—where police know a killer was taken off the streets, but also know that someone did their job for them. They totally hate that."

"Plus the fact that murder is murder," I added. "Even if the guy killed was guilty, that's not how our justice system is supposed to work. People deserve their day in court."

"Which this guy is never going to get now. Our dear, Mister Alleged-Stalker took a bullet to the chest sometime last night and was discovered about seven o'clock this morning by a dog."

"And all this takes place in Pleasant Grove?"

She shook her head, sitting across from me. "The two murders are in two separate cities. After Amanda Carson's murder, Blaine Adkins—the guy who was killed last night—moved to Salt Lake to get what he considered a fresh start. I don't know how that's possible when you're thirty minutes away from a town that considers you a killer, but it's what he did and I'm guessing that's why he's dead today. He didn't move far enough, and someone took it upon themselves to make sure he paid for the life he took."

Sounded like she had her narrative set. Whether there was an ounce of truth in it remained to be seen. "It sounds like if you find the connection you solve both murders by default."

She nodded. "A total two-for-one just begging to spill its secrets. I swear the ghost of Amanda Carson was at the crime scene today. There was just this crazy vibe, you know? Like the crime scene was a jack-in-the box that just needed someone to spin its handle for something explosive to come out."

I didn't doubt her impression, but it did raise an obvious question. "Well, if her ghost was there, wouldn't it imply that it still wasn't at rest? You'd think if Adkins was her killer she'd be at peace."

"Not if he's still presumed innocent. Or maybe he *is* innocent and a killer has struck twice. Point is, I have to know. I'm totally getting to the bottom of this." She took a bite. "Want to play, girl? This is going to be fun."

I hesitated.

"Straight fun, no work," she added. "I could use a lackey who can send out some tempting press releases for me. No investigation stuff. Just PR. Elliott can't take issue with that, right?"

Could he? She had a weird sort of logic going on there.

"Besides, it might be the last time we're able to play with each other on something like this before your big thing goes down. You need the distraction, Rhea. C'mon. It'll be fun."

Had she been talking to Dahl? That morning he told me to focus on anything but my problems and suddenly here Kay was with a bona fide distraction? Was that providence or conspiracy... and did it really even matter?

Next to me, Kay sighed at my obvious hesitation. "Do you want me to ask your ceiling for you?" Then, without waiting for an answer, she looked up at the ceiling and changed her voice to more of a chanting drone. "Dear-magical-ceiling-that-Rhea-thinks-is-bugged-with-very-high-tech-equipment-by-a-near-omniscient-ex-boss-who-apparently-has-nothing-better-to-do-than-watch-her-every-move. Can Rhea please come out and play with me on this very intriguing story? I promise I will make sure she doesn't get a dime for it, and I won't ask her to do anything I wouldn't ask a college intern to do. If your answer is no, almighty invisible microphone in the ceiling, please give us a sign right now. A bump. A knock. A phone ring. Or maybe get fancy and blink the lights or something. We both know she will heed your wishes like a trained puppy, so speak now, or forever hold your peace."

I froze, part offended, part terrified, and fully expecting to see the lights blink or to hear a phone ring.

"Nothing?" she said after a few beats, then sent me a beaming smile. "Then it's a yes."

"It's a maybe," I corrected, stabbing at my food while I considered playing intern to Kay.

She smirked at me. "When was the last time you wrote a press release?"

I had to laugh. "Junior year?"

"I'm pretty sure I remember that assignment." She took a bite, and sent me a smug look. "For once I could finally school you."

"I'll think about it," I said. But we both knew what that meant.

CHAPTER 4

Kay crashed in my guest room that night. We stayed up late inventing my new identity as her shady intern, Abby Straightway. An alias wasn't really necessary for the task at hand, it was more of a habit and a cue. Being called Abby on a track phone would help me remember who I was talking to and what my role was. Acting out of character was much easier when someone was calling you by a different name—a name like Abby. It was a peppy, enthusiastic name. Kind of blonde and optimistic. And Straightway... I wasn't really sure that was even a name, but somehow it had come up and stuck.

Abby, we'd decided, was in her senior year at the University of Utah, and had a little bit of a valley twang when she spoke. Her dream was to become the female Ryan Seacrest. And because her interest lay in entertainment media, she was never quite fully aware of the relevance of legitimate news. She was the type to thoughtlessly let explosive facts slip out while indulging in light gossip.

In short, Abby was the perfect person to leak key facts to national media that local media might be pressured into quashing. In Kay's mind, the only thing worse than getting scooped was letting people with special interests call the shots of what was allowed to be reported. Protecting the privacy of the innocent was something she understood, but everything else was free game in her book.

It was also free game for blabbermouth intern Abby Straightway— official pot stirrer and ambitious lackey of Kathryn McCoy—who just didn't quite comprehend that national news was not a gossip column.

In addition to writing press releases, Abby would field all incoming national calls and emails while Kay focused on the story.

It had been a long time since I had woken up excited for the day to come. Not even the biting cold of the dark morning could dampen my mood as I ran a quick five miles before logging in to see if Abby had any responses to the press releases she had sent out the night before. The east coast was two hours ahead, which meant news professionals were definitely checking their inboxes.

Two replies had come in while I was on my run, both of which Kay had already seen and responded to in Abby's name. Apparently she'd checked email before hopping in the shower. Of course she had.

I read through her responses, which promised an update after the press conference that would be held that day at 11:00 a.m. Mountain Time. I smiled, knowing that's where we would really hook interest, by dropping some details that wouldn't be broadcast anywhere else.

This was going to be fun. Way fun.

Stepping away from my computer, I went to the kitchen to make my morning shake before stealing Kay's phone and linking it to my own. I was just loading the dishwasher when Kay came in dressed for work in the spare suit she kept in her car.

"We're synced," I said, pointing to her phone on the table. "I can hear all your calls on that phone and get all the texts. Technically it's a mic full time, but if you want to make sure I'm listening in, hit the red button."

She left the phone where it was and headed to the cupboard. "Coffee," she muttered. "If I'm going to stay over here again, I need to stash coffee and a pot here. O.J. doesn't cut it."

Her southern drawl was much more pronounced in the morning, but I didn't mention it. Not when she was already visibly annoyed.

"Sorry," I muttered, sipping my shake. "You could try nutrients instead."

She sent me a death stare over her shoulder. "Yeah. Not the same." She moved her glare out the window. "If it weren't a hundred degrees below out there, I would have ventured out to the coffee shop down the street. But only an insane person would go out there if they didn't have to."

Yes, she was referring to me—the insane person who ran on icy sidewalks in freezing conditions. Next time I would have to remember to run by a coffee shop on my way back. It was the least

I could do to thank Kay for giving me something to do that day besides obsess over the unknown.

Today I was going to be a journalist. A seemingly inept one, perhaps, but a journalist nonetheless. It would be a thank you, if nothing else, to a friend who deserved more than this simple favor.

Kay took the orange juice out of the fridge, looked at it a moment, then put it back. "Too much sugar," she muttered, then faced me, frowning. "I give up. Give me some of your neurotic shake. Just don't tell me what's in it."

I pointed to the blender. "Made extra for you, just in case."

She muttered something like, "Of course you did," as she poured the remnants into her glass. Then she sat down across from me, eyeing me suspiciously. "You sure you're up for this? Being my intern? Doing this isn't going to push over some invisible mental ledge you're dancing on?"

"No ledge," I said easily, but I dropped eye contact and she noticed.

Kay hesitated then nodded, accepting me at my word before taking a swallow of my shake. She pulled a face and promptly dumped the rest of the contents of her glass back in the blender.

"It's good for you," I said.

"Yeah, well so is meditation, and I don't do that either."

It was hard not to smile.

"Oh, and in the interest of full disclosure, you won't be able to reach me between six and eight tonight," she added. "Ty and I are going shooting."

The disclaimer actually got a flinch out of me. Even worse, I avoided looking at Kay when I said, "Fine."

The fact that she and Ty were still besties and she split time between us was hardly "fine." It sucked—as did the fact that Kay was teaching Ty to shoot at my request. Ty had already fired a gun once on my behalf. True, it hadn't been a *real* gun, but the gun he'd been facing off against certainly had been real.

Fact: Because of me, Ty needed to know how to use a gun.

Another fact: There wasn't a better teacher in the state to show him the ropes than Kay.

I should have been grateful that she was taking time out of her busy schedule to give him lessons, but for some reason that gratitude was trying to manifest through me by throwing my glass at her and demanding she tell me what he was up to.

Which, of course, was not a nice way to say thank you.

Her eyes narrowed on me again. "Don't think I don't see you freaking out right now."

"I'm fine," I said, taking a swallow.

"Yeah. 'Fine' seems to be your word of the day." She put her glass in the dishwasher and grabbed the phone off the table. "Remember I need your game face on this. Last chance to back out. If you're not feeling up to it, I can whip out one of my other alter egos."

"I'm fine with it—*really!*"

She arched an eyebrow at me, and I realized I'd just said it again. *Fine.*

I could see why Kay was nervous.

"Game face on," I said. "Promise. In truth, it's nice to have something else to think about for a day. So I'm in, Kay. One-hundred percent. No hesitation, no balking, no break downs."

"Good," she said, standing. "Then I'm off. Keep your ears tuned, because things are going to move fast. Police like to hoard cases like this, and we're about to create a very hostile hoarding environment, my friend."

"Sounds good," I agreed. "Consider me your second set of ears. I'll be keeping pace and texting you updates."

"Counting on it," she said, shouldering her purse. Then she was out the door.

CHAPTER 5

That morning I did what any intern might do: I familiarized myself head-to-toe with the facts of the Amanda Carson murder.

As it turned out, the facts weren't overwhelming to remember. No physical evidence, no murder weapon, no motive, and no true suspects. Yes, Blaine Adkins was listed as a man who had expressed a little too much interest in an enhanced personal relationship with Amanda, but that was hardly reason to kill her. Plus his alibi overlapped the time of death.

Amanda's husband, Nathan, had about an airtight an alibi as a person could hope for: he was on an airplane that hadn't landed until two hours after the time of death. The son, Jeremy, hadn't killed her either. His entire basketball team could vouch that he'd been playing at the time of death, a fact that probably haunted Jeremy to this day.

Jeremy also had an alibi for Blaine Adkins murder, seeing as how he was currently attending UNLV.

If ever there was a cold case with no leads, it was Amanda Carson's case. Whoever had killed her had gotten off scot free. So why kill again? Or *had* he killed again? Did Nathan, Amanda's widower, have an alibi for Blaine's time of death? I texted Kay to check on that, to which she replied, *Duh.*

Yes, she was truly treating me like an intern. You could call Kay many things, but not someone who broke her word.

I kept my word, too, not using any of the connections I gained through Elliott to do background checks. That limited me largely to watching interviews of Amanda's friends trying to make sense of the tragedy in front of cameras and reading articles that dropped personal tidbits as a way to embellish the facts of the story. I read through them all, listing each quality in little thought bubbles around Amanda's name on a sheet of paper. The resulting picture was one of a flawless, selfless, much-loved and universally missed mother and friend. And while I was sure she was all those things, everyone had a skeleton in the closet. Everyone made mistakes.

Had Amanda Carson made a mistake that had cost her her life?

I picked up my phone and texted Kay again. *Can you request the case files for the Amanda Carson case from the Pleasant Grove police?*

Her response was almost immediate. *Negative. They consider it an open case.*

Of course they did. *Any information would be helpful.*

Copy that, she replied.

Also, is Nathan Carson on the menu today, or is he skipping interviews?

He's skipping. Aren't you eavesdropping on me through my phone? You'd know this and more if you did.

Okay, a not-so-subtle hint. *I listened for a while but then I remembered why I've never had an 8-5 job. I'll tune back in.*

And I did. It would save us time and update me real time. Meanwhile, I needed to figure out how in the world Kay was supposed to get a head start on this case with no leads, no witnesses, and no suspects.

I needed an inside scoop. I needed to talk to Amanda's son. He was only in Vegas—less than an hour's flight. I could pop out and back before the end of the day, except for the fact that plane tickets and day trips went way outside the scope of being an intern.

No, I needed to think closer to home. Amanda's friends. The neighbors. Her Relief Society president. And luckily enough, all of those were as close to me by car as Vegas was by plane—totally within the scope of being an intern.

On my way to Pleasant Grove, I texted Kay before grabbing my keys and a portable recorder, then heading out the door.

CHAPTER 6

Blaine Adkins had killed Amanda. That was the consensus.

Somehow everyone on my list had agreed to having an interview with me. It was quite unprecedented not to have anyone walk off in a huff. Everyone wanted to talk, as if doing so somehow atoned for everything else they couldn't do. And with everyone proving so helpful all day, I felt lucky enough to try the Pleasant Grove police department to see if they had anything to share.

They showed me the door moments after I walked in.

Still, I had a lot more to go on than I'd had that morning.

Amanda Carson had been a devoted mother and part-time wage earner. The latter had been her choice. Once her only child had started school, she'd wanted to be part of something that took her out of the house. That had led her through multiple retail jobs until she finally settled on her last job at a local health food store.

It was there she'd met Blaine Adkins. It was interesting to discover that Blaine was quite a bit younger than her. Amanda had been close to forty when she died and Blaine had only been twenty-four and a Master's degree student at BYU. They were both Mormon.

All of Amanda's friends were adamant that there had not been an affair or anything close to it between the two of them. They'd worked together, that was all. Amanda never saw Blaine outside of work—at least not that Amanda had told them.

But really, would Amanda have shared such a thing with her neighbors?

As for Amanda and Nathan's marriage, there had been no red flags—not even according to Amanda's most loyal friends. Perhaps routine had replaced passion but Amanda had been devoted to Nathan and Jeremy—who, as it turned out, had been something of a miracle baby.

According to her friends, Amanda had conceived Jeremy on their honeymoon and carried him full term with no incident. Once Jeremy was two, they had tried for another child, and after a year of trying they went to a specialist and learned something Nathan Carson should have known all his life: he had Klinefelter syndrome. It was a condition where males inherit an extra X chromosome from one of their parents, resulting in lower testosterone and less masculine physical development during puberty and beyond. By everything Nathan's doctor could see, he was infertile, and had been his whole life.

So rather than giving Jeremy a younger brother or sister, they got him a dog and counted their blessings.

Despite—or maybe because of the Klinefelter syndrome—Nathan was very active and enjoyed hobbies like tennis, running, and martial arts. I could understand that. Having low testosterone levels didn't mean you had to be a wimp if you didn't want to be. There were millions of women who could vouch for that.

When I asked if Nathan had returned to the dating scene since the passing of his wife, the answer was a universal no. Nathan Carson hadn't sought out women, and he hadn't accepted attempts at blind dates. He wasn't ready, he said. Maybe in another year or so.

Based on what I'd heard that day, there had been no insurance policy, no dispute, no affair, and no skeleton in the closet that would have given Nathan Carson a reason to murder his wife, even if he hadn't been on a plane at the time. They'd been friends and devoted mates. Nothing Amanda's friends had said spoke to any kind of heat or passion in the marriage, but they'd definitely been faithful partners.

Which brought the focus back to Blaine—a college student just seven years older than Amanda's son, Jeremy.

Had there been heat there? Passion? A thirteen-year gap in age wasn't unheard of between two people. Had they fallen in love? Even if they hadn't acted on it, had feelings been there and strong enough to lead to a crime of passion?

Amanda's neighbor, Mary, had been the only one with remote insight there. She'd mentioned that Blaine had shown up at one of Jeremy's basketball games a few weeks before she'd died. Nothing had happened, she said. The two of them hadn't even sat by each other or even said hi, but Mary knew she'd seen him and had all sorts of theories as to why he was there. In her mind Blaine had been an obsessed stalker with a pot farm in his garage. Never mind that a little digging showed that a year ago Blaine had been living with five other guys in an apartment with no access to a garage.

Outlandish suspicions aside, I did believe her claim that Blaine had shown up at one of Jeremy's basketball games before Amanda died. And if he'd been spotted there once, it was likely he'd been there other times as well.

Why attend a high school basketball game in another city if not for Amanda? Had Blaine known Jeremy? Had Jeremy invited Blaine to a game after dropping in on his mom at the store one day?

That was the problem with gathering information a year after the fact. It frequently led to more questions than answers. If only I could talk to Jeremy Carson, even on the phone. But no. I couldn't do that unless Kay came up with the number. I was an intern, not an investigator—even when it came to the stupid, little things.

We need to interview Jeremy, I texted to Kay, then picked up a racquetball to throw at my wall while I filtered through all I'd heard that day. When I didn't get a snarky text back within a few minutes, I took at look at the time.

6:15 pm. Kay was at the shooting range with Ty. My boyfriend.

My *ex*-boyfriend... or ex-fiancé, if you wanted to get technical about it.

They were talking now—likely taking little snipes at each other like siblings separated at birth. Sharing stories. Talking about their days. Maybe about Mindy.

My next toss against the wall was a bit harder than it needed to be, and sent the ball flying across the room. I was done thinking, and I didn't care if it was freezing. I needed to go for a run.

I started toward my room before catching a glimpse out the window and seeing that snow was silently spilling from the sky. I still needed to adjust to the fact that you knew it was snowing based on the vacuum of silence it created, not from the percussion the flakes made. It was unnatural. I hated it.

Then again, at that moment there were a number of things I hated.

Might as well take it out on a punching bag.

CHAPTER 7

After a solid session of unleashing on my punching bag, I realized something. I hadn't heard anyone defend Blaine Adkins all day.

*Every*one thought he was guilty.

But surely that wasn't case. Someone had to believe in his innocence. Everyone had a devoted mother, a longtime friend, a naïve neighbor who went on the record saying that there was no way so-and-so could be guilty.

Skipping a shower, I threw on a sweatshirt and cued up my DVR. I'd recorded all the local news casts just to get a feel for how the story was developing and the level of interest each station had.

For now the interest was high. It was the leading story for each of the evening newscasts. The headline essentially, *Suspected Killer Found Shot in Home*. Every station mentioned the Amanda Carson tie-in, and every station mentioned that they had both been shot. No suspects.

I saved Kay's broadcast for the end, knowing her narrative would be a little bit different than all the others. Her sense of pride demanded it.

Her lead was the same. She painted the picture of an otherwise quiet apartment complex waking up to flashing lights and yellow police tape. There were the obligatory sound bytes of neighbors expressing their shock and fear that such a thing could happen in the very place they lived.

No one had heard any shots, according to her news report. The body had been found when a neighbor took her dog for a walk that morning. Cut to a twenty-something woman named Melanie Cunningham, sitting on a faux-suede couch with a Jack Russell terrier on her lap. The camera didn't miss a thing as Melanie described how the door to Blaine's apartment had been slightly ajar that morning, and how her dog had sprinted straight out her door and to Blaine's apartment before she could even put a leash on him.

Melanie recounted how she'd known Blaine, but not really been friends with him. She'd known about his past and the accusations against him. It had made them all nervous to have him living there, she said, but with no criminal record there weren't really grounds to force him out.

Still, watching her face, I could see that she was sad. She was traumatized, too, but the way her eyes dropped when she said Blaine's name, the way the corners of her mouth pulled down when she stated that she'd never really reached out to him in a neighborly way, bespoke a sense of guilt.

Up until that very day the accusations against Blaine Adkins may have made her nervous around him, but as of the moment of taping her interview with Kay, I was certain that I was looking at a woman with a few regrets.

About what?

It might be a good thing to follow up on.

After that interview, the story cut back to Kay standing in front of the taped-off complex and doing a short Q&A with the news anchors back at the station.

"Well, this is certainly not an ending any of us saw coming," Veronica, the female news anchor, said. "Have the Pleasant Grove police made any statements on whether or not they consider the Amanda Carson case closed at this point?"

"I asked them that very question earlier," Kay replied. "And for now, the case is still open even though Blaine Adkins was, and always has been, their only person of interest in the case."

"Well, we certainly will be looking to you for updates on this tragic story," Veronica said sadly.

The male news anchor came on screen then to give the details on a fatal car accident. I pressed pause and picked up my phone.

Did you tape the interview with Blaine's mom? I typed, knowing that she was still with Ty, and would be for another hour. By the time she got back to me it would probably be too late to drop by the mother's place, but I knew exactly where Melanie Cunningham lived. There was a chance that she wouldn't be there that night. The instinct of most single woman would be to stay away from a murder scene the night after it happened.

But it was worth a try.

CHAPTER 8

Thirty minutes later I was in front of the apartment complex where Blaine Adkins had lived for the past eleven months. The place where he had been killed. Quietly, with a gun.

Quietly and *gun* didn't usually go together. Despite what Hollywood showed in the movies, gun silencers weren't so silent. Someone in the compact apartment complex should have heard.

I wasn't sure which apartment Melanie lived in, so I just walked up to the first available door and knocked. A few moments later a college-aged guy answered the door. I gave him a blank look, then glanced to the number on his door.

"I'm sorry," I said. "I think I have the wrong door. I'm looking for Melanie." I was female and Melanie's age. There was every reason for this guy to believe I was just a friend looking for a friend.

"2D," he said, pointing to the floor above us. "But I don't know if she's back yet."

I shook my head. "I know. This is all crazy, isn't it?"

He nodded slowly, and I could see his guard go up a little bit. That was my cue to either get gone or to do some talking of my own. I chose the latter.

"It's just freaky that no one heard anything, you know? I mean, you can hear a person sneeze here from one apartment to the next. How could a gun go off without anyone waking up?"

The question was rhetorical, but the guy nodded his head. "We're all asking ourselves the same thing. I think that's as freaky as knowing someone was murdered just a few feet away."

His face definitely looked haunted. This guy wasn't running away to sleep somewhere else for the night, but he was definitely shaken.

"I'm Rhea, by the way," I said, holding out my hand.

"Chris," the guy said, gripping it in his.

"Chris," I repeated, sending him a slight smile. "You comfortable staying here tonight?"

"Yeah," he said, releasing my hand. "I mean, it sucks, but what do you do, right? I treated that guy like crap the entire time he lived here. I can't even count how many times I said that he needed to go down for killing that woman in Pleasant Grove, but now that he has, it feels weird, you know? Wrong. Can't explain it, but for the first time I'm thinking he might have been innocent, and I owe the dude a huge apology. Weird, right?"

I shook my head. "Not at all. In fact, I think that feeling's going around."

His eyebrows shot up. "Did Melanie say the same thing?"

"Not in so many words," I hedged, but it was enough to get Chris to keep talking.

"She knew him the best, I think. Not because she wanted to, but because Prince liked Blaine so much. It drove her crazy that of all the people who lived here, her dumb dog liked Blaine the best."

"Because dogs are supposed to have instincts about people," I added.

"Exactly, right?" he said, slightly exasperated. "Here she has this dog for an added sense of protection, and the dog's favorite person besides her is a suspected killer. It was so awkward every time Prince made their paths cross—but I don't need to tell you that."

I shook my head, even though I was technically lying. Melanie wasn't my friend. I didn't know a thing.

"This morning when Prince raced into his apartment she was totally freaked. I heard her call the dog for almost a minute before going into the apartment. She kept calling the dog, then saying Blaine's name and asking him to bring the dog to the front door. She told me after that her imagination had gone wild and she thought he was baiting her into his apartment so he could attack her."

"Yeah, this is all going to play with her head for a quite a while," I said, not because I knew Melanie, but because I knew people.

"For sure," he said, his expression showing that Melanie wasn't the only one who would be dealing with everything for a while.

"I should probably get going," I said, gesturing to the stairs.

"Yeah," Chris said, straightening. "Didn't mean to hold you up."

I smiled again. "Not at all. It was good to meet you."

"Same," he said, glancing at the yellow police tape near the entrance. "Be safe out there, okay?"

"You, too."

For some reason he was reluctant to shut the door, but I heard it slide closed after I reached the top of the stairs. I turned to the right and knocked on 2D. A yappy dog immediately charged the door in a barking frenzy. Prince. Melanie's guard dog. The dog that liked Blaine. I wasn't really a fan of dogs, but at that moment I would have loved to be familiar with the basics of dog psychology—if there was such a thing.

What made a dog like one person and not another? And maybe more to the point, why would a dog like a person its owner hated or feared? Wouldn't Prince pick up on Melanie's fear of Blaine and become aggressive toward him? That was my understanding of how dogs worked—that they were extensions and enforcers of the mentality of their owners.

So why did Prince like Blaine?

The door swung open as I pondered that, catching me off guard. I looked up, expecting Melanie and finding a blonde woman in her forties. Melanie's mom, maybe?

"Hi," I said, not flinching at the suspicion in her eyes and smiling at the spazzy Jack Russell bouncing up and down at my feet like a batch of popcorn. "Hey, Prince. Is Melanie here?"

The woman blinked, clearly not sure whether I needed a friendly or rude dismissal. Her hesitation was all I needed, as I gave Prince a quick pet and looked at her again.

"I know it's not a good time, but I promise I can help if you just give me a minute with her."

The woman's head started to shake just as a younger voice called out behind her.

"Who is it, Mom?"

"No idea," the mom called back, her expression still wary.

In her eyes was the unspoken request that I introduce myself, but I knew that would end in failure. "Two minutes?"

Just then Melanie's face appeared over her mom's shoulder.

She gave me a quick look over, her eyes lingering on my jacket for a moment.

"Can I help you?" she asked.

"Actually, I'm here to help you," I said.

"Not interested," he mom said, swinging the door shut.

I stopped it with my foot, earning a scowl from her.

"Whatever you're selling, we don't need it," her mom said. "What my daughter needs is some privacy."

"What your daughter needs is to know what happened last night, and who Blaine Adkins was," I replied, earning surprised looks from both women. "And what I can tell you is that if Melanie can give me a few minutes of her time, I'm the person who can give her those answers. If she wants them."

Melanie said nothing for a moment, then glanced at her mom. This was the moment they would both decide whether to trust me or not. It was also a time when a pint-sized girl worked in my favor. And maybe, just *maybe*, I tilted my hand to flash the CTR ring I'd taken to wearing since taking off my engagement ring to see if that would work in my favor as well. The move felt kind of jaded, but I wanted in more than I wanted a clear conscience, apparently.

After a moment of unspoken communication between the two of them, Melanie motioned into her apartment. "Two minutes."

"Thanks," I said, stepping in. Prince ran circles around me, yapping until Melanie picked him up and handed him to her mom. "Take him into the other room, will you?"

Her mom nodded and sent me a protective look before heading down the hall.

Melanie turned to face me, arms folded, face frowning. "So you have answers? Why aren't you talking to the police?"

"I will," I said. "But first, tell me what you liked about Blaine."

She blinked, clearly taken aback. "What do you mean? I barely knew him."

"But there were things you liked about him," I said, following my gut. "And deep down, you don't believe he killed Amanda Carson."

The way her breath caught before quick blinks pushed back tears let me know I was on to something, even as she evaded answering. "How… what makes you say that?"

"It doesn't matter what makes me say it, if it isn't true. So why don't you tell me? What made you doubt that Blaine Adkins was a killer?"

She couldn't blink fast enough to stop a tear from falling then. "I don't know. I mean, it was pretty obvious he was, but it was just so hard to see it, you know? You like to think that you'd feel it if another person was a killer, but he just had such nice eyes. Like, sweet eyes. And sad. He knew why we all avoided him—why *I* avoided him, but he never seemed mad about it. Just sad. He could tell I hated it when our paths crossed—that I didn't want to look him in the eye even when my dog was all but dragging me across the street to see him."

"Did you ever figure out why Prince liked him so much?"

She shrugged helplessly. "I don't know. I got to thinking it was because he cooked so much. Blaine was one of those all-organic guys who thought that microwaves were evil. He did everything in an oven or on the stove, so his apartment always smelled really good."

It was a logical explanation. "Did Blaine ever feed Prince?"

Melanie hesitated, then shook her head. "No, but let's back up. Who are you? Why are you here? I thought you said you had answers, not questions."

"I *will* have answers," I said. "You don't know me, and it's probably best things stay that way, but I can promise you that if you answer a few questions for me, the next time you see me you'll find out who killed Blaine Adkins and why."

She laughed then. "Well, someone sounds sure of herself."

I shrugged. "I may sound cocky, but the truth is that I can only fulfill that promise if people like you cooperate with me."

"Are you a cop?"

I shook my head. "No. But if you want to help me, all I need you to do is tell me, honestly, what you thought of Blaine Adkins. Just let it spill."

She hesitated, clearly wary. Her mother had rejoined us and was giving her daughter a look that said, *Just say the word…* For several moments I wasn't sure if I was going to be thrown out.

"He was cute," Melanie finally blurted. "I think that's what I hated most about him—the fact that I was attracted to him. The chemistry was just there, you know? And it totally weirded me out. The guy I most wanted to go out with had apparently killed the last woman he dated? What in the world does that say about my judgment of men?"

Her mom blinked in surprise, and I knew that Melanie hadn't told her that particular tidbit.

"And he was just so nice to Prince. Patient. Gentle. And *funny*," she added, as if that last fact infuriated her. "He had this thing where he would pretend to narrate Prince's thoughts while Prince was wigging out and trying to get Blaine to pet him. And he was just dead on, you know? The voice, what he said, all of it. I mean, I knew who Blaine was and it freaked me out, but every time I was around him he made me forget all that, which only freaked me out more. I was actually planning on moving when my lease was up, because of him."

"Not because he freaked you out?" I asked.

She shook her head. "Because he *didn't*."

"Mel," her mom whispered in alarm.

"I know, Mom," she said on a tired sigh. "I know, okay? I don't need a lecture about it."

She wasn't saying it straight out, but Melanie was saying it as best she could: she'd had a crush on Blaine Adkins, suspected murderer. That definitely had to be tying her brain in knots right about then.

"Do you think he liked you?" I asked, not because I needed the answer, but because Melanie did.

Her throat clenched once, then twice. Then she gave one quick nod.

"How do you know?"

"He stopped trying to make eye contact," she said. "He tried to, at first. He tried to be friendly through the awkwardness. But there was this energy whenever our eyes caught, so I always looked away whenever he looked my way. It messed with my head too much, so I just avoided it. Then, after a while, he made it a point only to look at Prince or the ground when our paths crossed. He was still nice, but I could tell he was sad. Then after a while it didn't matter because he started keeping such strange hours that our paths never crossed anyway."

That sounded promising. "When did he start keeping strange

hours?"

"Five months ago, maybe. September-ish? All of a sudden it was like he didn't live here anymore. If his car hadn't been parked outside every once in a while, I would have thought he had moved."

"No visitors? No nothing?" I asked.

She started to shake her head before saying, "Well, once, last month. Some teenage kid came to his apartment with him one day. I heard them coming up the stairs, so I peeked out, only because it was so weird, you know?"

I nodded. "Did the other guy seem to know him?"

She hesitated, then nodded. "They were talking about something, and it was serious, but it sounded like they were mostly agreeing. Not arguing. Kind of like how we're talking right now. It's not happy, but it's not an argument. Like that."

"Can you describe the other guy?"

"Not really," she said. "They were facing the door when I poked my head out. Brown hair, tall, skinny. Hair cropped really short. That's all I saw, really."

"A basketball build?" I ventured.

She nodded. "That's one way to describe it, yeah. I'd be surprised if a guy like him didn't play basketball."

I wasn't sure what Jeremy Carson looked like, but he was the first person who came to mind when Melanie spoke, so I would need to follow up on that.

"But that's it," she finished. "That's the only person I saw Blaine talk to since September."

I heard the sadness in her voice. So did her mom, from the looks of it. The angry mama bear looked more like a cautious mama bear as she processed what her daughter was saying.

Blaine Adkins had been nothing but nice to her daughter, and he had died alone and friendless, with everyone around him believing he was a murderer. And while everyone else might be okay with that, Melanie Cunningham was not.

"I've spent months wishing Blaine would just disappear from my life," she said, her voice catching. "And now he's gone. Totally gone, and it feels awful. Like I made a huge mistake and I'll never be able to fix it."

Suddenly she was sobbing and not caring that she didn't know me as her arms crashed around me. "I don't think he did it," she cried against my shoulder. "I really don't think he did, and it's killing me to know that I felt that way for nearly a year and never told him. I should have told him."

I watched her mom's hand move to her mouth as she pushed back tears of her own and tried to find words of comfort. Our eyes met as I hugged her sobbing daughter, but it seemed neither of us knew what to say.

Or maybe I did.

"Well, Melanie, if Blaine was guilty, I'll tell you. And if he was innocent, I'll make sure everyone knows, okay? I specialize in finding the truth, so get ready either way. Your mom will tell you—and rightly so—that a woman who lives alone has to protect herself. For as long as Blaine was the only suspect in Amanda's murder your hands were a little tied. You were wise not to flirt with him. But if the same person who killed Amanda just killed Blaine as well?" I let the question hang.

"Then someone needs to take that person down," she said fiercely.

I nodded against her. "And not to sound cocky or anything, but that person is me." I pushed away from her and reached into my pocket to pull out a business card. "So if you think of anything, let me know."

She took it without really seeing it, and I stepped away.

"Thanks," she said, wiping at her face. "I needed to say some of that. It was clawing inside of me, but I just didn't know who to tell."

"Glad it was me," I said with a smile. "Now I'll get out of your hair. I promised two minutes, and it's been a bit longer than that."

Melanie nodded while her mom regarded me suspiciously. And why shouldn't she? I'd just promised her daughter something I had no business promising at all. Truth. Justice. Answers. I hadn't meant to. It had just slipped out like a foregone conclusion. I didn't have a track record of failure, and I certainly didn't plan to start failing on this case.

Story, not case, I corrected, as I showed myself to the front door. Things were different this time. Everything I had access to thanks to The Fours was off limits. No background checks, no looks at phone records, no nothing.

That was a problem.

Neither Melanie nor her mom tried to show me out, which I was glad for. When I shut the door behind me I heard Melanie start crying anew.

Her current state of loss was the worst kind—the kind where regrets far outweighed anything else. Someone she had cared about had died having no idea she cared. It made me think of Ty and how I would feel to find out he'd somehow died in a car wreck or something with things being how they were with us at the moment. And if I was the one to discover his body?

The mere thought took my breath away, and suddenly I was losing my own battle with tears. It was just a hypothetical situation, but after feeling how broken up Melanie was with how things had turned out for Blaine, it all felt a little more real.

But Ty knew I loved him, right? I may be keeping my distance from him, but he knew why. He knew it was because of The Fours, not because I didn't love him.

Right?

I missed him so much in that moment that I actually had to give myself a hug as I made my way to my car. Once inside, I paused before turning the ignition.

I needed to find out who killed Blaine Adkins. I needed to find out if Blaine really killed Amanda Carson. It didn't matter if I had my usual resources, it needed to happen. And even more importantly, the evidence wasn't even a day old. I could do this. Because a part of me knew something that I wasn't quite ready to say out loud yet. It knew that Melanie and her dog had good instincts. And not once when she had talked about Blaine had there been fear or concern in her voice. She'd been told to fear him, but she hadn't.

And that, more than anything, spoke volumes.

My phone vibrated with a text message and I turned on the car to get the heater started before looking at it. It was Kay, of course.

Where are you? I'm at your place with the mom interview.

Headed there now, I typed back. *10 minutes.* Then my phone rang, showing an unfamiliar number.

"Hello?"

Sniffle. "Rhea?"

It was Melanie. "Yeah."

"You didn't ask and I'm not supposed to tell," her voice said. "But he was shot in the heart. The police said he probably died really fast, but there was a sign of a struggle. I don't know if anything happened before he was shot, but he definitely moved around after being shot."

She took a slow breath that sounded a bit like a machine gun. I waited, not knowing if she would spook if I pushed her.

"There was..." She hesitated. "You could tell where he was shot, because there was splatter on the wall behind him. And a hole. I didn't know bullets could do that, you know? Go right through someone's chest like that and just keep going."

That was definitely unusual—unusual enough that I wasn't sure if a special kind of bullet would have to be used to make that possible. Kay might know.

"They say he died quickly, but I'm certain that he got his hands on his killer after he was shot. The blood... I would bet anything that his killer had it all over him when he left because it was all over the spot where he got shot, and then there was hardly any of it anywhere else except where his body was laying on the other side of the room. And he was shot in the heart. It wasn't like he stopped bleeding while he crossed the room. I've been playing it over and over in my mind, and I think he threw himself at his attacker after he was shot and bled into him, instead of the carpet. I don't know if that's one of the reasons the killer didn't make sure the door was totally shut behind him, or what. But somewhere out there, someone has clothes with Blaine's blood on them. I'd bet anything on it."

That was huge. I didn't know what to do about it, but I was really glad to know it.

"Anything else?" I prompted cautiously.

She hesitated, and I let her. This was her show. "I'm pretty sure the base for his PC was missing."

"Missing?" I echoed.

"Yeah. In his living room. There was a computer desk and a computer screen, but the computer part was missing. I might not have noticed, but there was about an inch of dust outlining where it used to be. I think whoever killed him took his computer."

"That helps a lot, Melanie," I said, even though I wasn't quite sure how I could use the information. "Thank you for telling me."

"Don't thank me," she snapped. "Just keep your promise. That's how you can say thank you."

"Will do," I said, promising her yet again something I had no business promising at all.

But I meant it. This case was under my skin now, too. I wouldn't stop until I had the same answers Melanie was looking for.

CHAPTER 9

After talking with Melanie Cunningham the night before, it was definitely time to talk to the people who thought Blaine was innocent.

The obvious place to start was Blaine's mother, Susan. After watching the interview Kay had done with her the night before, I understood why it hadn't been aired. The woman was clearly having a breakdown. She just kept on repeating how her son had been killed because he was so close to getting proof that he hadn't killed Amanda Carson. Of course, the mom didn't know the details of how, exactly, he was planning on doing that, but she was adamant that Blaine had been on the threshold of putting all the rumors about him to bed forever.

If she would have been able to say as much without screaming and sobbing at the camera, she might have had her moment of prime time. As it was, however, Kay wouldn't have been doing her any favors to use any of the footage she'd gathered.

So while I was starting the day getting to know Blaine Adkins better, Kay was making it her job to find out what caliber of bullet had been used in each shooting.

This was a detail the police were never going to release, of course, but if I knew Kay, she'd get her answer one way or the other. It helped that her years of hunting helped her narrow down the options without so much as a Google search. As for Blaine's computer, we both decided to keep that quiet, just like the police obviously were.

That didn't mean that Abby Straightway couldn't leak such details to national media outlets, though.

The intent was not for any of the outlets to pick up the story based on these facts. The intent was to get them to care. The intent was to get pickups on the story when it actually became a story. Because however this ended, I was fairly certain it would be worth the headline.

I used the morning hours to create a press release with enough details to hook in the memory of its recipients, then pressed send. Then I simply stared at my screen for a minute.

I'd worked on murder cases before, but never like this. Something was different about this one. Something doubly wrong. I wasn't sure what. Maybe it was just that the idea that Blaine Adkins could have been innocent the whole time and died trying to prove it sat in my stomach like a boulder.

Based on the raving interview of his mother, he'd been on the path to vindicate himself, but he hadn't shared any of the details with her. He'd kept them to himself, and taken them with him when he died. That had to be torture for a parent.

But how would things be any different with my father if things went wrong when I faced The Fours the next month? As far as my dad would know, one day I was alive and the next I was dead, and he wouldn't have any answers as to why that was.

I owed him more than that. Way more than that.

Before I knew what I was doing, my phone was in my hand and I was calling him. I just needed to hear his voice. I just needed to tell him I loved him. It had been too long. I couldn't discuss something as important as next month with him over the phone, but I could at least—

"Hello?" a sleepy voice said. A sleepy *female* voice. I blinked and looked at the clock. It was 7:15 in the morning in Utah, which meant it was 6:15 in California. It was early, but my dad was up.

Only this wasn't my dad.

"Rhea?" the woman's voice said, a little less groggy this time. It was Meredith. I'd spoken to my dad's business manager many times before, but never at six in the morning, and never on my dad's cell phone.

"Hi, Meredith," I said, keeping my voice neutral. "Did I catch my dad at a bad time?" Just act normal. Pretend it's noon. Pretend your dad's cell phone didn't just wake her up.

"Yes, he's away from his phone, but I'll let him know to call you as soon as he gets back." Her words were professional, as always, but her voice was totally tense. I'm sure mine was, too.

"That'd be great," I said. "Thanks, as always."

"Of course," she said, and I hung up before things could get any weirder.

My dad and Meredith?

The thought had me frozen in my chair. Not because there was anything wrong with it. Hardly. It was just that in all the years since my mom had died, I wasn't aware of one time a woman had spent the night at my father's place. This was the first. And the woman who had stayed over was his office manager.

My dad never mixed business and personal relationships. Never. That meant at a minimum, my dad was breaking two longstanding rules for Meredith. And that meant... well, it meant that I wasn't the only one who had something to talk about next time we got together.

It was going to take a minute to wrap my brain around that. Yes, I was happy for him. It was *way* past time he have a new love in his life, but...

But nothing! He deserved any happiness he could get. My mom would want it for him, so I just needed to get over my juvenile knee-jerk reactions of rejection and betrayal and give them my blessing.

In the meantime, however, I was more than happy to have a full day of distractions ahead of me. Some things were easier to accept if you didn't think about them too hard.

CHAPTER 10

It wasn't hard to find Susan Adkins later that morning since she was picketing the press conference. When I arrived, I spotted her *Who killed Amanda and Blaine?* sign immediately.

Susan was just as manic as she had been in Kay's interview the day before, which was scaring away more ears than it attracted. I parked on the street, paid the meter, and made my way over to her.

"The police *never* looked at anyone but Blaine!" she was screaming. "They never even tried to identify another suspect, and because of that, my son is *dead*!"

To her credit, Mindy, a perky Fox reporter Kay hated, was there trying to get a sound byte.

"Do you feel a suspect was overlooked in the investigation?" she asked into her mic. "Who should have the police looked into?"

"The husband!" Susan roared, her voice cracking. "Nathan Carson killed his wife! Not my son!"

"But the husband was cleared," Mindy said into her mic. "He was thoroughly investigated by the Pleasant Grove police department."

"They covered up for him!" she accused. "Yes, Nathan Carson was booked on the flight arriving at nine that night, but he took an earlier flight! The flight he really came in on landed three hours before Amanda died, not two hours after! Look into it—not just at the ticket he booked, but the flight he came in on!"

Mindy looked at her cameraman and gave him the cut sign. It was discreet, but Susan saw it.

"I'm not crazy!" she wailed. "Look into it, and you'll see!"

"I will," Mindy said tightly as her cameraman gathered their stuff. I waited until they were inside and focused on the press conference before approaching.

"Susan?" I said softly before she could scream in my direction. She blinked at my use of her name. "Mind if just you and I talk for a minute?"

"I will not be silenced!" she cried out. "I am on public property, and I have the freedom to speak my mind!"

I nodded, keeping my voice low. "I just wanted to talk to you about what Blaine had found out these past few months."

She blinked, as if trying to figure out if she heard me correctly.

"Like who was the guy who was helping him?" I asked.

"Helping?" she scoffed. "No one was helping him! Everyone was too busy accusing him!"

I shook my head. "No, there was someone. A young man. Tall with dark hair. Skinny."

Her body language changed and she faced me. "You mean Jeremy? You know about the DNA test?"

It was my turn to be surprised. "Why don't you tell me what you know about it?"

"What's there to tell?" she said, her face ugly with anger. "Last month Blaine finally got the test to prove they were brothers."

"Brothers?" How was that even possible?

"Yeah," she said before turning to face the police station and screaming, "Just *ONE* of the things police decided to cover up!"

I touched her arm, pulling her attention back to me. "So you're saying Blaine told police that he and Jeremy were brothers?"

"Half-brothers," Susan corrected. "And yes, he told them all the way back when she was killed last year—about two seconds before he became a suspect himself. He went in trying to help, and became their prime suspect instead. They said he was lying. Then, when he asked for the DNA test to prove it, they got his request thrown out. It would be too emotionally traumatizing for Jeremy they said, to have to have a DNA test with the man who almost certainly killed his mother. They said he was maliciously trying to inflict emotional distress or some nonsense. And Jeremy was a minor then, so it was his dad who had the final say. It took more than a year for Blaine to get a DNA sample and have it sent off for testing."

"And he got the results back?" I asked.

"Yep," she said, turning to scream the rest at the police station. *"Test results showed a 99.8% chance that they shared the same father!"*

"You saw the results?"

"With my own eyes," she said, only to me this time. "He didn't show me everything he found. He said he wanted to keep me safe, but he did show me that. Mostly because it helped prove that leaving his father was one of the best things I ever did."

"But I don't understand," I said. "Jeremy was born almost exactly nine months after Nathan and Amanda were married. He's a honeymoon baby. How could your ex-husband be Jeremy's father?"

This time she didn't yell her answer. This time her voice dropped down to match mine. "Because my ex is a bad man, and he did the same thing to Amanda that he did to me before making me believe I had to marry him. He raped her."

Talking to this woman was like taking a series of unexpected punches. Jeremy and Blaine had been brothers because Amanda had been raped? The claims were so outlandish that it was almost impossible to take them seriously.

"How do you know this?" I asked.

Her eyes narrowed on me. "If you're asking if Amanda Carson ever told me she was raped by my ex, the answer to that is no. She never said anything like that. But it doesn't change the fact that when Blaine mentioned his father's name while he and Amanda were at work together, she totally flipped. According to Blaine, she went ghost white and kept asking questions about his dad, what he looked like, where he went to school, all that. She even asked if he was in prison, since she knew he was. And when Blaine asked why she was asking so many questions she totally broke down." She stared me down as if daring me to contradict her. "So, no, Amanda may not have told me herself, but Blaine told me about that conversation almost a year-and-a-half ago. Then he asked me if I cared if he met his half-brother."

This. Was. Huge.

Yes, Susan Adkins came across more than a little crazy, but her claims were verifiable. A DNA test? One that Jeremy allegedly knew the results of? It would only take one phone call to verify that.

I needed to find Kay.

"What about the plane ticket you mentioned?" I asked. "How do you know Nathan took an earlier flight?"

She frowned. "Blaine didn't tell me how he found that out."

Still, that could be subpoenaed. I'd add it to the list for Kay to pester the police about.

"Why did Nathan kill his wife then?" I asked. "Why take an earlier flight home and kill her?"

She shook her head as if I had it all wrong. "He's not that smart. I think he just took an earlier flight home because he could. Then, when he got home he finds a wife who's asking him to help her tell their son that he's not really his father—that the father is someone else, and Jeremy had a brother. I think that's where things went downhill. That's what I think!"

It wasn't the worst hypothesis ever, but she'd had a year to come up with it. Or maybe she hadn't thought it up at all. "Is that what Blaine believed?"

Her face puckered when I said her son's name. "All he knew for sure was that Amanda had said she was going to tell her husband about it him, and see how he felt about introducing him to Jeremy."

"And Blaine told the police this?"

"Every word. Several times. And the more he told them, the more he became their only suspect. They called him 'obsessed' and 'imbalanced' and things like that."

"And they never looked to see if her husband took an earlier flight?"

"They *said* they did," she spat. "They said that when they looked into it, that records showed him on the flight that landed at nine, not the earlier flight. But that's a *lie!*"

I could see where she was losing the media. The claim that police were covering for a wife-killer? I was pretty jaded and even I couldn't swallow that one.

"It's a whole fraternity thing," she accused. "Those guys have each other's back. They cover for each other, and that's what they did for Nathan after he killed Amanda. They covered for him!"

Oooookay. Maybe we were done here. Sure, I'd look into her other accusations, but it was best I walked away before she talked me out of doing even that.

"You don't believe me!" she accused.

"I have my doubts," I corrected. "There's a difference."

"Why won't anyone listen!?" she wailed before launching

back into the rant she'd been screaming when I'd arrived.
　　I needed to talk to Kay.

CHAPTER 11

I stopped short when I spotted Kay and Mindy from the Fox station talking as I walked into the press conference area. Since when did those two talk? Whatever the two of them were saying, they were both flashing the fakest smiles ever. Then the awkwardness was over and Kay beelined it back to Nick.

"What was that about?" I asked sliding in next to her. She jumped, clearly seeing me for the first time.

"Oh, nothing," she said with fake perkiness. "Mindy there just wanted to know if she could get Ken's number from me. She has something she wants to ask him."

Oh, wow. The girl had real guts. "And?"

"I said I'd pass her number along."

"Uh-huh," I said, glancing Mindy's way. "It's like the curse of Mindies."

"Huh?"

I shrugged, feeling suddenly self conscious. "Never mind."

She squinted at me until a light went off in her eyes. "Oh, you mean Ty and his friend Mindy, and now Ken with Fox Mindy?"

"Forget I said anything."

"No, you actually referenced Ty in a conversation. That's progress—and *way* past time, by the way. I told you I'd answer your questions if you had the guts to ask them."

"It's better not to know—"

"Yeah, because then you can imagine whatever you want, right? Then you can justify whatever you want."

Wow. That conversation had derailed quickly. I had to get it back to a manageable place. "So are you really going to pass on her number?"

Kay's eyes narrowed. "Nice evasion. And yes, I will. Because unlike you, I let my men make their own decisions. I don't make up my mind for them and then force them on a path I think is best."

Not fair... or at least not nice. "And if Dahl calls her?"

Her face stayed impressively blank. "We'll cross that bridge when we come to it. But remember, unlike you and Ty, Ken and I are not technically dating, so there's no reason for him not to take out someone else."

"That's awfully mature of you," I said just as Nick walked up to us.

He gestured toward the door. "So you survived crazy town out there?"

He was referring to Susan Adkins. I turned back to Kay. "About that, you're going to look into her claims, right? That Blaine was Jeremy Adkins half-brother?"

She rolled her eyes. "And how am I supposed to do that at this point?"

"Ask Jeremy."

She laughed, then paused. "You're serious? You honestly want me to call Amanda's son and ask him if he'll take a DNA test to see if he's related to him mom's accused killer?"

"According to her, Jeremy's already taken the test and seen the results for himself. At this point, it's more of a yes/no question than a court-ordered test. Someone just has to ask the question."

"So now I just need to call a college kid and ask him if he voluntarily took a DNA test to see if he was related to his mother's accused killer?"

"Yes."

For a moment there was a bit of a standoff between us. "Rhea, she's crazy. She's desperate. She's a mother who will believe anything she needs to believe to convince herself that her son is innocent."

"Which is no reason to discredit her claim that Jeremy and Blaine actually completed a DNA test to prove that they were brothers."

She shook her head, moving over to her purse. "We can't talk about this right now."

"If you won't do it, your intern will," I warned.

"Better her than me," Kay said, pulling out her lip gloss. "At least her reputation doesn't matter. People like me need to pick and choose where they lose face. But for now, either stay and watch the press conference or get out of here and stop distracting me."

It was clear she would have preferred option two, but the decision was made for me when a barrel-chested man in uniform stepped his way up to the podium. The hum of the room died instantly as the red lights on all the cameras blinked on and started recording.

I'd never met the detective on the podium before, but I'd seen him on TV more than once doing a press conference similar to this. Detective Tony Knight. The guy had the highest closing rate for cases in the state, according to Dahl. They called him the Bloodhound, because he always seemed to know exactly where to poke his nose and when. If nothing else, Blaine Adkins was getting the best SLPD had to offer, even if he had to die to get it.

If Blaine was innocent, it was going to come out.

"I have a prepared statement, after which I will not be taking any questions," Detective Knight said, his tone a bit south of cordial. "As you all know, the Salt Lake Police Department is taking the death of Blaine Adkins quite seriously, and there are several pieces of information that, if shared, could compromise future legal proceedings or invite bias. Given that, the only information I have to share with you today is the autopsy report confirming that Blaine Adkins' cause of death was from a gunshot he sustained to the chest. There were no eyewitnesses to the event, and we are still sorting through all the physical evidence obtained at the crime scene. I know many of you have questions about what we found in Adkins' apartment, and while I don't have answers for you today, I can say that I do believe we will have answers for you in the near future."

The clicks of camera shutters became much more audible as Detective Knight looked over the gathered reporters. "Unfortunately, that's all I have for you folks today. As always, I'd like to thank you all for the work you do, and I promise to bring information to your attention as soon as it becomes available, either by press release or conference such as this. As a reminder, I will not be taking questions today. Thank you for coming, and drive safe on those roads out there."

Then, as quickly as he'd arrived, Detective Knight was off the podium and back behind closed doors.

I turned to Kay. "That's it? You all came down here just for that?"

Kay's eyes were trained on the door Detective Knight had disappeared behind, a frown fixed to her face. "Apparently."

"Huh. I feel better about asking you to get Jeremy Carson's phone number for me now."

She looked at me in surprise. "Me? Why do you need me to get it?"

"Because I'm your intern. I don't get to use my resources, remember?"

She rolled her eyes. "You're so weird, you know that? Like Elliott cares if you look up a phone number."

"You set the rules," I said. "I'm just playing by them."

"And if I don't get you his number?"

I squared off against her. "Then you might not get some things you want, either."

Her eyes narrowed. "Fine. Whatever. It's not even worth arguing about. I'll track it down."

"Thank you."

"Like I said. Whatever. Now go do something useful, okay? Something besides digging into crazy conspiracy theories. Something that gets me on the phone with people in New York, preferably."

"If it's there to find, I'll find it."

"Good. Now if you'll excuse me, Nick and I need to find a way to turn this joke of a news conference into a leading story at noon."

Happy not to have any such demands, I made my way back to my place to keep digging.

CHAPTER 12

Jeremy Carson wasn't answering his phone. Every time I called him, I went straight to voice mail. The one thing that was fully within my power to do—call Amanda's son—and he had his phone turned off.

My dad called while I was trying to get Jeremy, and for the first time in a long time I purposefully let his call go to voice mail. I was fine with him and Meredith. I totally was, but I was also still processing and he would hear that in my voice. I'd rather wrap my head around it all and then talk to him when I could be 100% sincere about giving them my blessing—if they were even in a place in their relationship where they wanted it. Maybe they weren't. And those were the kinds of mental landmines I wanted to work through before I blurted out something all of us would want to forget.

For now, I needed to help Kay, although I wasn't sure how much of a help I was anymore. Not now that I only had media clips and secondhand accounts to work with. And I'd already spent the morning and early afternoon reviewing those again. Nothing new had popped out from the fray.

So, what else was an intern to do? Eavesdrop on her boss? Drive back down to Pleasant Grove and poke around again? Drive back to Blaine's apartment complex to see if anyone felt chatty?

In the end, eavesdropping on Kay at work won out, so I put her phone on speakerphone and went to make some lunch.

For ten minutes all I heard was the clack of manicured nails on a keyboard. Exciting stuff. And she wondered why I didn't listen in more often. There was the mutter of voices in the background, but nothing I could make out. It didn't matter, though. Kay wasn't talking to anyone and she wasn't making any calls. She was right where I was. Stuck. Not that she would ever admit it.

Not letting her know I was listening, I picked up my phone and texted her. *Son's phone is off. Straight to voice mail all morning.*

I turned her back on speaker phone just in time to hear her mutter, "I could have told you that. The kid's totally off radar."

Did she know I was listening, or just muttering to herself?

The clacking started again, more staccato this time, until I finally heard her chair roll back and the clacking stopped. She didn't move for nearly a minute. Then her phone rang.

"Hi, Carla," she said picking up. There was a beat of silence, then, "Yep. Be right there."

Well, this should be juicy. Kay and Carla weren't exactly known for getting along, but to date I'd only heard their conversations secondhand. Luckily for me, Kay couldn't walk out of eyesight of her phone or her purse, so this time I would get to hear the fireworks.

I turned up the volume until I could hear Kay's footfalls on the hallway floor. Then they stopped.

"Shut the door behind you?" Carla's voice said. Moments later there was a click. "Any movement on your leads?"

"Do you see me running around like a mad woman?"

"No."

"Yeah, so that would be a no," Kay grumbled. "No movement."

"I didn't think so, so I'm making the executive decision to have Red do a one-liner on it in the opening segment with some B-roll. No live broadcast and no clip from this morning. It's basically useless."

The fact that Kay didn't argue with her was kind of big deal. It meant she knew that she literally didn't have a scrap to stand on.

"So I'm switching you over and you're—"

"Going down to Bluffdale to do a story on the new NSA center?"

"No—"

"It's the perfect day for it," Kay argued. "Nothing big, unless there's some fatal pile up during the afternoon commute."

"A little girl was just flown to Primary Children's due to injuries from a sledding accident—"

"Seriously? A sledding accident?" Kay scoffed. "A junior Utah congressman lobbies for, and *wins,* the right to build Big Brother in a Salt Lake suburb, and we're seriously not going to do a single story on it?"

"Well, *you're* definitely not," Carla quipped.

"Why? Because I care?"

"Because you're so clearly biased. If we cover it, we're sending someone who can do the story with a smile on their face."

Kay let out a bark of laughter. "Yeah. Like having someone smile while they tell the story isn't its own type of bias."

"There's no reason not to smile.," Carla argued. "It's a huge boon to our community. It will add billions to our economy and provide thousands of jobs."

"And the fact that Big Brother is going to be built in the middle of Zion, and essentially be staffed and run by Mormons? That's no never mind to you? Nothing about that strikes you as a little off?"

I could all but hear Carla groan. "First off, it's not Big Brother—"

"No," Kay interrupted sarcastically. "Just the second-largest technology building in the world, solely devoted to intercepting every phone call, every private email, every chat, every networked computer file, every vocal, physical, and digital fingerprint of each American citizen, along with a number of other things that aren't even disclosed."

"In the name of national security," Carla countered. "If people aren't doing anything wrong, they have nothing to fear."

Kay laughed, although it sounded a bit angry. "Oh, wow. You're kidding me, right? Although I guess if everyone around here believes that, I can see why the government chose to build it *here*. Because Mormons are so good they don't think they have anything to fear. Only bad people do, right?"

Carla let out a slow exhale, probably a calming one. "I'm not getting into this discussion with you again, Kathryn. We're doing the sledding accident. And the girl might die, by the way, so try not to be too glib when you get there. She ran into a wood pile and got her lung punctured. It's bad."

"I'm going," Kay said. "But off the record, exploiting a family in time of tragedy and filming them as they fall apart and pray for a miracle is *not* news. It's opportunistic fear mongering that we'll end up tagging with a lame headline like *Sledding day turns fatal. Are your children safe?* And at the end of the day we make a bunch of moms afraid to let their kids go sledding tomorrow, when they should *really* be more afraid of the fact that no phone call or electronic correspondence is private anymore. Not one. And in the near future, Utah is going to make billions making sure of that fact."

"So noted," Carla said, sounding tired. "Now out. You've got just over three hours before we go to you live up at Primary Children's. Make it good."

"Always," Kay said before I heard the click of a door closing. Several seconds later I heard a light knock and Kay say, "Saddle up."

"Yeah?" Nick's voice said. "Primary Children's?"

"Primary Children's" Kay echoed. "Let's go warn the world about the dangers of sliding into piles of chopped wood."

"I called around a little when I got Carla's email," he said. "I actually don't think the kid is going to make it. Not according to the consensus."

That apparently gave Kay pause. "Well, let's at least expand the story out to include safety tips for the most common sledding injuries. It's pretty much the most dangerous activity on the planet, so give me a few minutes to do some research before we head out."

"Roll out in thirty?" Nick offered.

"That'll work," she said, and I heard her footsteps move away.

Well, at least I knew what she was up to. I turned off our link, not needing to hear anymore.

Kay was officially off the Adkins story until later that night, but maybe that wasn't the worst thing ever. Sometimes distraction was good. I certainly needed some distraction.

Just then a text came in. From Kay. A little surprised, I opened it.

Let me know when D. Knight contacts you. I hunted him down after the press conference and sold you up. If we're lucky, your phone might ring.

Was she serious? *I can't help him,* I typed back. *You know that. Intern duties only.*

Never say never until you know what he wants, was her reply.

Hopefully nothing, I replied.

Text me with updates.

Updates? Like what? The fact that I could no longer sneak peeks into things like airline databases or people's financials? Or that getting a copy of Detective Knight's hard drive on my computer was off the table?

I was a normal person with normal person assets. That meant that even when someone told me a potentially groundbreaking fact, I had no way to fact check them and follow up. My hands were tied.

For the first time, I was legitimately no help whatsoever—especially to the Salt Lake police. I was totally stuck. Good for nothing and nobody.

My eyes glanced to Ty's house before I could stop them. No truck. He was at work, but I'd already known that without looking. But I'd come to depend on him when I got stuck in a mental rut. Somehow Ty knew just what question to ask, what button to push. He didn't do it on purpose. It just happened any time we spoke, like a natural synergy.

But I couldn't call him. Not about this. It wouldn't be fair... to either of us. Not unless I was willing to open the door to talking about more. Which I wasn't.

Was I?

No. Because I was doing the right thing. If things worked out in March, *then* we could talk about us.

Just thinking about March had an invisible vice tightening in around my chest. I hadn't worked out that day. Not really, and I hadn't studied in days. A solid run, then a trip to the library—that's what I needed to clear my head. Then I would be able to focus on the Adkins murder a little bit better.

CHAPTER 13

It was just after 8:30 when Kay poked her head in my basement and dropped a folder next to the gym door. "Can't stay. But thought you could use this."

I nodded, sweat dripping down my face despite the cool of the basement as I leaned against my punching bag and took a breath. "Thanks. I'll look through it."

She studied me for a moment. "You know, I've been thinking that if you really are going to stop investigating, you should teach me some of your tricks. I hate just waiting for the news to be handed to me by someone else. It's not my style. I want to pull the camouflage off of the corruption of those pristine press releases I get."

"Sounds dangerous," I mused.

She let out a short laugh. "Oh, please! If there was ever a time when a pot was calling the kettle black, this would be it."

"Just speaking from experience," I pointed out, even though I also knew from experience that once Kay got it in her head to do something, she was going to do it. With or without my help.

She rolled her eyes. "Well, then, I'll promise in advance not to pledge my loyalty to any psycho secret societies when they ask for my soul. I'll just turn and walk the other way. That work for you?"

"Ha ha," I deadpanned. "It doesn't exactly work that way."

She frowned then, leaning against the door frame. "Have you figured that part out yet? How they reeled you in, I mean? How they allegedly have claim on you?"

We didn't talk about my former employers very often for more reasons than one. But no matter how much we did or did not talk about it, it didn't change the fact that the whole situation was a bit beyond my understanding. Somehow I'd become the only female in a fraternity that had existed for generations. As near as I could tell, it all came down to my old boss, Elliott Church. He'd taught me the ropes on the investigation and security business, and I'd worked with him for over six years on high-end cases.

"Elliott never made you swap bodily fluids with him or made you confess weird things to him on tape during your apprenticeship?"

"Never," I said. "Not even a secret handshake."

Kay considered that. "I just don't get where they're coming from if there's no contract or no oath they can site."

"That's the thing with secret societies," I said with a shrug. "They pretty much just have to site the fact that they're willing to kill you."

"So messed up," she grumbled right as my phone chirped with a new text. Glad for a distraction from the conversation, I walked over to my phone only to feel my heart clench unexpectedly when I saw the name attached to it: Ty.

My expression must have shown my shock, because Kay came over and looked at the screen. "I thought you two were incommunicado."

"We are," I said, annoyed at the pounding in my chest that had nothing to do with beating up a bag.

"Obviously," she drawled. "And speaking of Ty, he's getting better with a gun. This last time he grouped solidly in the first three rings. If you're not careful he'll be better than you sooner rather than later."

Good to know. Although for Ty's sake, I hoped he did get better than me sooner rather than later. Because of me, his life might depend on his ability to make a shot. I knew everyone thought I was being overly dramatic for thinking that, but something in my gut told me it was a possibility. And if it was a possibility, that meant I needed to address it—overly dramatic or not.

Turning the phone's screen away from me so I couldn't see it, I put the phone back down. I couldn't respond. I shouldn't. One of us had to maintain the boundaries.

"You're not going to look at it?" Kay asked. "Not even a little curious?"

Oh, I was. Absolutely.

"I am," she said reaching for it, but I blocked her hand. For a moment we were caught in a battle of wills.

"Reading it won't fix anything," I said.

"Who says it's meant to?" she replied. "If it was personal, I'm pretty sure he would take the fifty steps it takes to get over here and say it to your face. You know that as well as I do. So you've got to ask yourself what in the world he would choose to text you about."

She was right. Ty wasn't a texter. He was a face-to-face kind of guy. And the fact was that not reading the text meant I would be making up text messages from him in my mind and responding to them all night. So I gave in, picking up the phone and angling it so I got to read the message before Kay could get a look at it and start sounding off about it.

Pretty sure you're being watched, it said. *A guy is hiding in the shadows along the south side of your porch.*

I squashed the impulse to look at the south window in my gym and quickly typed back, *On it.*

My heart pounded in my chest, but I wasn't quite sure why. Was it because Ty was secretly watching over me or because I was about to take down a peeping tom?

"What did he want?" Kay asked, reaching for my phone.

"Nothing," I said, voice casual. "He's still trying to talk me into going to that concert."

Kay's head tilted in confusion. Then she blinked and I saw a flash of realization flicker through her eyes. "I thought he sold those on Craigslist."

Message sent. Message received. There was no concert and no tickets. Talking nonsense was our signal to each other that a phone was tapped. But since we clearly weren't on the phone, Kay seemed to make the next logical leap. Her eyes glanced around the room, looking for something, anything, that was out of place.

"Apparently not," I said.

"What are you going to do with that boy?" she asked, her voice not quite as calm as she was trying to make it sound. "Are you serious about making your break permanent?"

I let out a sigh and started to the kitchen. "If we're going to talk about that, I'm going to need a drink. Want one?"

"Whatever you're having."

I nodded before moving up the stairs, through my kitchen, and cutting out the door that led from the kitchen to the back yard.

Some idiot was looking through my windows? Not for long.

The back door didn't give the slightest squeak as I slipped out into the still night wearing my workout clothes and grappling gloves. It had stopped snowing, and yet I didn't see any tracks in the fresh snow. Only mine. Using silent footsteps to bring me to the side of the house, I debated my options once I reached the corner that would take me to the south side of the house. If I peeked around from where I was, I might be seen and give the person a head start. Conversely, it was highly likely I was faster than whoever it was. I also had to assume that Ty was out here with me somewhere. He wasn't the type to watch something like this go down from a safe distance. I hadn't waited to ask him where he was via text, but I could assume that he was near my property line on the opposite side of the house. If the person Ty had spotted made a run for it, he'd have both Ty and me on his tail. The question then was, did I want to catch the peeping tom or just scare him to the point he wouldn't come back.

I was still debating when I heard an owl call from the rear part of my property. My eyes moved to the source of the sound and I thought, *There are no owls in the Avenues,* just before I saw silhouette move from the tree to my neighbor's yard. A very human silhouette. I glanced back to the front of my house just in time to see a man vault over my neighbor's seven-foot fence as if it was nothing and the world went quiet again.

For a moment I was stunned into inaction. Two men? Watching my house? Using an owl call to warn each other once they were detected? This was no peeping tom. And just as I realized that, I saw Ty's figure sprint across the gap between my house and the fence then vault over the fence with the same ease the other man had, albeit a little less silently.

Seeing Ty on the move snapped me into action.

Knowing Ty had the other guy, I ran in the direction of the human owl, using the tree to leverage myself onto the fence. White snow covered the area beneath, but there were no footprints. There was literally no trace of the guy I'd seen, or indication of which way he had gone even though I knew he had disappeared to the west, whereas his friend had gone due south. Logic said their rendezvous point would be to the southwest, but I hesitated, instinct drawing my eyes to the north, toward Ty's house.

Grown men who moved silently in the night, didn't leave footprints in the snow, and used animal calls to communicate? Chances are they did other cliché things like lead pursuers away from their safe zone before doubling back. Besides, Ty was running to the south and he actually had eyes on his guy. I should take the north. Sure, it was a wild card, but I'd learned long ago that ignoring instinct nearly always led to regret.

As I returned to the ground and ran to my front yard, the familiar hum of adrenaline began its journey through my system. This was what I trained for—what I lived for. It was one thing to maintain a heart-pounding pace while you ran up a mountain. It was another thing entirely to run into the night with all six senses on high alert knowing that somewhere in the shadows you had an enemy.

I'd lived in the Avenues for nearly nine months. I knew every car, every motion detector, every empty house, and as I ran, my eyes searched for anything new. Anything out of place. An unfamiliar car. An idling car. A light on where it shouldn't be. Footsteps where they shouldn't be—although my guys had already proven that they could cover them when they wanted to. Neat trick, that. I'd have to look into it.

I reached the first intersection to the north of my house, my eyes scanning east and west to the cars on the road. I'd seen them all before. And besides, these guys weren't the type to park a few hundred yards away. Given how they moved, I'd guess at least four blocks stood between me and their getaway car. *If* they had a getaway car. One could hope.

I kept moving, making my way to the next intersection and again taking stock of all the cars. There was one new car, a red Chevy Cobalt. I memorized its plate number and kept moving up the next block. The recent snow made my job a bit easier, since I only needed to look at the cars with the snow brushed off. Cars covered in snow clearly hadn't been moved in the last day.

By block five I was getting a little nervous about my choice to go north. I should have gone with Ty. If he caught up to those guys it would be two against one, and these guys were clearly not beginners. What had I been thinking? Ty could be hurt. Or worse. When I reached the next intersection, something in me calmed when I looked east and saw LDS hospital.

Where better to park than in a place where no one paid attention to who came and went because it happened all day? My system calmed as I took in the tiered parking structure. They wouldn't have parked there because of the cameras, but on the street? Definitely.

I had to move slower here, since all the cars were new and none were covered in snow. Most of the cars on this street were visitors. There were a lot of license plates to memorize. Unless, of course, I wanted to take a gamble and stake out the area in the hope that it would pay off. I pressed my fingertips on the hood of a nearby car as I debated. It was cold. Not my guys. But this was by far the most strategic place to park a getaway car to the north of my house. No one would take notice of a new car or an unfamiliar face on the street since they were a constant there.

Sometimes logic matched instinct, sometimes it didn't. This time, both were telling me the same thing. I needed to stay right where I was and wait for two urban ninjas to get into the same car.

Slipping into the shadows, I moved to the edge of a nearby hedge and squatted down. It wasn't easy to do when my body itched to keep moving but I reined it back and settled in, breathing slowly in through my nose and out my mouth to lower my heart rate. After a minute I realized my sweat was freezing. Yet another thing you didn't need to worry about in California. Freezing sweat. Still, I didn't move.

Five minutes passed. Six. Seven. After eight minutes a lone man strolled from the direction of the hospital and got into a Toyota 4Runner about a block and a half away. A moment later exhaust rose from the tailpipe like a pillar of frozen smoke while the headlights stayed dark. He was warming up his car. Most Utahns did that in the winter. They let their cars idle for several minutes before actually driving them, a habit carried over from in the days when cars actually needed to warm up. Technology had changed to the point where cars really only needed thirty seconds, but much to Kay's chagrin, most people in Utah still gave their cars five or ten minutes of idle time before actually driving them in the winter.

A minute later a couple made their way from the hospital, the woman's arm linked through the man's as her shoes skidded along the slippery sidewalk on their way to their car. Despite the cold, the man opened the woman's door first, letting her in before walking around and getting in himself. They were in the car a matter of seconds before two taillights on the street were spitting exhaust into the sky, only this second car wasted no time in getting on its way. Its lights flipped on and it pulled onto the street, moving past me.

I looked back to the idling 4Runner. Black. I couldn't see the plates, but it had been idling over a minute. The crunch of feet sounded behind me along with the jangle of a dog collar. A few seconds later, a bundled up woman passed me on the side walk, neither she nor her dog paid me any attention. The four-legged creature just pranced by with a daft look in its eye, nearly dragging its owner in its effort to get somewhere—anywhere that was a change of scenery, probably. For my part, I was just glad that it had tunnel vision and didn't spot me.

The 4Runner was still idling and did so until the woman and her dog turned to the right at the next corner. As soon as she disappeared out of sight, the lights turned on and the SUV casually pulled from its spot, moving to the intersection that lay between us and stopping. Was there a stop sign? I wasn't sure. A tree stood in my way, and before I could adjust and check, a dark figure sprinted down the sidewalk from the passenger side. My feet were moving before I was fully aware of what was happening, moving on instinct and sprinting to the intersection as the passenger door swung open and the second figure jumped in the SUV.

The blaring headlights made it impossible to see the license plate, which meant I needed to get the rear plate as it left. No matter what direction it went, I should be able to see it.

Before the door even shut on the passenger side, the SUV was making a U-turn and moving back toward the hospital and revealing a rear plate that had been strategically covered by snow. The entire car was completely snow-free except for the bumper, where snow had been packed directly over the license plate. Perfect.

I pushed my pace, needing to get closer if I wanted a shot at even a partial plate. I burst into the intersection just as the 4Runner completed its turn, and based on how it suddenly accelerated, they had spotted me. The wheels spun, slipping on the packed snow in the road before gripping and lurching forward. That momentary halt gave me the break I needed as I reached the car and smacked the plate to clear it off.

Gotcha, I thought as the SUV sped away, two darkly clad men in tow. Three seconds later they had turned and were out of sight.

I slowed my pace, not needing to chase them anymore as I repeated the license plate in my mind, creating a mnemonic device to remember it before turning and heading back the way I'd come. Just then Ty sprinted around the same corner the second man had emerged from. He lost his footing for a moment when he spotted me, his feet sliding on the slippery street before he recovered and righted himself. Somewhere in the back of my mind I realized this was the first time we had been alone since we'd decided on our break. It could have been awkward. It might have been under other circumstances, but the situation itself was too odd for extra awkwardness to carry any weight.

He looked good. Perfect, really. He wasn't dressed for the cold. He'd just come from the gym based on his warm-up pants and pristine Nikes. He looked down the street, realizing the man he'd been chasing was long gone before jogging up to meet me.

"How'd you get here so fast?" he asked, not exactly sounding frustrated but not sounding pleased either.

"Took a shortcut," I said, digesting the fact that the man Ty had been chasing had outrun him. That was no small thing. Ty ran like the wind and was an advanced gymnast. I couldn't outrun him over mixed terrain. Dahl couldn't either. I didn't know a non-professional athlete that could.

Yet someone just had. And that told me I wasn't dealing with amateurs.

"You okay?" I asked, looking him over as he closed the distance between us.

"Physically? Yeah," he replied. "But that guy just schooled me. Kind of embarrassing."

"How did he get ahead of you?" I asked. "No way he's faster."

His eyes narrowed, as if he wasn't quite sure if that was true or not. "He's a free runner, for sure. Used a lot of roofs on his way over here. Roofs, trees, fences. He could literally run a half-inch of fence top like it was flat ground. Crazy!"

That was crazy.

"What's going on here, Rhea?" he asked, his voice both

concerned and annoyed. "Is this about your friends?"

He meant The Fours. I'd been wondering that myself while lurking in the shadows and had an answer ready.

"No," I said, voice confident. "Nothing fits for their MO in this. They never send a person to do what technology can. Plus, they don't train like this. Military, sure. But not urban ninja stuff. Not free running."

Ty considered that, reluctantly nodding as he sent one last look down the street. "Yeah."

"Plus that 4Runner is about ten years old and local," I added. "The Fours would get hives at the thought of driving something so middle-class. These guys are different."

"Dare I ask what you're into now, then? Gosh, I leave you alone for a few weeks and now ninjas are after you? What's next?"

He stepped in as he spoke, close enough that I could feel the heat of his body radiating off of him. He smelled of *Pure Blanc* and sweat—a mixture I would recognize in my sleep from our more recent work out sessions before I'd put us on a break.

For a moment my body went into autopilot, stepping in to wrap my arms around him and hold on before I reminded it that we weren't currently on that page. No touching. No kissing.

I took a small step back.

"I actually don't think I'm the one who needs to answer that question," I said, thinking of Kay's recent arrival at my house. Was it possible they'd been following her? She'd been asking me about teaching her how to investigate. Did that mean she'd already started experimenting on her own and set of a few alarms that got her some extra attention?

"Urban ninjas are scouting out your house, and you don't think they were after you?" Based on his tone, Ty was far from convinced.

I shook my head. "No, but I think maybe it's time to have a little chat with Kay."

He all but rolled his eyes. "Of course. Because free runners are known for tailing reporters."

Well, well. Someone was feeling sarcastic. And maybe a little bitter. I deserved that, for sure, but it didn't mean I had to take it.

"Doubt me?" I challenged. "Then join me. And we'll see what Kay has to say about all this. Hundred bucks says she brought them my way."

At last his mouth curved into a smile. "If there's one thing I learned from you two, it's never take a bet. Somehow I never win."

It was in that moment the awkwardness of being on a break crept in. There we were, standing in the middle of the street about a half a mile from our houses, neither wearing a coat, both freezing our butts off but pretending we weren't so we would have an excuse to stay and talk. Then I'd added an invitation back to my place and he was accepting.

What now? Were we going to walk home? Race to avoid conversation? If we did talk, should we venture into personal territory or blatantly avoid it?

More than usual, it sucked to be on a break as I took the initiative and started walking back to the sidewalk.

"Where's your coat?" he asked, falling in step beside me. "You must be freezing."

"I didn't know the search of my property would turn out to be quite so eventful when I headed out." I glanced at his t-shirt. "Looks like you didn't either."

Then, as natural as can be, his arm wrapped around my shoulder and rubbed my upper arm as he pulled me against his side. The heat was immediate.

"Let's get you inside," he said, picking up the pace a little bit.

The contact was casual—brotherly, even—but the reaction shooting through my body was anything but. I missed this. I'd tried not to think about it but at the moment there was nothing else to think about. Then, of their own accord, my feet stopped moving causing Ty's to stop unexpectedly as his arm tensed around me rather than letting go. Still, he moved forward a little, his body swinging slightly to face me.

"What?" he asked, his eyes searching my face. "What is it?"

I love you. No matter what I happens, I want you to know that. It was the perfect time to tell him, to thank him. And I would have said it if his eyes hadn't dipped to my lips.

Oh man, I wanted him to kiss me. It was actually quite alarming how badly I wanted to feel the pressure of his lips against mine and the feel of his arms around me. But if I let that happen, then where would we be?

"I'm freezing. Race you back?"

"Definitely," he said, and started off without warning. I let him go, falling into a steady second-place pace. There were worse views to have while running down the street in the freezing cold.

CHAPTER 14

A solid punch in the arm greeted me as I stepped into my house.

"Twenty-five minutes!" Kay snapped. "You disappear for twenty-five minutes without a single word? You could have at least taken your phone." Her eyes snapped to Ty as he stepped in behind me. "Ty!" In a flash her arms were around him in a happy hug.

I got a punch, Ty got a hug. Go figure.

"Kay," he said, hugging her back with one arm while shutting the door with the other. "Word is someone in this room is already on Santa's naughty list."

She stepped away from him, so she could glare and stab a finger my direction. "Yeah? This one. You two nearly gave me a heart attack."

"Sorry," I said while I rubbed my deltoid. "The situation... escalated."

"And word on the street is that the guys we just chased weren't here looking for Rhea," Ty teased. "They weren't here for me either, which leaves..." He wiggled his eyebrows, letting Kay finish the accusation herself.

"Me?" she asked. "Yeah, right. And there was more than one? Where are they?"

"They got away," I said, appreciating her look of disbelief.

Just then a car pulled up in front of my place and it only took a glance to realize it was Dahl's. "You called reinforcements?"

"Of course," she said, chin high. "You two disappear into the night and I read a text that says there's an intruder on the property? You'd better bet I'm going to call in some protection."

"Yeah," Ty drawled. "Never mind the 9-mill you carry in your purse at all times. That's certainly no form of protection."

She scowled at him. "Whatever. If I want to call a sexy man to keep me safe, that's my choice. Besides, he might know something helpful, okay? Rhea here is trying to act like a girl scout these days, and it's giving us a fat lot of nothing to work with."

Ty regarded me doubtfully. "You? A girl scout?"

Why was he being nice? Why was he joking around? He should hate me. After all, I broke up with him, allegedly stomping on his heart. But he didn't look all that heartbroken. Was that because he wasn't?

Suddenly I didn't feel so well, but chose to focus on Dahl's arrival over obsessing on the subtext of Ty's amiable behavior.

"Come in," I said, opening the door as Dahl approached. He didn't look too surprised to see me and gave Ty a little man nod before moving straight to Kay.

"You alright?" he asked, framing her face in his hands.

She leveled Bambi eyes on him. "Better now. Thanks for coming."

"Definitely," he said, letting one arm slide around her shoulders as he turned to face Ty and me again. "What's going on here? There was an intruder?"

"Two," I corrected. "Watching the house."

Dahl's arm tightened around Kay ever so slightly, and she followed his lead by leaning against him. "What did they want?"

"We're not sure," I said, looking at Kay. "Where did you go after work today?"

She rolled her eyes. "They weren't following me."

"Rhea tried to get me to bet a hundred bucks on it," Ty offered, arms folded over his chest. What a pair we made, him pinning his hands with his arms, and me with my hands shoved in my pockets while Kay and Dahl openly held on to each other.

"A hundred?" Kay's eyebrow popped up. "Please, this has Rhea written all over it."

"The bet's still open," I said. "And you didn't answer the question. Where did you go after work today? You get off at 6:00 and you got here at 8:30. Where were you between here and there?"

"Nowhere," she said. "At work, putting together that folder for you. I got done just after eight and headed over here. That's it."

It didn't make sense.

"Maybe they were just common criminals," Dahl offered.

"No," Ty and I said simultaneously, which was awkward for some reason. Maybe because you weren't supposed to emphatically agree with the guy you were currently broken up with.

"I was the one who spotted them," Ty said when I didn't add anything. "I mean, maybe they were casing this place, but at 8:30 at night? It may be dark, but that's still way early to take a risk like that. Plus these guys were in crazy good shape. They out maneuvered both me and Rhea, which means that they've definitely been around the block."

That got Dahl's attention. "Did you get a good look?"

Ty shook his head. "They were guys dressed in black."

"Probably in their twenties, based on how they moved. Six-ish feet and 180 pounds, give or take ten."

"We basically saw what a person could see of another person in the dark, from behind," Ty added.

"Although there should be some shoe prints hanging around."

"Yeah, if we dig them up," Ty said. "Did you see they were doing that trick where they get the snow to fall back and fill in their tracks?"

I looked at him in surprise. "You know how to do that?"

He gave a little shrug. "Kind of, but not like they do. It was a thing we played around with back boy scouts. It only works in fresh, dry powder, but they're like crazy good at it."

"You'll have to give me a tutorial," I said, and everything grew silent and I realized what I'd done. I'd crossed the line. I'd overtly invited Ty back into my life.

"Sooo," Dahl ventured. "Did I miss the memo? Are you two back together?"

"No," Ty and I said in unison. Again, glancing at each other as we did so. I know what I was looking for as I looked at him, but I had no idea what he was hoping to see as he studied me.

He looked good. Really good. His hair was styled different—a little less choir boy and a little more bad boy. Was that Mindy's doing? Had she talked him into it? If so, I hated it. But if it had been Kay whispering in his ear, telling her I would like it? Well, then she had been right on the money.

I didn't dare ask, though.

"Well, okay," Dahl said, tone casual as Kay stepped away

from him.

"This isn't about me," she said with confidence. "I've been obscenely well behaved lately. It's kind of sad, actually."

"Well, that definitely wasn't anyone from my little clan either." I purposefully didn't use The Fours name. They still liked to pretend that they were a big secret, and I knew they were listening in. "And I haven't taken on a case in months."

"Which means either one of you is wrong about keeping her nose clean, or this was random," Ty said.

I sent him a look. "This was far too weird to be random."

"Agreed," he said even though Kay and Dahl didn't look as convinced.

"Seriously, you didn't say or do anything different today?" I asked her.

"Not a thing!"

"What about yesterday?" I pressed.

"Just my job," she snapped. "You know that as well as I do."

She was right. So what was I missing?

Dahl cleared his throat. "Not to be awkward or anything, but is it cool if I make an exit? I was kind of at a... thing. It would be good to get back to it."

Kay aimed a suspicious look at him. "A *thing?*"

"Yeah," he replied, suddenly uncomfortable. Well, now so were the rest of us as Dahl and Kay had a momentary conversation with their eyes.

She studied him for an awkward beat before walking to her purse. "Speaking of *things.*" She reached in and pulled out a business card, turning to hand it over to Dahl.

"What's this?" he asked.

"I promised I'd pass it along," Kay said sweetly. Too sweetly. "Mindy would like you to give her a call."

"Mindy?" Ty asked in surprise.

"Not *your* Mindy," Kay snapped. "His Mindy."

"From Fox?" Dahl asked, taking the card.

"That's the one."

He flipped the card over, not really looking at it. "Huh. What does she want?"

In answer, Kay folded her arms and smiled. "I dunno, Ken. Who really knows what a woman wants when she gives her phone number to a man. It's quite a mystery. Don't you think, Ty?"

Ty held his hands up and stepped away. "I'm staying out of this."

Frowning, Dahl shoved the card in his pocket. "If you don't want me to call her, I won't call her."

"Why not?" Kay said with a shrug. "We're not dating, right? Just friends. And you like her. There's chemistry with the two of you and you're both Mormon, so what's the issue?"

"It just… I…"

"Unless you want to start dating me," she offered. "Then of course, I would insist you not call her."

Dahl looked uncomfortable then—as uncomfortable as Ty and I hypothetically should have been standing in the same room. For some reason, however, having Ty in the room felt right. Good. Just like it always had, and always would.

What was I going to do about that?

"Kate," Dahl said, glancing our way as if there was something he might say if Ty and I weren't present. "You know how it is."

She nodded. "I do. So call her… after you finish your *thing*."

Moments ago they'd been hands on and holding on. He'd been the hero who showed up when Kay called only to turn around and ask to be excused. It always astounded me how quickly things could implode between the two of them.

"It's not what you think," he said softly.

She raised an eyebrow. "It's not a work thing?"

"Well…yeah."

"Then it's exactly what I think," she said with a curt nod. "Get back to it. And if it's not too late when you're done, give Mindy a call."

Dahl sent Ty the look of a drowning man looking for a lifeline.

"Eject, dude," Ty said softly even though all of us could hear. "Do as the lady says, or go down in flames. There's always tomorrow."

Dahl let out a sigh. "Don't make things awkward, Kate. I came here to make sure you were safe, and you are. But I did have other plans tonight, and there's no reason to get icy with me for wanting to get back to them."

"None at all," she agreed.

"We've got it covered," I said, needing to diffuse the tension.

"But thanks for making it over here. We'll let you know if we figure out what in the world was going on tonight." I stuck my hand out to shake his, just so he would have something to do besides have a stare off with Kay. He took it, using it as an excuse to move toward the door.

"I really do wish I could stay, but I have people waiting for me."

"Of course," I agreed, opening the door.

"Good to see you, man," Ty said, joining us at the door while Kay hung back.

"I'll ask around to see if these guys fit the description of anyone the cops are looking for."

"Great," I said, flinching when I saw him look over my shoulder to Kay.

"Drive safe," I heard her say.

"Yeah." That was all he said before turning and moving swiftly to his car. I watched him until he was in his car before shutting the front door.

"*Why* do I like him?" Kay wailed the moment the door clicked shut. She turned to face Ty. "Tell me I'm not overreacting here."

"He wasn't smooth," Ty conceded.

She rolled her eyes. "There are washboards smoother than him. But I just don't get what he's thinking, you know? He spends almost every evening with me, but he says we're not dating. He loves to make out, but says we can't have a romantic relationship. He insists there's no future with us, but then asks me if it's okay if he asks someone else out. How in the world am I supposed to process all that?"

"The biggest difference between me and your non-boyfriend is that I'm smart enough to know not to even to try answer that question," Ty said before jerking his thumb toward his house. "And luckily for me I have an excuse not to hang around and let you pester me about it since Mindy—*my* Mindy just drove up. So I'm outtie, too."

He was leaving? Just like that? No meaningful looks, no silent plea to get back together, and no backhanded comments? Well, unless you counted the "my Mindy" reference.

He turned to me. "I'm glad you're safe, though. That was kind of crazy. Let me know if I can do anything else."

I gave a weak nod, noting that he was close enough to touch me but making no attempt to do so. For some reason that hurt.

"Then I'm outta here," he said, reaching for the door. "You know my number if you need me."

"Yes. *We* do," Kay said.

He gave a quick wave and was gone. I stared at the door, listening to his steps move down the porch.

"You're an idiot," Kay said from behind me, then started over to the couch.

I turned to face her. "Me? As far as I can tell both of our men just walked out the door."

"Yeah. The difference is that one of those men wanted to stay." She flopped down, picking up the remote. "Did you DVR the evening news?"

"Aren't we going to talk about the guys Ty and I just chased down?"

She shrugged. "You'll figure it out. I got nothin'."

That must have been going around, because neither did I. Even worse, I almost didn't even care about them anymore. All I could think about was Ty with Mindy, and how comfortable things had just been with him just then. Loose. Relaxed. No anger, no tension, and no pressure.

Like he was happy.

Which, of course, was what I wanted for him. It was the exact reason I'd told him we needed to break up—that he would be happier without me.

And he was.

My stomach felt hollow, my lungs felt like they'd been topped off with cement, and I had to fight the urge not to rub the vacuuming sensation around my heart. All the while Kay eyed me from the couch.

"You ready to talk about it?"

I shook my head. "No. I'm good."

It was a lie, and her snort of laughter told me she knew it. "Whatever you say."

Then she cued up the first recording of the evening news and pressed play.

CHAPTER 15

I needed resources. That was all there was to it. A girl had a right to defend herself when dealing with intruders. The Fours had to understand that.

Leaving Kay to lecture her colleagues on the TV screen, I made my way over to my bedroom and called Elliott. We hadn't spoken in months, but somehow I knew he would answer my call.

"Rhea," he greeted on the first ring. There was no background noise, which was odd. Usually Elliott was out and about during the evening and night hours. "I was thinking you might call."

At least he didn't pretend that I wasn't under twenty-four hour surveillance in my own home. "I'm assuming you know what just went down here."

"Of course."

"Is it you? If so, I'll leave it. But if not, I need you to let me deal with it... however I need to, without you guys hanging it over my head when we meet up next month."

For a long moment there was only silence. Then came a chuckle. "Rhea, you'll never be able to walk away from this business. It's why I recruited you. Just come back. That's the answer here."

"You know my answer to that, Elliott."

He sighed. "Our relationship is perfect. You help us get what we want, we help you get what you want. Why walk away from that?"

"You know the answer to that," I said.

"Maybe," he said. "But do you? Why divorce yourself from true power, Rhea? Why make enemies with the powerful in exchange for permission to pose as a sheep. Because you're not a sheep, Rhea. We both know that."

"Nor am I a pawn," I shot back.

"Please, Rhea," he said on a chuckle. "When have I ever

treated you like a pawn?"

Okay. Never. But that wasn't the point.

"Look," I said, my voice much less thoughtful. "Personal labels aside, I don't know the rules right now. No one sent me a handbook here on how things should play out while I wait for March, but I've been doing my best not to step on any toes or send mixed signals. I'm turning over a new leaf, but that shouldn't mean I lose the right to find out why I'm being watched. Because if it's not you, who is it?"

"A good question, indeed."

He knew. All the way in California, he knew who those guys had been tonight. How?

"Whatever," I snapped. "This is just a courtesy call. Do your friends have any vested interest in what I'm looking at here? Are there toes to be stepped on your side if I look into this?"

"None," he said without hesitation.

"Then I'm going to assume that I have free reign. It's personal, not business."

"You've always had free reign, Rhea," Elliott said sweetly. "When have we ever asked you to be anything other than your best? We like you the way you are. You're the one all hell-bent on changing and leaving your best parts behind."

"No, I'm trying to live in a way that has some sort of moral compass. You want me to stay the girl who gets things done, no matter the collateral damage."

"Because that's who you are, Rhea," he said forcefully. "We didn't make you into that person. We empowered that person. So if you don't like her, don't blame us."

He was twisting my words—twisting my thoughts until I wasn't even sure what to say.

"Next month doesn't need to happen, my dear. We can even have you work from Utah. You can get back together with your little boyfriend, and we'll feed you cases that will help you save the day right there in Utah. We're willing to be flexible for you."

"Save the day?" I scoffed. "Yeah. You point me at bad guys who aren't cooperating with you anymore so I can take them down and you can replace them with people who are more willing to cooperate with you? Tell me, how is that saving the day again?"

"A bad guy goes to prison."

"Yeah, a 'bad' guy who's committed the unforgivable sin of trying to get out of your net—kind of like I'm doing right now. So who are you going to aim at me once you're sure I'm done cooperating, Elliott? Who's going to take me down, and how? You going to plant some drugs? Frame me for something? Or is it something a little more imaginative that you've needed these past few months to set up?"

"I guess you'll find out," he said.

If we would have been in the same room, I would have punched him. "I guess I will."

A soft chuckle came from his side of the line. "It's been a while since I heard that tone from you."

"Get used to it."

"Oh, I am. Trust me. And Rhea? Some free advice."

"No thanks."

"Do what you can while you can."

What in the world was that supposed to mean? I didn't get a chance to ask, because he hung up.

It took a moment to realize my heart was pounding, shooting adrenaline through my system.

Do what I could while I could? It was a warning, no doubt about that. But I couldn't think about that. As much as I hated to heed Elliott's advice, he was right. I needed to what I could, while I could. And right then I had a license plate and the make and model of an SUV that had just transported two men who were spying on me for whatever reason.

I was back in business.

CHAPTER 16

The black Toyota 4Runner I'd seen that night was registered to one Trevor Baxter—a twenty-six-year-old everyman with no tickets or citations on record. Local and college newspaper articles showed that he had been a star high school football player in Pleasant Grove who ended up second-string in college, which was surprising based on the level of athleticism I'd seen that night. His occupation also seemed to be a mis-fit. Trevor worked at an auto parts store in town.

A college-educated urban ninja doing basic customer service in an auto parts store? That piqued my interest as much as where he had grown up: Pleasant Grove—the same Pleasant Grove where Amanda Carson had been killed the year before.

Coincidence? I was going to take a leap and assume that no, it wasn't.

About an hour after I hopped on my computer, Kay got on the phone with Nick then cut out without filling me in. It didn't matter. I was happy to have her out of the picture and the TV off while I started building the profile on Trevor.

Young. Athletic. Law abiding. Underemployed. Attractive. Strategic. Intelligent. Disciplined. The more I learned about him, the more his profile painted the picture of a man who was either legitimately good, or a man so bad he looked good on paper.

Either way, what business did he think he had outside of my house on a winter night?

Just before midnight I decided to make the drive to the address listed on his registration. On the way out I couldn't help but notice that no silver Subaru was parked on my street. That should have made me feel better, but somehow it just made me mad.

Mindy shouldn't be at Ty's at all! Or at least not more than once or twice per week. Certainly not daily. Yet she was. No one spent that much time with another person. Not even friends. Mindy needed to back off.

The drive to Trevor's was made to an internal soundtrack of me laying down the law with Mindy. The mental conversation looped and repeated in different variations, all resulting in a victorious me, until I pulled onto Trevor's street. The house he rented had a closed one-car garage and three cars in the driveway, which told me he had roommates—one of which was possibly the listed owner. I recognized Trevor's 4Runner right away, but checked the plates just to be sure.

Jackpot.

A few of the windows in the house still glowed, telling me someone was still up and about. That made sense if the place was a bachelor pad.

My hand itched at my door handle as I fought the urge to go do some peeping of my own. There had to be a window I could peek through or a door I could sneak through. The problem was the snow. Trevor and his buddy had proven themselves to be students of detail that night, and I was fairly certain that no matter how stealthy I was, I would leave a trail leading right back to me.

I knew where he lived. I knew where he worked. That alone was way more than Trevor Baxter would ever assume I knew, and I needed to make that work for me.

That decided, I fired up my car and headed back home.

CHAPTER 17

Dahl canceled on our session at the pool the next morning. I didn't blame him, but it did throw me off my game. By the time I decided to hit Mount Olympus again I was about fifteen minutes behind schedule, and when I stepped outside the first thing I noted was that Ty had already left for work.

For some reason this stopped me in my tracks. Or maybe it was the arctic wind. Either way, I made it about half way to the end of my porch before turning and walking right back in my front door. No mountains for me that day. No jogging. No swimming, and I was too emotionally wiped to start hitting something.

Yoga?

No.

P90X?

Meh.

Hot cocoa?

Yes.

I hated hot chocolate.

What in the world was wrong with me? All I wanted to do was sit in front of a fire wrapped in an afghan. I didn't even *own* an afghan. Ty did, although that had nothing to do with anything since it wasn't like I was going to break into his house and steal it. Besides, I was dressed to sweat. I needed to push myself a decimal further than the day before. And yet somehow I ended up sitting cross-legged in front of a crackling fire about five minutes later. It was completely unacceptable as far as morning workouts went, of course. I should have at least been doing sit-ups or something. A hundred sit-ups, minimum. So I started doing sit-ups, only to stop counting at thirty-two so I could lie down.

All I wanted to do was stay right where I was and have an afghan magically appear over me.

Was I getting sick?

Statistically speaking I was probably due, but I didn't feel sick. No cold symptoms, no flu symptoms. All systems were normal except for the fact that I felt... unmotivated. Like a car that wouldn't start because the alternator had died overnight.

Not feeling like I had much of a choice, I went with the impulse to stay right where I was until my phone chirped with a text. For a moment I did nothing more than glare at my phone, but when it chirped again I reached out for it.

Text #1: *Jeremy Carson has released a public statement through his lawyer stating he never participated in DNA testing with Blaine Adkins.*

Text #2: *Nathan Carson's itinerary from last December also released in response to the accusations by Blaine's mom. They show his flight landing at 9. Press release for this morning postponed until SLPD is ready to make a large announcement. Maybe tonight, maybe tomorrow morning. Word on the street is they will be closing the Amanda Carson case.*

What? Could they do that? I wasn't a cop or anything, but that seemed awfully premature.

The one good thing about the news was that it had me feeling slightly more proactive.

There was no question that Nathan Carson's scheduled flight landed around nine, but the claim was that he'd moved himself up a flight and gotten home earlier. As for Jeremy's claim that he'd never participated in a DNA test, a test like that wasn't exactly something a person needed consent for. All Blaine would have needed was some hair, some spit, some blood. Anything.

Of course, I had to assume that Blaine's mom was totally wrong as well, but I'd been around long enough to be wary of carefully worded statements released by lawyers and itineraries being used for alibis. Maybe I was being paranoid. After all, I was used to dealing with fairly sophisticated criminals, not middle-class single parents, but still... I wasn't buying the alibis and I certainly wasn't convinced that the Amanda Carson case should be closed entirely.

Maybe that wouldn't be the announcement. Time would tell, but suddenly I wanted to head back down to Pleasant Grove and take the temperature of the situation. If, indeed, the announcement later that day would be the closing of the case, did the Pleasant

Grove police have the community support to make that decision stick? And if they did, who were they saying killed Blaine? They would have to name a suspect in his case to pull focus from closing Amanda's cold case based on circumstantial evidence.

It felt wrong... too fast. Or maybe that was just my ego on overdrive, since I usually got to an answer before the police did.

Whatever the case, I was in my car and half way to Pleasant Grove before realizing that I was still in my running clothes and wearing exactly no makeup.

CHAPTER 18

The gossip mill was abuzz in snowy Pleasant Grove. Small towns being what they were, it wasn't too hard to find out that Kay's guess about what might be announced later that day was also the guess of common citizens. It was kind of hard to loiter in any one spot too long in a no-Starbucks town like Pleasant Grove, but the local ice cream parlor, neighboring grill, and famous grease pit worked in a pinch. All I had to do was kill time at the local library until those places opened.

Three stops, three food orders, multiple conversations, and one consensus: *It was about time!*

The citizens of Pleasant Grove were ready to have Blaine Adkins declared guilty of murder, but the verdict was mixed on whether his killer really needed to come to justice. One elderly woman went so far as to call Blaine's killer a good Samaritan. I simply nodded and kept on listening.

Kay's dream of this story generating national interest was clearly dying on the vine, but as her intern, I felt it my duty to keep any of her national contacts ahead of the curve. Who knew if they would even open the press release, but I sent it anyway with the lead of *Police Expected to Name Murder Victim as Killer in Cold Case*. I built the story out, even using some of the comments I'd heard as quotes, then pressed send.

Through it all, my phone uncharacteristically silent which meant things were moving on Kay's side. I would have listened in if my ears weren't otherwise occupied, but just after 1:00 I got a text that read, *Press conference 4:30.*

Poking around in PG. Might not make it, I typed back.

Pointless. Head back.

Since when was Kay one to tell me how to do my job? Okay, maybe since the day I decided to be her intern. But still, I'd go back to Salt Lake when I was good and ready... which I had been right before she demanded it. Now all I wanted to do was call her and tell her she wasn't half as good at her job as she needed to be before she added telling me how to do mine to her list.

Seriously, what was up with me? Was it all that surplus energy I hadn't burned in the morning trying to find an outlet by picking a fight?

I tried to shake it off, turning instead to my information on Trevor from the night before. If he was working that day, it was getting to be the perfect time to catch him at work. It would also be a perfect time to slap a tracker on his 4Runner and see where the blinking lights took me. That would mean I'd have to take a pit stop past my house, but that wasn't a huge deal. It might delay me by twenty or minutes, or so, but it would be worth it as I saw where Trevor would lead me and who he would introduce me to.

I listened to Kay's phone on the way back, which was just in time to miss all the business conversations and hear her meet up with Dahl for a late lunch. In less than twenty minutes they went from *Ask Mindy out* to planning an official date and sealing the promise of it with a kiss.

Maybe some other development happened between them after that point, but I didn't tune in to find out. I was through being happy for them when they got back together, given their track history of falling right back apart again. If they were still together next week *then* I would be happy for them. For the moment I was just happy to drive in silence, so I didn't have to hear a song on the radio that reminded me I was single.

Single by choice. At least initially. But after seeing so much of Mindy at Ty's place I had to wonder if our relationship was really as solid as I'd always thought.

By the time I got back to my place I was a bit of a tornado. I went straight to my shed to grab a tracker, then picked up a receiver so I could test the batteries in both. Nothing drained a battery like temperature fluctuations, and there was no reason to go through the effort of putting a tracker on a car if it didn't have any juice.

After changing the batteries in both, the signal checked out and I was just about to power down when my eye was drawn to a secondary signal the receiver was picking up. At first I thought it was my phone until I realized my phone was in my pocket, not in my car. But the secondary signal was definitely coming from my car.

I blinked, willing myself to stay calm until I knew for sure what I was picking up on, then I grabbed a bug detector and headed to my car. It took thirty seconds to find the stupid thing. They'd actually had the gall to stick the thing under my hood, where there was less chance of it getting caked with snow.

Trevor had put a tracker on me when he visited.

I fought the urge to crush the thing with my shoe. That was clearly the emotional choice. The tactical choice was to let them think I didn't know about it, then allow them to track me when I wanted to be tracked.

They knew, for example, that I had spent the morning and early afternoon in Pleasant Grove so no warning flags would go off if I appeared to be parked in my driveway for the next few hours. Meanwhile I could be spying on Trevor. The down side? Placing a tracker on his 4Runner would be useless. They would detect my bug as quickly as I had detected theirs and they might reassess my skill level.

Pulling the batteries out of my equipment, I headed back to my car and moved Trevor's tracker to the underside of the railing on my front porch. Unless they drove by, they'd have no idea that I wasn't home. In the mean time, all I could do was thank my lucky stars that I'd tripped over the bug before staking out Trevor. That could have been awkward, to say the least. As it was, pure dumb luck had saved me from making one of the rookiest of mistakes. And what was all the high-end training in the world worth if I forgot to follow up on the basics?

Annoyed with myself, I headed to Trevor's work to see if I would find him there.

CHAPTER 19

Saving you a seat.

The text came at 4:15, and I glared at it. I wasn't coming, and she knew it. In my nearly two-hour stint hiding out in the strip mall across from Trevor's work, I'd deduced that he worked the day shift, not the night. Other employees had showed just before 3:00, which meant Trevor would be getting off shortly.

Where, oh where, would Trevor boy go?

There was a huge chance I would lose him at some point during the tail. An Audi R8 wasn't exactly a car that blended, but depending on how dark it was when Trevor left, I might have a bit of a shot at tailing him. I would need to hang back—way back—and just hang in there for as long as I could before an ill-timed light separated us.

A tracker really would have come in handy right about then. Maybe I had been premature to ditch it. Maybe they—if there even was a "they" outside of Trevor and his buddy—wouldn't have picked up on the signal with all the millions of other signals interfering.

I considered that a moment before rejecting my regret. Ditching the tracker had been a good idea, but that didn't mean I should disregard similar ideas like cloning his phone. That would give me access to all his calls and texts in addition to his location. All I needed to do was pair and sync our phones.

Easier said than done, obviously.

Skip the seat, I typed back to Kay. *I'll just listen in.*

Where r u?

Was about to tell her when it struck me that I might not be the first to think of the clone idea either. Someone might be watching our texts.

Doing some research.

A few moments later she popped back with, *Hate to say it, but*

I'm pretty sure it's a waste of time at this point. They have a suspect in the Adkins case, and are going to announce the Carson case as closed. Nice press release, btw. Saw the one you sent out earlier.

Well, someone was in a good mood. She and Dahl hadn't broken up again yet, it seemed.

Thanks. Does that mean we can look at the Carson files in PG tomorrow?

I can put in a FOIA request tomorrow and find out if they don't put the story to bed tonight.

No way, I typed back. *It's still going.*

We'll talk l8r. Gotta get to work on this side.

I let her get to business on her side, putting her on speaker so I could listen in while I watched for Trevor's exit.

The press conference started right at 4:30, but with all the cameras clicking on Kay's side, it was actually hard to hear. I found myself closing my eyes as I tried to focus in on what was being said as they announced that a spokesman from the Pleasant Grove police department would be addressing everyone first, followed by the spokesman for Salt Lake.

Even only catching the occasional word, I got the picture. Weighing in evidence that would have been inadmissible had the charges gone to court, the Pleasant Grove police felt confident in naming Blaine as Amanda's killer posthumously and would be closing her case.

Detective Knight spoke next, alluding to several "key" witnesses who had stepped forward in the Adkins case. Things went a bit crazy on Kay's side of the phone when he announced that they were having a composite sketch made, and I basically didn't hear anything after that.

Witnesses? A composite sketch? I had clearly missed a few key spots in my investigation. Not a huge surprise, given that I'd only been both feet in for less than a day. Still, I didn't like being behind the curve. I may not have been the first to get a description of a suspect, but I could definitely make it my goal to be the first one to find said suspect.

Across the street there was still no movement from Trevor when the press conference moved from prepared statements to reporter questions. I had to listen carefully, but I could make out what was being said again.

Reporter 1: *"Are you releasing any details about the suspect today?"*

Knight: *"No. We feel it best to release all the information at one time. We feel that's the best approach to apprehending them."*

Them? Was that a plural or gender-neutral reference?

Reporter 2: *"Will the case files in the Amanda Carson be made public?"*

Knight: *"Not immediately. Some of the information could compromise the Blaine Adkins' case if released, so we will wait for a resolution in that case before opening Amanda's files."*

Reporter 2 follow up: *"So are you saying that the murders are connected?"*

Knight: *"In a fashion, yes."*

Reporter 3: *"When can we expect the composite sketch?"*

Knight: *"Our hope is to have it released to the press within the next twenty-four hours."*

Reporter 4: *"Closing the Carson case seems premature, given that there wasn't enough evidence to even name Adkins as an official suspect while he was alive. How are the departments justifying the closing of a case based purely on circumstantial evidence?"*

Good question.

Knight: *"That is hopefully a question that will be resolved once the files are made public. If the citizens look at the evidence and believe that Adkins was not guilty of murder, I'm sure the Pleasant Grove police would be more than willing to address those concerns."*

Pure evasion. I crossed my fingers, hoping for a follow-up that didn't come. Instead I heard Kay's voice pipe in.

"And Detective Knight, during the course of your investigation, has the department seen your long-term friendship with Nathan Carson, Amanda's widower, as a conflict of interest?"

I sat up straight in my seat. What had she just said? Was that why my phone had been so quiet all day? She'd been sitting on a bombshell, and she hadn't even told me.

Detective Knight's response came without hesitation. *"No."*

"Really?" Kay followed, powering over the other reporters

who were trying to chime in. *"You're the lead investigator in the murder of a man who Pleasant Grove police now claim killed your best friend's wife, and that's not considered a conflict of interest?"*

The cameras went crazy, but voices were silent as all the reporters awaited the answer. *"Again, Kathryn, no. Justice is justice, and I have no problem arresting killers, regardless of my feelings toward their victims."*

He'd used her name. Usually doing that was a way to initiate intimacy, but sometimes it was a form of intimidation. For some reason the way Knight said her name it felt more like the latter.

Knight fielded two more questions I couldn't quite make out before the press conference was called to a close and I listened as Kay's peers swarmed her. At least that's what it sounded like on my side. She was ready for them, magnanimously sharing how she had discovered that Nathan Carson and Tony Knight had joined the National Guard together in 1983. That discovery had followed after she'd learned that Tony Knight had been raised in Pleasant Grove himself, right along with Nathan Carson. There was every reason to believe that the two men could have known each other their entire lives.

She didn't tell them anything else, but she didn't need to. All she did was reference the records where she'd found the information and go on her merry way.

Nice job! I texted her.

I know, right? Felt good to drop a bomb. We'll see if it goes anywhere.

It should, I typed back. *Good digging.*

I figure if you're getting out of the business, I'd better start stepping up.

☺

It was probably best that I not tell her that I'd cracked last night and started digging in myself. That said, I hadn't gotten so far as looking into shared histories between Nathan and Tony. What had gotten Kay on that path, I wondered. I'd have to ask her.

Just then Trevor walked out the front doors of his work and headed for his SUV. Using his keychain, he deactivated the alarm before unlocking the driver's side door.

At last. Now I could see where he headed in his after hours. There was still enough sunlight to force me to keep some serious distance, but I could at least get a direction. North. It was a start, although not a big one. All of downtown was to the north. His home was to the northeast. The heavy afternoon traffic allowed me to stay within three or four cars of him as we made our way downtown.

We passed Liberty Park, making our way to the shopping district. Then we passed that, too. He was aimed solidly at the Avenues when horrible realization hit me.

Trevor was headed to my place, and he had a GPS tracker showing him I was already there.

Crap, crap, and triple crap. I had exactly eight blocks to somehow get ahead of Trevor, park, replace the tracker, and get out of sight if I didn't want Trevor to know I was on to him. He was headed to South temple, which meant he was probably planning on taking E Street up to Fifth and approaching from the north. It was what he'd done the night before, which—scratch that. He'd done that the night before and gotten caught. He definitely wasn't doing that. But if he took Second, I was screwed. He would totally see me.

Crap.

Whatever. I couldn't worry about it. All I could do was my best.

As expected, Trevor passed through the 100 South light and got in queue to turn left at South Temple, so I took a left at 100. The lights were timed and the traffic wasn't as thick, so that was to my favor since I was now weaving through it. If the light was green, I went through it. If the light was red I pulled into the right turn lane and waited until I could blow through it. Yes, I got a few angry honks, but less than a minute later I was headed up B Street. Trevor was likely just turning onto Second. I couldn't see him, but I would have bet money on it. Even better, the rise of the street between E and B completely blocked his view of the intersection I was passing through.

I was clear.

I was half way out of my car before it was even in park. I grabbed my bag, popped the hood, and replaced the tracker before locking the car and jogging up to my front door. No 4Runner. No Trevor. Wherever he was parking, he hadn't had a look at my house yet, and that was all that mattered for the moment.

CHAPTER 20

I kept the tracker on my car when Kay asked me to meet her for celebration drinks. The day had given her a bit to celebrate, after all. The station was giving her latitude on her angle of the ethics of Detective Knight being the lead investigator in Blaine's death. She'd recorded it that afternoon, and it would play in the ten o'clock prime time slot. Add that to her and Dahl being on-again instead of off-again, and the evening's brand of celebration involved cheesecake rather than alcohol.

It took all of five minutes for Kay to tell the tale of how she had uncovered the connection before she started treading into other territory she apparently wasn't ready to talk about yet.

"You can trust us," Dahl said, his arm draped comfortably around her as he gestured my direction. "What else are you looking into?"

The tone in his voice gave the impression that he didn't really care if she answered or not. He was just happy she was happy.

"Not saying," she said, stabbing her fork at me. "Rhea never opens her mouth about anything until it's a sure thing, so that's what I'm doing. Not a peep until the bomb is ready to drop. Fair is fair."

I couldn't fault her logic, even if I found it a bit annoying. Then again, it's said that the people who act the most like us are the people who annoy us the most. Maybe that's why I liked Ty so much. The guy was nothing like me... in all the best ways.

In the meantime, I was the third wheel at a celebration dinner where Kay and Dahl came closer to sitting in each other's laps with every bit of cheesecake they took from their shared plate. I was so over it.

"I think I'm going to head out," I said, dropping some money on the table.

"You're going?" Kay pouted while Dahl picked up the money

and handed it back to me.

"I've got it covered," he said, and for some reason I wanted to choke him. I could pay for my own dinner. He wasn't my boyfriend.

"Then add it to the tip," I said, dropping it again.

He frowned. "That's kind of a lot."

Yeah. He *definitely* wasn't my boyfriend. "Then keep it, if you think you deserve it more."

Kay bit back a smile before turning to press her lips to his. "I think our Rhea is in a bit of a mood. What do you think?"

"Just a little," he muttered, before being distracted by her lips.

I left before I screamed, *Yeah, have fun while you can, you two, since we all know you're going to break back up in the next forty-eight hours!*

I didn't even notice the cold as I headed out to my car. All I could think of was how happy the two of them looked every time their eyes caught. Their whole relationship was doomed, and yet they chose to ignore that fact and fight for it anyway. Kay was never going to become Mormon, and Dahl wasn't going to marry outside the temple. Kay was always going to push the physical part of their relationship, and Dahl was committed to keeping a sexual relationship within marriage. The common ground between them was next to nonexistent, yet they were still pretending those little islands of common ground could be enough.

They were like the opposite of me and Ty. We had a continent of common ground with the occasional island on the outskirts. The problem was that my particular islands were lethal and I had spent quite a bit of time there. Exposure to me meant Ty was at risk.

It was a conversation I was sick of having: Was Ty any safer now that I had broken up with him? Not necessarily, but that wasn't the point. The point was that if he had his way, we would be married next week. And if we were married, that meant he was legally tied to me. That meant anything that happened with me directly impacted him. If we weren't married, he was protected—which was something he didn't claim to care about. So naïve. But that naïveté was the same reason we were currently on different islands, rather than together.

Ty didn't want me to have an easy exit out of our relationship when things got tough, and I didn't want him to be tied up.

The compromise? Just keep dating until it all blew over, right? Wrong. Not with Ty. It was get married or bust.

I chose bust. He'd chosen...Mindy.

Her stupid Subaru was parked in front of his house again when I pulled onto my street. Why didn't she just move in? Or had she? Might as well at this point.

In a flash, I was furious. Who did Ty think he was? Honestly. He said he loved me, but what about having another woman at his place—the *same* woman—every night since the day we broke up spelled love?

Up until that very moment I had been willing to accept the blame for our break up. It was *my* baggage—*my* issues that got in the way. It was The Fours. It was the fates conspiring against us. But no, it was none of those things. It was Ty's insistence that we get married before the seventeenth of March. It was his ridiculous notion that I wouldn't come back to him unless we were married—that when things got tough, I would bail on him. And while there were situations where that might be a possibility, it was my right to protect the people I loved in any way I chose. If leaving Ty would save his life, I would leave in a heartbeat. Whether he had a ring on his hand or not.

Getting married before March seventeenth was a plan for failure. I'd told him as much, and how had he responded?

With Mindy.

Well, screw that. I was done with pretending I was okay with him flaunting her under my nose. I was done playing nice. I didn't care what Mindy was doing over there, if Ty really loved me he would kick her out.

I don't know how long I stewed in my car before coming to that conclusion, but when I got out I didn't head to my front door. I headed to his. And I didn't knock.

When I burst through his front door, the TV was on and Ty was sitting on his couch and looking at some papers spread on his coffee table.

"Where is she?" I asked before I could think of anything more sophisticated to say.

His face didn't look half as surprised as it should have been. "Rhea. Come in."

He sounded...amused, which did nothing to improve my

mood. "Seriously, Ty. Get her out. We need to talk."

He stood. "That, we do. You want to shut the door?"

"I'll shut it behind Mindy," I snapped as he calmly walked over to stand across from me and placed his hand on the door over mine. It shouldn't have felt good. My entire body shouldn't have let out a sigh at the contact, but it did and I hated him for it.

"She's not here," he said, looking into my eyes. Hand still on mine.

I ignored the sensations stirring in me and scowled at him. "Is that why her car is—"

"Parked out front?" he finished with a nod. "She parks here on nights when I'll be home then sneaks out the side and has Connor take her where she needs to go. It's been a pain for them, but what can I say? I have good friends."

If I hadn't been embarrassed, I would have been impressed.

"They're engaged, by the way," he added. "Mindy and Connor. It happened on Valentine's."

"Mazel tov," I grumbled, snatching my hand out from under his. He responded by shutting the door. I reached out to open it again.

"Oh, no you don't," he said, gripping my arm this time. "No running away now that you know the truth."

I sent a pointed look at his hand. "Remove your hand, or I will remove it for you."

Not surprisingly, his hand stayed right where it was and he smiled. "I don't think I've ever seen you look so bad."

I twisted out of his grip and he let me, moving forward as I stepped back. "Bad being a relative term, of course. You always look good."

"Stop," I drawled. "You're going to make me blush."

He used one of his Swiss-Army smiles on me, the lopsided one that had a bit of a pucker to it. His hand came up to my hair. "Unwashed hair that's spent some time in a ski cap? No makeup? Little circles under your eyes? You really didn't think things over before you headed over here, did you? Just kind of charged over."

"And I'd be happy to charge back, if you would get out of the way." As far as comebacks went, it was total weak sauce, but whereas I may have looked a mess, Ty looked quite perfect. Smelled perfect. His hair was washed, styled, and had spent exactly no time in a ski cap. There were no circles under his eyes and the scent of *Pure Blanc* had me noticing that he'd just licked his lips.

I needed out, and gracefulness of the exit was swiftly moving down on my priority list.

Just then my backside ran into a table. I hadn't even realized I was backing up.

"You came over to talk," he said, looking and sounding way too confident. "So let's talk."

"I was wrong," I said, making a move for the door. It was stupid move, really. Totally predictable, allowing Ty to use my momentum to twist our bodies flush against each other.

I'd taught him that move, just like I'd taught him exactly how I liked to be kissed. He used both lessons against me in that moment, his mouth capturing mine as his arms locked me to him. Something in me broke. What, exactly, I wasn't sure. All I knew was I was kissing him back and the world felt right. The anger might come back once we were back at arm's distance, but for the moment all my anger was gone and I was pressing in.

"Coat," I muttered, unzipping it. A second later Ty had pushed it off my shoulders then all the way to the floor. I leaned in, sighing at the feel of him without an inch of fluff between us.

His hands went to the curve of my hips before moving up as if mapping to make sure everything was just how he'd left it. My hands did the same, moving up the front of him as his hands slid along my back. Yes, he was just as I'd left him. From head to toe. And he was still the one guy on the planet who could make me stupid with a single kiss.

"I love you."

Ty froze the moment the words were said, and it wasn't until he broke away and looked me in the eye that I realized I'd been the one to say them.

Speaking of stupid...

"But that's not our problem, is it?" he said, stepping away. The room suddenly felt cold. "We've never been short on love. Just trust."

He licked his lips, pressing them together before turning away.

"C'mon, Ty, that's not fair."

He sat on the arm of the couch, arms folded. "Yeah? You don't think I've been fair to you in our relationship, Rhea?"

I rolled my eyes, bending over to pick up my coat.

"That's not an answer."

I straightened, coat in hand. "Yes, Ty. You've been more than fair, okay? I'm the unfair one. Does that make you happy? Do you want a trophy?"

His mouth curved. "If that trophy is you."

I threw my coat at him, and he caught easily.

"Although why I want you when you're so incredibly difficult, I'll never know," he said, setting my coat on the couch. "I seriously could not make things easier for you, and you still find a reason to run away from me."

"That's not—"

"So I started thinking," he interrupted. "Maybe that was my problem. I was making it easy for you. You didn't have to fight for me. I was just always there, no matter how lazy you were about keeping me happy."

I felt my eyes narrow.

"We both know I'm a guy with options, but I had to convince you that I'm a guy willing to take advantage of those options. No more safe break ups. No more pushing me off to the side any time you decided I was better off without you. I had to make it clear that I could move on." He grinned. "And it worked."

There was no point in denying it. "Congratulations."

He took a deep breath. "But this brings us to the hard part, Rhea."

"Yeah?"

He nodded, not meeting my eyes. "This is the part where I tell you that the next time I bring someone over here, it won't be a decoy. You and I are going to figure things out right here, right now. And if you make the choice to kick me out of your life, then I'm not going to wait for you to come to your senses. I'm going to move on."

My stomach fell so quickly, I literally looked for a chair to sit in. The nearest one was over ten feet away.

"But let me start the conversation by saying I love you, too. And if this conversation ends the way I want it too, you'll agree to marry me again. You'll let me help you. You'll let me love you. And you'll look me in the eye and promise me that you won't succumb to some martyr complex and run away thinking you're some hero who's saving me. You'll promise me that no matter how hard it is, you'll try to remember that guys have a thing for wanting to be heroes, too, and you'll give me a chance to save you if things get rough. That's what I want. But if all that is too much for you to swallow, then I guess you're right. We should exit now while we still can."

Ty and his way with words. Some days I loved him for it. At the moment, I would have paid good money to have a boyfriend who bumbled a little. Because when he put things like that, there was no arguing with him. I was the bad guy.

The only problem was, he had *no* idea what he was talking about.

"Ty..."

"Here it comes," he sighed. "Let's hear your excuse today."

I searched for an answer, realizing the only thing I really knew was that I was tired. I spent every day feeling like there was a band around my chest that grew tighter every time I took a breath. It was a suffocation so slow that I had learned not to fight it, but to just accept the gradual loss of oxygen even as I pushed to run faster.

"I'm tired," I finally managed. "I'm trying to make things work, but I honestly don't know what my situation will be in a month, Ty. Why do these guys need six months to get ready? Am I going to be a fall guy? Are you going to wake up one morning and find out that I allegedly shot some power player? Are they going to put a gun to your head and really make me shoot someone while you watch? I know you think I'm being ridiculous when I list these things as options, but they *are* possibilities. You can't blow them off and pretend to be serious about marrying me. Don't doubt it. What happens next month is very likely to tear us apart."

"If we let it," he snapped, standing.

I shook my head. "No, there are things that make it so two people never want to look at each other again, Ty."

"So based on the worst case scenario of what may or may not happen down the line, we shouldn't be happy now, right? We shouldn't roll the dice and see if we actually can make our way through this?"

"It's not that easy."

"So you keep saying," he said, turning away. "So you're not

budging then? It's you against the world? Let me make it clear then, Rhea. If you walk away and insist on facing all this alone, then just keep on walking. I don't want you coming back after it's all over and pretending you're ready to commit. Ready to trust. Even Christ asked a few friends to come with Him to Gethsemane. True, they weren't a lick of help, but He asked. He trusted them enough to bring them along and gave them a chance to step up. That's all I'm asking for here, Rhea. A chance to step up, not be pushed back. Because if I let you push me back whenever things get rough, then we don't have a future anyway. I might as well walk away right now and find some girl with a scrapbooking habit and dreams of a mini-van with automatic doors."

From Gethsemane to scrapbooking within a breath. Yes, the man had a way with words, and this time I actually got his point.

And he was right.

If I walked away, there was no walking back when I got all my ducks in a row. Ty would just be waiting for the day when I decided I needed to handle something else solo, and cut him out of the equation again. He would resent me for not trusting him. And he had every right to. He deserved better than that. He deserved a wife who went to him with her problems—a woman who trusted him with her hopes and her fears, and gave him a chance to slay her dragons when they got too overwhelming. In fact, it would be quite the waste of a perfect man not to point him at a dragon or two and watch the sparks fly.

For a moment, I could almost picture it. I could see him rising to the occasion and everything turning out just fine. Then I acknowledged it was just a fantasy.

Then again, so were the thoughts of all the ways he could be destroyed by The Fours. Those were just fantasies of a darker variety.

"Talk to me, Rhea," he said softly. "You always sit there and think. I'm a guy. I need you to say it all out loud."

Where to start? My mind was such a mess, I didn't know what to address first. To Ty's credit, he waited patiently, even if he wasn't smiling about it.

It took a while to filter through everything, but once I had I took a deep breath and leveled a tired gaze at him. "First off, I want to make one thing totally clear."

He tensed. "Yeah?"

Without saying a word, I crossed the distance between us and laid a solid one on him. After a stunned moment, his hands threaded into my hair and he was kissing me back, full force.

"First of all," I said against his mouth. "You're too good for me."

I felt him smile. "And if I didn't love you so much, I would totally agree with you on that."

That got a giggle out of me as he slid from the arm of the couch to the cushions, taking me with him.

He locked me against him. "You said 'first of all.' So what's item number two?"

I pulled away, tracing the line of his jaw as I looked into his impossibly blue eyes. "Number two is you win. I totally want to marry you, Ty Kimball. It absolutely freaks me out, but I want it."

The grin that split his face came in stages. "And since when are you one to turn tail and run because you're freaked?"

Touché. But being scared for myself and scared for another person were two very different things.

I rested my head on his chest, knowing that if I looked at him for one more second we would end up making out. There was still more that needed to be said. "Ty?"

"Yeah?"

"I really am scared."

He took a deep breath, and I rose and fell with it. "I know."

"What are we going to do? I mean, if you're still thinking you want to stick this out with me, how do we do it?"

"We," he mused. "I like the sound of that."

"Me, too. But it's scarier than dealing with things myself."

"I get that." His arms wrapped around me in a hug. "So where do we start? You tell me. Where can you let me in today?"

"Today? There's nothing. All I've got going to today is helping Kay out with her news story. Hate to kill any exotic image I might have, but right now life is dull."

"You don't need *any* help?" It wasn't a question so much as a gauntlet. "There isn't a single way I could help you out that would make your life easier?"

I thought through the case, my mind pausing on the late night run Ty and I had taken the night before. "Well, there is this peeping tom guy I kind of want to learn more about."

His arms tightened slightly. "Yeah?"

"Turns out when he dropped by last night, he put a tracker on my car. I typically don't like to let people like him get away with crap like that without finding what they're about."

"I could get behind that. What were you thinking of doing?"

"What would *you* do?" I challenged, then inched up so I could whisper in his ear. "There's a good chance that he's outside right now. He came by right after he got off of work."

Ty tensed beneath me. "Are you serious?"

"Totally," I said, resting my head on his arm. "So what to do, dragon slayer? He'll find any tracker I put on him just as quickly as I found his." Quicker, even. "What's the plan?"

"Besides pounding his face into the snow?" Ty bit out.

"Yep. Besides, that."

He was still tense. "Well, in that case, I would defer back to you. What's your ideal response?"

"Clone his phone," I said without hesitation. "I get eyes and ears on all his texts and calls, and use his own GPS against him."

"Man, you play dirty," he said with a light chuckle.

"I play how I need to play to get the job done."

He grinned at that.

"The trouble is getting it done," I added. "We both know based on last night this guy isn't stupid. He also knows what we both look like. I watched him for several hours through the windows at his work. He keeps his phone on him at all times, and I would need it for a minute or two while our phones synced."

He was quiet for a moment. "And if I told you that I had an idea on how to do that?"

I looked up. "A way to get access to his phone for a few minutes without him knowing?"

"Yep."

"Then I would tell you keep talking."

He grinned at me. "Well, it's like I said at the beginning of this conversation, I've got options."

I gave his chest a little slap, but I could tell by the look in his eyes that it hadn't exactly hurt. "Options that are officially off the table."

"But options that certainly have it within their skill set to distract a guy for a few minutes."

I grinned then, too. "Yeah? And do any of them happen to have tomorrow off and a thing for guys who know how to fix cars?"

"I'd have to make a few calls." He eyed me coyly. "It'll work better if I pretend I'm still single."

I shook my head at him. "You're already starting to think like me. It's kind of scary."

"So you're cool with it?"

I considered it. "Light flirting only, and don't lie to her. Don't make it a point to say you're single."

"And if she asks?"

"She won't."

He considered that, then nodded. "I know just who to call. She'll have a blast with it."

I couldn't help it. I planted another kiss on him. "It always works out better that way."

"Yeah. It does." He slid out from under me, waiting until he was standing before adding. "And, Rhea?"

I snuggled into the heat he had left behind. "Yeah?"

"We're still on for next Saturday."

For a moment I missed his meaning. "Next Saturday? What's—"

Then it hit me. Our wedding. Back in November we had scheduled the wedding for next Saturday.

"Kay made that point that we would lose the deposits whether we canceled a month in advance or a day in advance, so she talked me and your dad into waiting until closer to the date before we made any final decisions."

"You *and* my dad," I stammered.

"Yeah. He didn't like lying to you, but I guess he knows you as well as the rest of us do. Anyway, point being that the party is still on and all the guests invited for next Saturday."

"But Meredith—"

"Didn't send out the cancelation notices," he said with a shrug. "So I guess she's in the know, too. Nobody else with an invitation to the wedding knows that we've been on a break for the past few weeks."

Well, that explained a lot.

I was glad I was lying down. Some news is easier to take when you're already grounded. "It's like a full-on conspiracy with you guys."

"Well, sometimes dealing with you requires a bit of a conspiracy," he replied, his tone not exactly joking. When he realized I wasn't going to hit him, he reached down and took my hand in his. "This is for real, Jensen. You, me, and a wedding next week, followed by a big ol' weeklong slumber party on an island with no cell phone towers. If you want out, you've gotta say so now."

I gave his hand a light squeeze, realizing that the pressure around my chest was gone for the moment. "Nope, you can count me as a plus-one. Wouldn't miss it."

.

CHAPTER 21

Bubbly, curvy, and blonde. That described Ty's "option," named Courtney. She was the kind of girl Ty had dated before me. And the fact that she had made herself available the moment Ty called her did not escape me. Nor did her outfit. She knew exactly how good her butt looked in those jeans, and the amount of cleavage she was showing in the chilly weather was no accident.

She'd dressed up for Ty, just as she'd forced him to catch her flying embrace when she'd met up with us. Ty shot me an apologetic expression as he tried to politely push her away. I kept my expression neutral, pretending to be indifferent Courtney's exuberance.

Girls like Courtney were the reason I had originally offered to give Ty space. The man did have options when it came to women. Lots and lots of options. Bubbly options with bodies that actually needed the structure of a bra to support them while they celebrated his every word and smile.

Yet he was with me. He wanted me. I knew that even as jealousy fisted in my gut at the contact between them. It was all part of the game plan—my game plan. But still, the urge to grab the other woman by the hair and threaten her wellbeing was overwhelming. Even after Ty pushed her away.

"Thanks for helping us out here, Court," he said brightly. "And perfect outfit, by the way. You're just going to make this too easy."

Courtney beamed. "You said you needed a distraction." She held her hands out, simultaneously thrusting her chest his way. "Ta-da!"

Yeah. *Ta-da* was right. She'd probably dropped about ten grand for "ta" and "da." Those babies weren't real. I'd bet money.

"Perfect," Ty said, taking my blood pressure up a notch. I'd told him keep things light and fun for her, but "perfect"? If that was his version of perfect then there was no way he was content with what I brought to the plate.

"So where is this guy?" Courtney asked, her voice both flirtatious and conspiring. "You said he was hot?"

Ty indicated me with a bob of his head. "Well, she seems to think so."

Cue: me.

"Seriously, thank you *so* much for helping us," I gushed, stepping forward.

"Totally!" she beamed. "And I know what you mean about planning the perfect surprise party. Is it his birthday?"

"Half birthday," I said. "Real birthdays are too predictable for surprise parties, if you know what I mean."

"They totally see it coming," she agreed, taking the story without hesitation. And with such perk. It was like having a conversation with an *Old Navy* commercial. "So what's my role in all this?"

"I need to get his phone," I confided. "Just long enough to get a few phone numbers. We've tried to get it when we're together, but he never takes the stupid thing out of his pocket. I need a distraction." I gestured to Courtney and glanced at Ty. "When I told Ty what I was trying to do, he said he knew the perfect girl to keep any man distracted."

Her grin was wide and confident. "Yeah?"

"Uh-uh," Ty said, keeping his tone light as he wagged his finger at her. "This doesn't change a thing between us, Court. I'm staying out of your tangled web."

Her bottom lip pouted out but the coyness stayed in her eyes. "It's not such a bad web. I'd be gentle, I promise."

Ty made a cross with his fingers. "I'll pass, my little cobra. I'm familiar with too many of the casualties you've left in your wake."

She touched a playful finger to his bicep in invitation. "And every one of them would do it all over again."

The nervousness in my laugh was authentic. "Hmmm. Are you planning on breaking Trevor's heart?"

This time her coy look was aimed at me. "Depends how hot he is." She winked. "Just kidding. So you just need me to distract him while you sneak his phone and grab some numbers?"

"Yeah," I agreed, fighting the urge to look at Ty. "I'll wait until he's focused on helping you before grabbing his phone—"

"From his pocket?" she interrupted. "How are you going to get it without him noticing?"

I sent her a knowing smirk, all but winking at her. "Trust me."

An evil twinkle lit Courtney's eye and I knew she was going to have fun with all of this. Ty really had chosen the perfect girl.

"It'll just take a minute. Two tops. I'll slip in behind him once you two start talking. As soon as I'm done, I'll return the phone and we'll be good to go."

"Huh. It almost sounds too easy."

"With you, it will be," I said, knowing she would take the praise well. In this case it was also the truth. Without a decoy this plan was a no-go.

"Well, I'm totally in," she said, this time beaming at me and not Ty. "Where does he work?"

"In an auto parts store."

Her nose crinkled. "Nothing's wrong with my car, though."

"Just ask him how to change your own oil, or something. Maybe a tire. Tell him you want to be more self-sufficient and just let him do all the talking."

"Oh, that'll be cake," she said with a little wave before offering Ty a flirty look. "What do you think, Ty? Should I pull a *Marco Polo* or a *Fly Trap*?"

"*Marco Polo,* for sure," he said.

Whatever that meant. I'd have to ask him later.

Her hands clapped together. "Okay. Lead the way."

I pointed to the other end of the strip mall. "He just a few doors down, actually. Can't miss it. I'll wait for you to go in first. Just position him so that he's not looking at the entrance so I can get in and out."

"Easy, peasy," she said, tossing her hair. "Does he have a nametag on?"

"Yeah," I said. "But just look for the only hot guy working there. That's him."

"Perfect," Courtney said, then flitted out of the bagel shop.

Watching her go, Ty stepped to my side. "Sooo... should I be worried at how easily you use truths to create a false impression?"

I shot him a dry look. "Part of the package, my man. Kind of like you having hot blondes at your beck and call."

"Hey, you're the one who asked me to—"

"I know," I interrupted. "I asked you to call her. But still, I hope you enjoyed that hug she gave you. Because once you marry me, filled out C-cups are not in your foreseeable future."

"C-cups? Hadn't noticed."

"Mm-hmmm," I drawled thinking I should give Courtney at least another ten seconds.

"Seriously, I don't remember the hug so much," he said, reaching across me to grip my hand and turn me to face him. "But the look on your face when I got it, though? Not forgetting that any time soon."

It was impossible to not to take a step closer to him. "Yeah?"

He nodded, a hand coming up to push a lock of hair behind my ear. "Oh, yeah. I don't see you jealous often. Definitely not often enough."

I shrugged, finding it hard to meet his eyes all of sudden. "What can I say? She's everything I'm not. Blonde, peppy, curvy—"

"Psychotic, manipulative, a man trap," he added.

"She wants you," I said, watching him closely.

"Never going to happen," he said, dropping a kiss on me. "Not even in a moment of deep self-loathing." He kissed me again, this time taking his time with it. "You're it for me, Rhea. Get used to it."

I was. I couldn't believe it, but somewhere deep down, I was absolutely used to it. That fact still freaked me out a little, but there was no denying it.

I pushed to my toes and gave a quick kiss of my own. "Ditto. Now wait here while I go be dastardly for a few more minutes."

His bottom lip pouted out, clearly imitating Courtney's favored expression. "You mean I don't get to oversee while you stick your hands into another man's pockets?"

"He won't feel a thing," I promised. "Stay out of sight. No unnecessary risks."

"Yeah, yeah," he said. "I'll babysit the bagel shop. Make sure it doesn't go anywhere."

"Good boy," I said and gave him one last peck before releasing his hands and heading to the door.

Courtney was nowhere to be seen when I stepped outside. That meant she was in the auto parts store and had likely already made contact with Trevor. Perfect. I made my way to the first window of Trevor's work and glanced in to see what I could see. It didn't take too long to spot Courtney's blonde locks. She was standing at the cash register, talking to Trevor. She needed to get him out from behind the register, but I had no doubt she could pull off a move like that. It would be child's play for her.

Sure enough, thirty seconds later Trevor was walking around the register and leading Courtney to one of the aisles. That was my cue.

I slipped in the front door, letting the bell ring even as I slipped into an aisle and walked to the end. Trevor had been leading the way when he took Courtney down a parallel aisle, which meant his back would be facing the direction of the register. I needed to approach from the opposite direction.

There were a few other customers in the store, which helped mask my presence.

"I just never get what the whole 5W, 10W thing is all about, you know?" I heard Courtney say as if she were talking about the greatest riddle in the universe. "And how do you know if you need 30 or 40 oil? Isn't oil just oil?"

The fact that I couldn't hear Trevor's response from my aisle told me that I had moved behind him and had chosen the right approach. As long as Courtney kept asking questions with a volume that assumed everyone in the world cared what boggled her mind, I should be able to pick a window of approach easily enough.

Once I reached the corner of the aisle Courtney and Trevor stood in, I stopped and did one little peek around the corner. Courtney looked at me in reflex, just like I knew she would, which was why I slipped back out of sight before Trevor could glance my way. When he looked over his shoulder to see what she had looked at he would see an empty aisle. In turn, Courtney would pick up on her tactical error and not repeat it. Or I had to assume she would.

I waited until I heard her say, "Viscosi-what?" before making my move.

Coming around the corner, I walked casually toward the two

of them as he explained why different types of oils were better for different seasons. I didn't look at Courtney as a cue to remind her that she shouldn't be looking at me.

"Huh, so cars are kind of like people?" she asked, her expression almost humorously daft. "Like how in winter I like hot chocolate, but in summertime I always want smoothies? Cars are like that, too? They want to drink different things when they're cold than when they're hot?"

"Basically," Trevor said as I came up behind him.

"And what about you?" she flirted. "What do you like to drink on a cold, winter night?"

"I, uh, hot chocolate's good." In the time it took him to utter those words I slid his iPhone from his pocket, into my hands and was heading back down the aisle.

"Yeah? What flavor?"

"I'm a traditionalist," he said. "Straight chocolate."

"Not me," Courtney said with feeling. "Hot chocolate isn't complete without a peppermint stick." She gave a moan of appreciation just as I turned out of the aisle and out of sight.

Thank heaven. How did blondes do it? Honestly. Sure I could whip out a banal, flirty conversation if need be, but people like Courtney somehow managed to do it all day long in the name of catching men.

Well, at least one guy was smart enough not to fall for such come ons and I was marrying him. But I could rejoice in that fact later. For the moment I needed to concentrate on syncing our phones. I brought up the app on my phone and got the ball rolling. All in all, it would take less than a minute, but nothing made time slow down like a watching a progress bar so I busied myself by looking at seat covers.

"Shut up!" I heard Courtney laugh. "Wouldn't that taste like toothpaste?"

I didn't even want to know.

While I waited for the progress bar to reach 100%, the conversation somehow migrated from hot chocolate to looking under Courtney's hood to see if changing her oil was actually required. Courtney was going to get Trevor bending over the hood of her car? Well, wasn't she just accommodating.

I heard the bell chime as they walked out the front and moved along the walkway to her car. In front of the bagel shop.

They're headed to her car, I texted Ty the moment the sync was complete. *Stay out of sight.*

As I made my way to the front of the store, an older employee sent me a dry, tired smile. "Anything I can help you find?"

"Just price checking," I said, heading for the exit. "Just wanted to make sure my mechanic isn't overcharging me."

He nodded. "Yeah, they'll do that."

"Thanks, though," I said, sneaking a peek out the window to make sure Trevor's back was to me when I exited. It was. He and Courtney were about half way to her car. I walked quickly, covering most of the distance to them before casually leaning up against one of the strip malls supporting posts and pretending to text so I would have an excuse to be out of sight while they popped her hood. I didn't want to walk their way until his head was safely under the hood. It was only moments before I heard the hood latch release and Trevor prop it up.

"Yeah, you're car isn't designed for easy access," Trevor said officiously as I stepped out of concealment. "It's one of the down sides of pretty, new cars. You pretty much need to be a professional to service them."

"You mean I can't learn to service it myself?" Courtney pouted.

"Well, ah, you could. But a girl like you shouldn't be self-serving her car."

How Courtney didn't laugh, I had no idea. All I know is that she did me the favor of leaning over her engine as I passed behind Trevor, thereby bringing *Ta* and *Da* to the party.

Trevor didn't even come close to noticing his slim phone slipping back into his pocket.

"It just gets so expensive, you know?" Courtney pouted to add to the distraction. "Mechanics just assume that because I'm a girl they can tell me I need a new air filter with every oil change or that brake pads need to be changed every ten thousand miles. I never know who to believe."

"Do you go through the dealer?" Trevor asked, his tone protective. That was the last thing I heard before slipping back into the bagel shop. Ty was nowhere in sight.

Where are you? I texted. A few seconds later Ty's head poked out of the bathroom behind me. I waved him out as I walked toward him.

"They can't see us from where she'd parked," I said.

"That was quick," he said as we came together. "Mission accomplished?"

I nodded. "Now we just need her to finish up with Trevor and we're good."

Ty glanced out the window even though we couldn't see Courtney from where we stood. "She was right, you know? This feels way too easy. Are you sure all this is going to lead to catching a killer? I'm not seeing it."

"Good," I teased. "If you don't see it coming then maybe they won't either."

CHAPTER 22

Life was good. I got to kiss my man as he got back into his truck and Courtney got to watch. She took it in stride, though. Especially when I slipped her a gift card to Nordstrom. Then she glowed.

Then Ty went to work, I went to work, and Courtney went shopping.

I checked to make sure the clone job was solid, then gave Kay a call.

"No suspect description yet," she said picking up. "Word is that they're releasing it end of business. No press conference, just a press release."

That was weird. "They probably don't want any rogue questions like the one you tossed out yesterday."

She chuckled. "They're smart, then."

"Yeah? You got something up your sleeve?"

"Not saying until it's a sure thing, just like my mentor taught me."

"Uh-huh. And has anyone told you that your mentor is obnoxious?"

"More times than I can count. Any news on your side?"

"Well, I'm no longer tapped into your phone. I needed to redirect my phone's brain power."

"No point at this stage in the game anyway. You're going to find out things on the same pace as I am."

"What about your little secret investigation? When will I be let in on that?"

"Right now a lot depends on who this suspect is. I don't know what kind of latitude I'm going to have until that card is shown. If it's someone solid, I'll get a choke hold slapped on me. If it's something vague and generic, then I get a bit more leash."

I nodded, even though she couldn't see me. "Well, just so

we're clear, I'm kind of invested in finding this guy, so I'm in for whatever."

"Him?" Kay echoed. "Why do you think it's a man?"

I blinked considering that. "I don't know. I guess the gun." And the scene Melanie had described of the killer carrying the dead weight of Blaine for several feet.

"Hmmm."

I knew that tone. "Hmmm, what? What do you know?"

"Nothing," she said quickly. "Nothing for sure. But one of my contacts said about an hour ago the description to be released may or may not be that of a Latino woman."

"What?" I gasped. "And you didn't lead with that when you picked up?"

"It's a rumor, not a fact."

A woman? Latino? No way. "What in the pool of evidence points to a Latino woman?"

"Eye witnesses, if my guy is telling the truth. He could just be messing with me."

"It *sounds* like he was messing with you."

"Hence my reasoning for not telling you straight out of the gate," she said, sounding a bit irked. "But at least now it will be fun to see if your instincts are wrong on this one."

"A single shot to the heart?" I said. "No way. That's not a woman's style."

"Some might say a shot to the heart is *exactly* a woman's style. If he broke her heart, she might subconsciously aim there."

"Yeah," I countered. "But to actually hit where she was aiming? No novice would do that, even from across the room. Nerves get in the way. Fear makes you hesitate and flinch. Even if an angry woman knew exactly where the heart was located and aimed straight for it, she probably would have hit Blaine in the shoulder and needed to fire again. Women are emotional. After she pulled once, she'd keep pulling. One, clean, precise shot is a man's move."

"As a woman, I resent that assessment," Kay said, even though she sounded like she was considering it.

"Yeah. Well everyone can't be you, babe."

"Very true."

"Whatever," I huffed. "I'll see what I can dig up about this

alleged woman."
"Ditto here. I'll call you if I get anything."
"Perfect."

CHAPTER 23

I spent the afternoon looking through Blaine's phone records. It wasn't that hard. Most of his calls were to businesses or to family in recent months, so as far as phone calls went I could definitively say that he had not been calling any women whose skin was not European white.

It was a bit of an iffy move, but around four o'clock I decided I needed to see Melanie again. I swung by her place, but there was no answer at her door and her phone went straight to voice mail. Could she be at work on a Saturday? I was fairly certain she might be less than comfortable to see me show up at her work, but I needed to ask some follow-up questions.

Finding where she worked was a snap, and twenty minutes later I was parked outside of the car dealership where she spent forty hours of her week. Parking in the front, I moved past the eager salesman and stepped into the main building, scanning the lobby and offices for Melanie and finally locating her at a loan officer desk. She looked tired.

Melanie spotted me a split second after I spotted her, her body stiffening as she stared at me, unblinking. She was totally freaked. I sent her a friendly smile to see if it would break the tension, but it didn't seem to get much of a response. Rather than smile back, Melanie slowly got to her feet and moved to the edge of her cubicle. It was as close as I was going to get to an invitation, so I met her half way.

"Hi," I said when we were a step away from each other. "I know you're working but—"

"There are cameras here," she interrupted, looking at one of the loan officers and giving him a tight nod. It was definitely a signal. "Everywhere."

I blinked, confused. "That's fine."

She frowned at my response. "Why are you here?"

"I have a few questions. I know that police are closing the Amanda Carson investigation, but I'm still not convinced Blaine did it."

"Of course he did," she quipped. "The evidence is overwhelming."

Wait. Was I talking to the same girl?

"But you told me—"

"Never mind what I told you. I was in shock. I was in denial that I could be that close to someone that evil and not sense it. I wanted him to be innocent because that would mean I was a person with good judgment."

That wasn't a conclusion someone came to on their own in a day or two. Someone had put those words in her mouth.

"I don't know," I said. "After talking to you I did some digging. I'm not seeing anything tying him to the killing."

Her eyes got big for a second, and I could have sworn that she was a breath away from slapping me. If so, I was probably saved by the fact that we were at her work place and I was technically a patron.

"What's changed since we last met?" I said, watching how her body knotted at the question.

"What's changed?" she laughed. "What's *changed*? Let's just say that I'm not as naïve as I was the last time we met."

"How so?"

"Well, I know Blaine was a killer, for one thing." Her eyes drilled into me then. "But you know that, too, don't you? This song and dance you're doing? It's all just a show. Admit it."

I studied her. "I would, if it were true."

She shook her head. "You know, it took me a while to believe the part about you, too. Even knowing how bad my judgment had been with Blaine, I looked into your eyes and trusted you. So did my mom."

Realization dawned on me so hard I was forced to take a step back. "Melanie. Who have you been talking to? Who told you what you're saying right now?"

Her face was the model of disgust as she shook her head. "It doesn't matter, does it. Because they were right about everything. Your downfall is your arrogance—your desire to investigate your own crimes. To stay close. To hug those are mourning even as you applaud yourself for being so good."

"No, Melanie," I said, taking another step away. "Who told you that? I need you to tell me who you've been talking to."

Just then my phone rang. Kay. My stomach felt like ice, and somehow I knew exactly why she was calling me.

Melanie's eyes glanced at the door behind me and I followed her gaze to a police car. Lights on. I definitely needed to speak to Kay while I still had a phone.

"Kay—"

"Rhea, it's you!" she all but yelled in my ear. "The sketch they're releasing is straight-up you. No question."

"I know. They found me here at Melanie's work."

"Melanie?"

"The girl with the Jack Russell? The one you interviewed?"

"The witness? What are you doing there?"

"Later," I said, just as two officers pushed through the door, guns drawn. All the hands in the building immediately went up, expect for mine and Melanie's. "I'm about to be taken down, but a hundred bucks says Melanie is one of the people who worked with them on the sketch after someone convinced her I killed Blaine."

"Are you serious?"

"Hands in the air!" the first officer yelled. "Drop the phone! Drop the phone!"

"You have my permission to do anything you want with this story," I said and clicked off the call.

He'd said to drop the phone, but I had worked too hard to get Trevor's information on it to chance damaging it with a drop, so I bent slowly and set the phone on the ground while turning it off.

"Face on the floor!" the officer yelled, as he circled around behind me while his partner stayed in front. "Hands to the side, palms down. Now! Now!"

I did as he said, calmly and without a word even as I fumed. Moments later a knee jammed into the small of my back and my hands were whipped behind my back, one at a time, and cuffed about two clicks past where was comfortable.

I watched Melanie's expression as the officer drilled my Miranda Rights into my ear. It held no regret, but the more I met her gaze the more she faltered.

Someone is lying to you, I mouthed her direction before being escorted out of the bank with an officer on each arm.

CHAPTER 24

I'd had my scrapes with law enforcement before, but being arrested was a first. I hated it. Then again, hate might be too mild a word. I was livid. Not just for the blemish on my record but for the fact that I hadn't actually been doing anything illegal at the time of the arrest. Of all the times in my life when I could have been arrested, it was when I was fully innocent. For some reason that burned.

A detective sat across from me, asking me questions and trying to get a response out of me. That wasn't going to happen, even though I did have one question: Why hadn't I gone to booking yet? I'd been brought to the jail and taken straight to the interrogation room. That's where I'd stayed for the past two hours.

The detective across from me held up the phone I had activated to act as Abby Straightway's in an evidence bag.

"It's really handy how you get a new phone for every client you work with," he said. "One phone, one client. And when you're done? No trace, right?"

I stared at him, at his wedding band. Someone was probably cooking dinner for this guy as we spoke. Maybe he was even late for dinner because of me.

That's what Mrs. Harston got for marrying a cop.

It was a hard life. No questioning that. The guy sitting across from me was dedicated to keeping his community safe. I could see it in his eyes... along with a few other things.

"Ms. Jensen, this will go a whole lot easier for you if you just work with us now. Life in prison isn't so bad compared to your other options."

I didn't flinch, I didn't smile, and I didn't blink. I let him do all those things while I watched. After all, of the two of us, he was the one who was lying, so he was the one with the tells. He'd spent the last twenty minutes explaining how they had enough evidence to convict when the fact was that they didn't even have enough to book me. If they had, they would have done it by then. But they hadn't, which explained why Detective Harston was the third person I had talked to since arriving in the room.

They needed me to talk—to say anything that give them an excuse to book me. It didn't even have to be related to Blaine Adkins. It could have been anything, which also told me they hadn't gotten around to looking in my car. I could certainly be arrested for some of the upgrades in there.

And yet here we were, Detective Harston and me.

Thus far Detective Knight had not shown his face, but I was guessing he was watching on the other side of the mirror. He was the one who started the manhunt for me, so it only made sense that he would be close by.

Detective Harston leaned forward. "We'll find the phone you used with Blaine Adkins. Don't you doubt that for one second. We have the number."

I did smile then. No doubt they did have *a* number, but it wasn't going to trace to a burner phone that had ever been owned by me. Bummer for Detective Harston. He really looked like he could use a win right about then. But still, his presence puzzled me. Why not Knight?

"Why are you here?" I asked, surprising him. It was, after all, the first time he'd heard my voice.

"I think you should be asking yourself that question, Ms. Jensen."

I shook my head. "No, I've worked with several detectives in the SLPD but so far only detectives from the Unified Police Force have been paraded in here. Why not send in someone who has a relationship with me? Someone I trust?"

He blinked then, leaning back.

"Ah," I interpreted. "You tried that, but they won't come in, will they? Or, at least, they won't come in and stay on script. Interesting. Well, that's good to know at least."

His eyes darted to the side before he focused in again. "You're being questioned by Unified Police because we are the ones who took you into custody."

"Got it."

The guy needed to lay off the fast food because his blood

pressure wasn't helping him with his poker face. He was mad at my power play and it turned his face a shade of pink.

"There's one thing you need to get through your head, Ms. Jensen, and that's that the little connections you think you have are not going to get you out of this. Once they all see the facts we have against you, you'll have no favors to call in, and no one in uniform is going to speak in your defense. You've betrayed us all with your actions, and we don't take betrayal well."

I raised an eyebrow. "Oh, there's evidence now? Not just accusations?"

The grin that slid into place was confident, eyes unblinking. "Building up as we speak. We didn't know where to focus at first on the victim's hard drive, but once we plugged your name in it was like winning the lottery."

This time I leaned forward. "Wait, you're saying that you have Blaine Adkins' computer?"

He leaned back, smiling discreetly as he folded his arms across his chest. "Of course we do."

I wasn't sure how to read the body language. Was he lying or had he simply realized he was over-sharing and that's why he was closing off his body language? I probably looked like a freak as I studied him, but I needed the truth.

"You are saying that the PC from Blaine Adkins' living room is in evidence right now? As we speak?"

He must have mistaken my intensity for fear, because his arms uncrossed and he leaned forward to speak directly in his face. "And your name is all over it."

Holy...word-I-couldn't-say-anymore.

According to Melanie, the killer had taken the computer, and now Detective Harston was saying that the police had it and it had evidence against me on it?

"When did you get it?" I asked, letting my voice sound afraid and rubbing my thumb against my other hand in a false self-soothing motion I knew he would pick up on.

"We've always had it," he sneered. "From day one. Bet you didn't consider how leaving that behind would be your fatal mistake."

The killer had. And the killer had taken the computer, only to have it show up in evidence the next day.

If I hadn't been absolutely sure that The Fours were uninvolved, I would have doubted it in that moment. Fabricating a computer history took savvy. I certainly couldn't do it.

This guy had done it overnight. Up until that moment Detective Knight had been the highest on my list of suspects, but this little update stalled me. This was specialized, high-end stuff that had to have been prepared in advance. That meant Blaine's murder was fully premeditated.

But to have my information on there the night of the murder? It was just ridiculous. I was on no one's radar a week ago. There would have been no reason to target me, unless... unless the information had been updated on it throughout the course of the investigation. Detective Harston had said that they had no evidence against me until my name came up as a suspect.

Maybe the information hadn't been on the hard drive a week ago. Maybe it had been added when I popped on radar as a viable scapegoat.

The train of thought again brought me back to Detective Knight. He would have access to the evidence, and he—or someone like him—were the only ones who could have snuck the computer into evidence the next morning after stealing and modifying it the night before.

It was all a bit much to believe of a Salt Lake City cop.

I was debating whether or not to chance one more question when the interrogation room door swung open. The man who crossed the threshold moved with the impatience of a person who had somewhere better to be. He was certainly dressed to be somewhere much classier than a jail. He didn't even look at me or Harston. He looked at his watch. A gold Omega Speedmaster.

"I'd like to speak to my client now."

I'd never seen the man before, and he definitely wasn't my lawyer. I hadn't called one, and I highly doubted Kay had either. Even if she had, I was looking at a man who had just stepped off a plane—probably from somewhere in the east coast. His watch read 9:47. Local time was 7:47. The fact he hadn't updated his watch to local time meant he probably wasn't planning on staying.

He was a Four.

Within moments my heart was pounding so hard I could feel it in my throat. I had to keep it together. I couldn't be like Detective

Harston and show it in my face.

The detective looked at me as if trying to find some good parting words. Before he could open his mouth, however, my "lawyer" snapped his fingers twice.

"Out."

His tone was akin to how most people would address a dog, and Harston's face pinked up again as he registered the complete lack of respect.

I smiled at him. "It's been fun."

"We're not done," he said.

"Yes you are," the lawyer said from behind him, his tone curt and efficient.

Clearly resenting it, Harston stood and exited the room.

My "lawyer" shut the door behind him then walked over to the interrogation table and set his briefcase down with a flick of his wrist. He'd done that move a time or two. Without speaking, he opened his suitcase and took out a gadget I knew too well. With the press of his thumb, the cameras and microphones in the room, and maybe neighboring rooms, ceased to function.

"I'm assuming you handled yourself," he said, offering me a dismissive glance as he identified a folder in his case.

I nodded.

"Good. We can't have any records of you falsely being accused of a crime now, can we?"

"You tell me," I hedged, to which he smiled.

He looked at me then—truly looked at me with eyes that looked like broken hazel glass. "You get arrested when we want you arrested, and you get accused of what we want you accused. Those are the rules for as long as you're one of us—and you still are, whether any of us want it or not."

He didn't blink once the entire time he spoke. It was almost serpentine.

"That said, after your little chat with Elliott the other day, it's been decided that we've been spoiling you." He slapped the folder he pulled out of his briefcase in front of me, but I knew better than to reach for it. "We've given and given and given, and you've responding by taking everything and then complaining about it. That ends now."

He pulled some clipped pages from his case and slapped them

on top of the folder.

"Behold your bank account," he said, then let the print out do the talking.

Forty dollars. That was the balance. Forty. Dollars.

"You've been living the high life out here on all the money we paid you over the years. Even bought yourself a pretty little house with checks you cashed. From us. All your skills, knowledge, and training? All those millions you had stashed? You had none of that before us and it's time to start showing you how life is going to be when we take it all back."

I could have balked. I could have claimed that half a million of that was money from my mom, but he would be ready for that and just up the stakes. No, I had to play the same game with this lawyer that I'd just played with all the detectives. I had to stick with my poker face.

"This extends to those around you," he added. "What has been given shall be taken away, and you, and those close to you, will never see it again. Understood?"

My answer didn't matter, so I didn't make one.

"Funding, favors, and relationships acquired during your employ will be removed. If you want it all back, you know what you need to do. Otherwise, we'll see you on the seventeenth."

The Fours were offering an olive branch? Officially? I hadn't been expecting that.

"Understood," I said, keeping my tone as cold as his.

"Excellent. Someone should come escort you out soon. All charges have been dropped," he said, pulling a set of keys out of his pocket and singling out a car key. *My* car key. "Thanks for the car. It's a beaut."

Then he walked out.

I reached for a place to sit down, only to realize I was sitting.

I had definitely not seen this coming. Everything The Fours believed they had given me was being taken away? That essentially amounted to everything I had acquired in the past eight years. I didn't even know how to process that.

CHAPTER 25

After having all my property returned to me by a clerk, I was released into the lobby where Kay was pacing while Dahl spoke to one of the guards.

Where was Ty? I went from missing him, to being relieved he wasn't there, to worrying *why* he wasn't there within a breath.

What would I tell Ty? What would I tell Kay? The man had mentioned taking back things from the people around me. Had The Fours been involved in Kay's career path at any level without mentioning it? Had they been the reason she'd been hired on back in L.A. or gotten the transfer here within months of me moving to Utah?

The Fours were delusional if they thought Kay needed a leg up from them, but that didn't stop me from feeling like I'd swallowed a lead brick when she spotted me from across the lobby. She nearly plowed me over with a hug while Dahl's approach was much more respectable. I waited until he was close enough to hear me before saying, "I'm going to need a ride home."

"Sure," he said from behind Kay. "Where's your car?"

But we didn't get any further in the conversation before Kay took over. "I officially turned this into a PR disaster for the police department, and Abby's inbox is overflowing. It kills me that tomorrow is Sunday. Why couldn't you get arrested on a weekday when we could take over morning programs and talk shows?"

"I'll try to time it better next time," I said with a wan smile.

Kay glanced at my hand. "What's that folder?"

Uh-uh. No way. "Where's Ty?" I countered.

"Oh, he was here," she said, smiling a bit. "Nearly got himself a holding cell right next to you until some richy-rich lawyer came and told him to go home. And for some reason he listened, but he wants you to head straight home. No detours. Those are our orders."

"Got it," I said, leading them toward the exit.

Dahl waited until we stepped out into the cold of night before voicing his thoughts on everything. "You didn't help yourself in there by not talking, Rhea. It made you look guilty."

I sent a glare his way. "All I did is what the arresting officer advised me to do. Stayed silent."

"Which is not something innocent people usually do," he countered.

"Yes, but most innocent people don't have cops framing them."

"It's not a frame job," he said in a huff. "It's an honest description from witnesses."

"Who were convinced by someone in a position of authority that I was a killer," I snapped back. "Someone told them a story, Dahl. And it was either a really good story, or it was a story told by someone people are trained not to question."

"You don't know that."

"And you don't know that I'm wrong!"

"Can we save the arguments for some place a little warmer?" Kay said, wrapping her arms around herself.

Neither Dahl nor I said anything.

"And by the way," she added. "You'll have to show me how to wire the money you gave me for bail back into your account."

I stopped in my tracks. "Bail money?"

She slowed. "Yeah. The fifty grand? I have no idea how you got it there so fast, but we obviously didn't end up using it."

I hadn't wired her any money. This was not good.

"What?" she said. "I know that look, Rhea. You're freaking me out here. What's going on?"

"That money... did you see that it was from me, or did you assume it was because of the timing?"

She hesitated. "Who else would it be from?"

She had assumed, and suddenly I heard the lawyer's warning echoing through my mind. Kay was one of the people on their list to become a have-not. I would have bet my forty-dollar fortune on it.

"Rhea? You're totally freaking me out."

I waited until we had reached Dahl's car to answer. "The money's not from me, Kay."

"What?"

I looked her in the eye. "I didn't transfer any money into your account."

For a moment we just looked at each other.

"So you're saying that it's just serendipity that within minutes of you getting arrested I get a deposit of fifty thousand in my account?"

I shook my head.

Dahl's alarm was immediate as he faced Kay. "Why didn't you tell me about the money?"

"I didn't think it concerned you," she said, too confused to put any real snark into it.

Dahl and I looked at each other, both thinking the same thing. He was the one who said it, though. "A one-time transfer of that much is going to be flagged by the Feds."

I nodded. "And investigated."

Dahl stepped in close, looking like he wanted to grab my arms and shake me. "Where did the money come from, Rhea?"

"I can't even begin to guess where the funds will be traced to."

"Meaning what?" Kay asked. "Rhea, what are you not saying?"

I cleared my throat, hugging myself against the cold. "It means what it means. You just got an unaccounted for deposit of fifty thousand dollars into your account that will almost certainly be investigated. Has anyone tried to bribe you lately?"

Kay looked from me to Dahl, then back to me. "Ken, would you mind warming up the car while Rhea and I take a little walk?"

He stepped forward, hand reaching for her. "Kate—"

"We need privacy," she said. "Just a few minutes."

Everything in Dahl's eyes said he objected, but after moment of hesitation he got in the car. Kay hooked her arm through mine and led me away, waiting until Dahl's door was shut before she spoke.

"What's going on?" she said when he was shut inside the car and we were a good distance away. "What are you not telling me?"

"I'll answer that, but first I need to ask if you have consciously tried to have a career trajectory that kept you close to me, or if things just unfolded that way."

Her eyebrows furrowed in confusion. "I'm not sure what

you're saying. I worked in L.A. because I lived there and transferred here when a job opened up. Sure, I wouldn't have taken the transfer in a billion years if you weren't here, but the job came up so I took it."

I didn't like the sound of that. "When you transferred here, was there anyone else who interviewed for your job that you heard about? Any other applicants?"

"You mean, did I see anyone else in the waiting room while I was interviewing? No, not really."

"And were there any internal candidates that begrudge that you got the job?"

She paused, not answering, not blinking. "Rhea, I'm officially nervous right now. Will you skip the part where you baby-step me to your conclusion and just jump to the punch line?"

I indicated the jail with a nod of my head. "I had a visit while I was in there. It was from a guy who said that since The Fours gave me everything, they were now taking everything back."

Kay visibly flinched.

"They have my car, and my bank accounts are a wash. The house will go next, and then every other asset I've acquired since I was eighteen. All of it. So what I'm asking you, Kay, is if you think there is any reason at all that The Fours might consider your career as something they gave you. If so, I'm guessing that money was invested in your account to frame you and destroy your career."

The cold meant nothing to either of us as Kay stood there and digested my words.

"I can report the deposit myself," she said at last. "I'll tell management the truth and that I have no idea where it came from—that I thought you gave it to me for bail only to find out it wasn't you."

"But they will investigate. And even if you're cleared, you have to think of the things they'll find that will kill your career with or without bribery charges."

She cursed, her head falling back as she looked helplessly at the sky. "This is for real, isn't it? Just the accusation alone is enough to blacklist me. Facts are no longer necessary in my industry, just an allegation. This is insane, Rhea."

It was. Never in all my imaginings of how things would go

down with The Fours had I pictured this. True, I didn't have any direct proof that The Fours were behind this, but I had worked for Elliott long enough to know that this was right up their alley. They were going to take her down just to show me how easily they could flex their muscles. And if I came crawling back to them afterward, they would get Kay her career back just as easily. That was how they rolled.

For the first time since the whole situation with The Fours started snowballing last Fall, I actually considered giving up. Life hadn't been so hard before. In fact, it had been really good. I'd had a job I loved that I was really good at. In exchange for helping rich people, I got rich. And while I had broken a lot of rules and laws to do it, that fact had never really bothered me on a moral level.

What was I trying to prove by walking away?

"Rhea? What are you thinking?"

I didn't answer right away, but my curiosity of her opinion finally won out. "I'm thinking what's the point of quitting? I didn't leave L.A. because I hated my job. I left to get away from Ben for a bit. It was a vacation that snowballed into this. Why shouldn't I go back?"

"You're kidding, right? We both know you could never respect yourself or your life if you went back now."

"Even if it saves your career?" I asked, feeling frustrated, cold, and useless.

She started to respond then cursed again. "They're narcissists if they think I am where I am because of them."

Neither of us pointed out the fact that narcissism wasn't a label any Four would balk at.

"This affects you, Kay. Your input matters to me on this one."

"I'm thinking," she snapped. She was silent for several seconds then, during which I glanced over at Dahl in the car. He was watching us closely while talking into his phone. I wondered who he was talking to. A moment later, Kay had her phone to her ear as well.

"Hey, Carla," she said when the other side picked up. "Kathryn McCoy here. Just had something odd happen and thought I should fill you in on it. I just checked my bank account and the balance is about fifty thousand dollars higher than it should be... Yeah, I'm sure... No, it wasn't there earlier today and I haven't made any deposits. As far as I can tell it was wired into my account... Oh, I'm sure it's nothing. I'll talk to my bank on Monday. I can only imagine that it's a mistake, but it seemed like something I should tell you, just in case... Yeah, I saw it about an hour ago... I hope so, too... Yes, I'll call them as soon as they open tomorrow to see what they have to say and I'll fill you in... Okay... Okay... I'll see you Monday."

She hung up and sent me a defiant look. "That may not save me, but it will buy me time."

I nodded, still not feeling right about it all. "When investigators tell her about the deposit she'll already know about it and tell them that it's under investigation. That's smart, but once pressure builds Carla will fold, Kay."

"Like a chair, but she'll be on my side for a while at least. We need a little time to figure this out."

She was in denial. I could understand that. Kay had always been a survivor and there was no way she was simply going to accept our situation for what it was. She was screwed—totally screwed—just like I was if I didn't go back.

"Now I'm freezing," she said. "Let's get to the car and get you home."

Car. I'd always taken having a car for granted before. Now I didn't even have money for a cab. What was I supposed to do?

"Sounds good," was all I could say and without another word we walked back to where Dahl waited.

CHAPTER 26

The lights were on in my place when Dahl pulled in my driveway.

My driveway. Not for long.

"Looks like Ty's waiting for you," Kay said from the front passenger seat. "Want us to come in?"

I shook my head. "Thanks, but no. You two get home."

What happened next was strictly for Ty and me, and it represented a first. I was going to go in there and tell him everything. I wasn't going to skirt an issue, I wasn't going to edit content. For the first time in my life I was going to look someone in the eye after a rough day and lay it all out on the table. It was a scary prospect, but Ty deserved nothing less. Not if he really was going to marry me in a week. He only had a week left to press eject on me. After that he would be stuck, for better or worse.

Kay reached back and gripped my hand. "It's all going to turn out right, okay?"

Her calm impressed me, and I took a deep breath in an attempt to follow suit. "Okay."

After thanking Dahl for the ride, I stepped out of the car and walked up to my front porch.

Ty had helped me paint the porch last summer. He'd helped me do pretty much everything else, too. There were a lot of memories in the house, and now that I was about to lose it I could confess that all the memories were the reason I hadn't sold it yet.

It felt like home.

But I couldn't think about that. Not if I wanted to keep my sanity.

Stepping through the front door, I braced myself for the inevitable conversation with Ty. It wouldn't be pretty. How could it be?

When opened the door, I found Ty standing in the living room, waiting. The expression on his face was unreadable.

"Hey." As far as opening lines went it was lame, but it was the best I had and apparently it was enough. Ty crossed the room and wrapped his arms around me.

"You okay?" he asked in my ear.

"A little chafing on the wrists never killed anybody," I joked, earning a tighter squeeze before Ty pulled away.

"So I get back together with you and you decide to test my stamina by immediately getting arrested?"

He wasn't freaking. He wasn't yelling. He was joking. I took that as a good sign.

"You're the one who signed up for this package deal," I reminded him as I stripped off my coat and hung it up. "I told you I'd get arrested. Also, there's a new development. I'm officially destitute. Everything I've acquired in the past eight years is being repossessed by The Fours. How exciting is that? Still think I'm a winner?"

He glanced to the front window, his smile immediately turning upside-down. "Is that why there's no car in the driveway?"

"Yep. And soon there will be no house either. Probably sometime tomorrow, or maybe Monday, I guess, when the banks are open."

He blinked, clearly stunned. "How can they do that? Just take everything that's in your name?"

I shrugged. "I'm about to find out, I guess. But whatever they do, I'm sure it will stick. The messenger I met tonight said that the only way to get it all back is to go back to work for them."

"I see. So they're upping the ante by cutting you off at the knees?"

"Basically," I said, handing him the printout of my bank account. "This is my current statement."

He let out a puff of air as he looked the statement. "Forty bucks? Probably not what you were expecting when you woke up this morning."

For some reason the way he said it got a smile out of me. "Yeah, I was expecting a few more zeroes, for sure."

He gestured to the folder still in my hand. "And that? Or dare I ask?"

I brought it up between us, my hands lightly shaking. "I don't know. I haven't dared to look yet."

"You don't know what's in there?"

I shook my head. "I figured that whatever is in here should be seen by the guy who thinks he wants to marry me, but if I looked at it first I may not have the guts to show him. So…"

"So…" He looked around the room. "What's you least favorite piece of furniture in the house?"

I blinked in confusion. "What?"

He gestured to the folder. "We're about to make a bad memory. Where do you want to remember it? In the kitchen? On the couch? Those Victorian chairs over there? I've always thought those were awkward chairs for awkward moments."

I stepped in and pressed my lips to his. "I love you, man."

He pressed his forehead to mine, looking into my eyes. "Back at you, babe. Now pick a spot."

"Couch," I said. "None of this is going to be mine in a few hours anyway, so might as well be comfortable."

"Sound logic," he said, leading me over and tossing the bank statement on the coffee table as we took a seat.

For a moment I just sat there, letting my hand run over the manila file folder without opening it. My heart was hammering, yes, but I also felt a strange calm. I wasn't alone. Whatever lay inside the folder, Ty was going to have my back. I could feel the support emanating from him.

"Ready when you are," he prompted.

I didn't hesitate then. I grabbed the edge and flip the folder open to see a picture of my dad clipped to a print out. My heart stopped, and my eyes locked on the picture as Ty pushed it to the side to see what was under it.

"What is it?" he asked.

I couldn't breathe. I was still stuck on the fact that my dad was part of the equation. How? What claim could they possibly have—

Then I saw it.

"It's a client list," I said. "The names are blacked out, but it shows services rendered and amount billed." I flipped through the next two pages to where the numbers were tallied to just over sixteen million.

"Wow. Your dad makes that much?"

"A bit more, but this would be about 80% of his annual

income, I would guess."

"And—"

"And these are the clients they're saying he'll lose if I leave." I didn't have to be told that was the case. "He always made good money, but he's certainly made a lot more in recent years."

"So they're basically saying they'll blacklist him if you get out?" He turned to the next page as he spoke, revealing a picture of Ben—the man I'd always thought I would marry until a year ago.

"What?" I said, immediately looking at their print out on him. It was a copy of the recording contract he'd signed along with my friends Isaac, Aaron, and Danny several months back. The next page was his touring schedule. All of it would disappear from under them if I got out.

I didn't comment this time. I just turned to the next page. Kay. Yep, she would lose everything she'd thought she'd earned. My Aunt Kathy, too. The next face was my tenant, Emily. She was going to be one of my bridesmaids in a week. I was about to object that The Fours hadn't done anything to help her until I saw the dates of parties I had brought her to—parties where she had met very important people and made connections that had led to her current employment.

She would lose that if I left The Fours, just like my dad would lose a minimum of 80% of his business, Kay would lose her career, Ben would lose his dream of being a rock star, my aunt would lose her interior decorating clients, and my uncle's business would absolutely disappear in smoke.

And I wasn't even half way through the folder yet.

"This is bad," I finally said, and for once the person I said it to didn't blow me off.

"It's unbelievable," he breathed. "Part of me doesn't want to believe that anyone could have this much power over such a large group of people." He turned the page. "Who's this?"

I took a slow breath. "A pro bono case I did about six years ago while I was still in college." They had the value of assets provided and billable time at just over $8,000.

"Are they saying you owe them, or these people owe them?"

I didn't want to answer that, because saying my suspicions out loud might make my suspicion true.

I laughed at the next picture I saw and Ty looked at me to see if I was snapping.

"Worst roommate ever," I said, tapping the picture of Camille. I didn't look at what they claimed she owed them because of me. It was all just water overflowing the edge of the cup by then.

Ty reached over for the folder. "Can I see this for a second?"

"Please," I said, glad to be rid of it. "Knock yourself out."

He grabbed, quickly leafing through every page until he reached the end. Then he grew still and grinned from ear to ear.

"A smile?" I said. "Are you seeing a silver lining here that I'm not."

His smile grew. "I'm not in here."

For a moment I forgot how to breathe, as our eyes locked on each other. Then I grabbed the folder. "Are you serious?"

He stood, punching both hands above his head as if he'd just won a world title. "I will never apologize for my male pride *ever* again. And I mean *never*!"

I leafed through the files, not seeing him. Then, not believing what I saw, started at the beginning again. "How is that possible?"

"Because from day one I made it a point not to let you do a single thing for me, that's why! Holy cow, I can't believe that these guys are actually acknowledging that. Say what you will, but they are playing by honest rules. I never took a client, a buck, a referral, or anything from you. I paid, always. I gave, always, and I stuffed your attempts to give back because I refused to let anyone accuse me of having a Sugar Mama." He looked at my ceiling, as if not knowing where to aim his voice for the mic in the room. "At least someone noticed."

I had no response. I was still reeling at all the names that were in the folder, but not having Ty in there? That was big. Huge, actually.

Abruptly he sat next to me. "I'll stop celebrating now. It's tacky. I know. But really, I can't tell you how good it feels to be me right now."

"You're allowed," I said, placing the folder on the coffee table. "Heaven knows I'm not going to turn my back on good news."

He took a steadying breath. "Gotta say I didn't see this coming, but I'll take it." He glanced my direction and bumped his shoulder against mine playfully. "And you. I'll still take you, too."

I didn't get it. How was he smiling? I was about to lose

everything. *Everything!* Oh, and then there was that little thing of just having come from jail. Any rational person would take issue with that.

"Ty—"

He silenced me with a kiss, then said, "Yes, you can borrow my truck if you need it. I paid for it myself."

"That wasn't what I was going to say."

"Yeah?" He brushed a lock of hair away from my face. "And what were you going to say?"

I didn't know how to process what was happening. Why wasn't he mad? Why wasn't he freaked out or yelling at me? Why wasn't he seeing what a completely bad investment I was as a life partner. "Ty, this is only the beginning. It's going to get worse—much worse—and I just can't let you—"

"Tut, tut," he said, placing a quieting finger over my lips. "Not this again. Do you think I didn't hear your I'm-born-to-face-the-world-alone speech the other hundred times you gave it?"

Against my will I smiled, then quashed it. "Ty, making light of all this doesn't change the gravity of what I'm—"

"We're," he interrupted.

"Fine, *we're* facing here. This is a whole lot more than I bargained for, and I'm not equipped for it, Ty. I can't pull a rabbit out my hat this time. The situation is what it is. If I'm out, the collateral damage extends far beyond me. If I stay…"

Neither of us finished the sentence and for several moments both of us were silent.

"You know," Ty mused. "As I really think about it, I think everyone in that folder will have your back no matter what you choose. I obviously don't know that for a fact, but that's the vibe I get." He reached out and took my hand. "The blast zone on this might be crazy big, Rhea, but in the end you still need to do what's right for you."

For some reason his words got a tear out of me. And that tear was followed by a breaking dam of its buddies. And unlike most men, Ty had been raised with all sisters and knew exactly what to do when a woman cried. He pulled me against him and let me have at it.

Part of me was embarrassed to sob on him like a baby, but the rest of me was glad to be held while I decompressed. And when I was all cried out, I stayed right where I was.

"You know, breaking up with you is pretty much one of the dumbest ideas I've ever had," I said against his shirt.

He ran a hand across my hair. "Aw, anyone could have told you that, babe."

I gave his stomach a light punch. "Seriously, though. My heart's glad you're here, but I'm still freaking out about it. It's not smart, Ty. The smart thing for you to do would be to get out while you're still in the clear."

"Sure," he said. "If I only cared about me, that would absolutely be the right move." He tilted my chin up to look in my eyes, which were no doubt a mess. "The problem is I don't only care about me. In fact, I care about you a whole lot more, and that means if I can help you in all this, I absolutely will. No questions. No exit strategies."

I shook my head. "Ty, you can't think like that. You can't—"

"Now it's your turn to confess the hard truth. And I know you're not as good at it as I am, so I'll give you a little help. Repeat after me: I need you, Ty."

My chest clenched in panic and I pulled away from him. "Ty, that's not the—"

He made buzzer sound. "Nope. Let's try that again. Say: Ty, I need you."

For a moment it was a battle of wills as we stared each other down.

"Four words, Rhea. Four easy words. How hard is that?

I tried not to roll my eyes, but my resistance clearly sounded in my voice. "Ty, I need you."

"Hmm. Needs work, but we'll move on anyway. Ty, I love you."

That one I could say and mean. I smiled. "Ty, I love you."

He grinned. "Much better. Now last but not least: Ty, I want you."

Rather than saying it, I leaned in and kissed him. Man, I'd missed him—all of him.

"Say it," he whispered against my mouth.

"I thought actions spoke louder than words," I teased, moving back in and not quite making it before he pushed against my shoulders to keep me out of reach.

"But sometimes a person needs to hear that they're wanted. It makes a difference," he said cupping my chin and looking into my eyes with a steely focus. "I want you," he said, then kissed me.

Okay. He won. It totally made a difference.

My heart was pounding in a whole new way. Who knew three words could be so dangerous? And who knew that I could be so easily distracted from the events of the night? Getting arrested, losing everything, having to break it to Kay that she may be out of a career sooner than later and realizing that because of me my dad's business might fold within the year? How had Ty made that disappear for even a moment?

I pulled away from him. "How are you not freaking out right now?"

He smiled, a secret hidden in his eyes that I knew he wasn't going to share. "I find that basing your actions today on what you fear from tomorrow is never really a winning combination, don't you?"

Of course I thought that. I was the queen of thinking that... until recently. When had that changed?

"Ty?"

"Yeah?"

I looked him dead in the eye. "I need you."

A smile slowly split his face.

"And you know what?"

"What?" he asked.

"I'm totally in love with you."

An actual blush crept into his cheeks. "Yeah?"

"Yeah. And there's one more thing."

His eyes dropped to my mouth and I actually felt his heart rate pick up in his chest. "What's that?"

"I've never wanted anyone more than I want you." My plan was to kiss him then, but he beat me to the punch, capturing my mouth with an urgency that made me feel a little bit proud. There was no calculation in his moves, which made them all the more personal.

Ty Kimball was mine. It sounded so territorial to say it that way, but it was what it was. He didn't belong to me in the same way my car had, or any of my money. I'd done absolutely nothing to deserve him. I knew that. Yet he'd chosen me just like I'd chosen him. I would do anything for Ty and it was about time that I accepted the fact that it was a two-way street.

Ty wasn't going anywhere. Kay wasn't going anywhere. I wasn't alone—not by a long shot. And realizing that made me optimistic for the first time in months.

"Marry me next Saturday?" he said, hands tracing my.

The question was asked and answered, but it was nice to hear the question again after everything. "Definitely."

He pushed my hair away from my face, gazing down at me. "Longest six days ever."

"Ditto," I said, pressing my lips against his.

CHAPTER 27

Once I turned my phone back on after my little heart-to-heart with Ty, the reality of what had happened that day sunk in a little deeper. Thirty-seven voice mails, and I didn't want to hear one of them. I was far more interested in who might have called or texted Trevor in the same time frame.

"They're probably mostly from ward members," Ty guessed when he caught me staring at the voice mail count. "You want me to get on that?"

"Please?" I said without hesitation.

He nodded. "Just make a list of who called from the ward and I'll call the bishop. I'll explain what I can to him and he can make sure the word gets passed along to everyone who took the time to call."

He made it sound so easy, which was exactly why I let him do it.

As it turned out, thirty-six of the calls were from ward members, including the bishop, and one was from my dad. I gave the list to Ty and he got on the phone with the bishop while I called up my dad then got right to work.

Blaine had found Amanda Carson's killer. That was my premise. And since his computer had been taken by the killer, I was also going to assume Blaine had found proof. Everything on the computer was almost certainly gone, which left only the dubious testimony of a grieving mother to go off of.

I would start there.

Trevor's text and phone record was of some help. He had tracked my car to the jail then to the airport, where he reported it being loaded onto a plane.

Seriously? Mr. Omega-watch had *flown* my car out of the state?

It was gone. Really gone. And while I knew that all spiritual teachings warned against becoming attached to worldly things, I really loved that car.

"I want the gear-shift handle back," I told the ceiling. "I'll send you the factory original handle, but Ty made me the one that's in the car right now. By your rules, that's mine."

Who knew if it would work, but I had to say it—had to say *something*.

But rather than going off on a rant or heading to my punching bag, I focused all my energy on finding out who Trevor was communicating with. In his phone book he had the two people he had been communicating with for the past few hours listed as *Link* and *Shodan*. The first one might have thrown me in its reference, but the second clinched the first as a video game reference. Link was from Zelda, and Shodan from System Shock.

While Trevor only texted Shodan once to report that the tracker was lost, that was the phone number I was most interested in. It was also a blocked number—not a huge shock for a person who had been named after technical mastermind in a video game.

Link, as it turned out, was one of Trevor's roommates. It made me wonder about the other two. Were they all in the same clan? I did a quick search then decided the other roommates were regular citizens based on the fact that Trevor had them listed under their real names.

That brought me back to Shodan. Was she a female, like the character in the video game? Although, technically the character was a computer program that had just assumed a female identity. She was also, undoubtedly, a bad guy.

Considering that, I did a sweep of my computer. I no longer had my usual assets, but I had picked up a trick or two along the way, and those tricks told me that my computer had not been hacked. No fake information had been planted, nor was anyone streaming my activity, which meant Shodan's nickname might be a little unwarranted. Or maybe he/she was a specialist in one particular field, or just an accountant who only had the all-seeing eye within their own group.

I could spend all night guessing and get nowhere so I focused back on my premise: Blaine had found the killer and found proof. Someone had found out and killed him for it. Add that to the fact that one of the first things that had been done after his death was closing the Amanda Carson case, and I sensed a bit of a trail. And while I may not have had access to Blaine's computer, there were certainly things I could look up online now that I was playing by my own rules again.

It was midnight before I realized that Ty had fallen asleep on the couch. Part of me was tempted to wake him so he could go sleep in his bed, but I knew if he'd wanted to be in his bed, that's where he would be. And it felt good to have him there. I wasn't in the mood to be alone in my house that night.

About one o'clock someone listed as *Yoda* called Trevor.

"Have you found out if she was on that plane yet?" the male voice asked. Older. Forties, maybe, with the tone of someone who was used to giving orders and having them followed.

"It was a chartered plane that was on the ground for ninety minutes. That's all I know," Trevor replied. *"Our usual connections have no insight on this. It's locked down."*

"Sonic drove by her place and says the lights are on. He only saw the boyfriend inside, but Shodan confirms her phone is pinging from there. You can head home for the night."

Trevor hesitated. *"Have you been listening to the news?"*

"Can't say I have," Yoda said, a hint of reprimand in his voice.

"It's playing on the radio over here while I try to track that plane, and they're saying she's innocent—that the police have totally blown it with her arrest."

"And you believe them?"

For a moment the line was silent.

"Altair, it's late. Get home and we'll talk tomorrow."

"Okay," he said, and the line went dead.

I wrote down Yoda's number along with the names of Sonic and Altair. One sci-fi reference and two more video game references. It made me wonder if the differences were generational. Someone Trevor's age might identify with video games more than someone who was born before the age of video games. At the moment that didn't matter, however. What mattered was that my cast list of bad guys was growing and their hierarchy was being revealed.

Yoda and Shodan were administrators while Sonic, Link, and Altair were footmen. None of them were Detective Knight.

Also, they were tracking my phone. Not on a constant basis, or they would have known I was home about five hours earlier, but they had the capacity to track phones when needed.

Good to know.

I kept my phone as it was, letting it ping its little heart out if it gave my watchers a sense of control. And while it pinged away, I reverse looked-up Yoda's number. It was a cell phone, no shock there. Part of me was nervous as I dug deeper. I was running out of accounts I could hack to look up information. Unlike Trevor's crew, The Fours were watching me and they were disabling accounts almost as quickly as I hacked into them. But I snuck through again, this time getting the name Mitchell Davis with a location of West Valley, Utah before the site kicked me out.

West Valley? Not really a place where the affluent lived, but then again Trevor had three roommates. Perhaps their line of work really didn't pay all that well… or at all.

So why do it? If it didn't improve anyone's standard of living, why invest so much time and effort? Why become a freaking ninja?

Maybe it was time to take a look through all of Trevor's text history with anyone who had a name from a video game or sci-fi/fantasy series. Before I did that I text Mitchell's name to Kay. I no longer had access to any of the accounts that would let me do a background check—I'd used my one shot into that software to look-up and get a print out on Blaine. But as a reporter Kay had limited access to similar software. She also had access to Dahl, who could possibly be swayed to use his assets as well. He wouldn't do it for me. I knew that without even asking, but if Kay didn't find anything she liked then she might be able to convince him for more.

In the meantime I honed in on Blaine. He'd had only two credit cards, one with a $3,852 balance and another at a zero balance. I bypassed the password for the first card using security questions until it let me in. From there I could see the email address he had his statements sent to and hack that. Not exactly Fort Knox.

All emails deleted.

I took a moment to process that. The account hadn't been closed by the person who hacked in before me, just emptied. I checked the Sent folder and other subfolders to see if anything had been missed, but the screen looked the same every time. Blank.

It kind of made sense. There was a paper trail leading to this as Blaine's primary email address, so to have it disappear when he died would be suspicious. So was having nothing in the Inbox, but one could argue that Blaine was simply paranoid.

There was a place, however, that most people forgot to scrub when trying to erase evidence: the address book. And sure enough, when I pulled Blaine's up it showed a count of 652 addresses he had either sent or received emails from. I copied all the addresses into a subfolder on my computer, deleted all the ones that ended .gov, and put the rest in the bcc: field in an email message from Abby Straightway.

Subject: *Did This Murder Victim Reach Out to You Before He was Killed?*

You are receiving this email because you recently had contact with Blaine Adkins, a man who was murdered in his home this week. Blaine had been actively investigating last year's murder of Amanda Carson, and some believe he was killed for getting too close to solving that murder.

If Blaine contacted you regarding the murder of Amanda for any reason, please respond with anything he might have shared with you. His killer has deleted all of his emails and all other information related to Blaine's investigation and Blaine has been posthumously convicted of her murder.

Help us put the killer(s) of Amanda Carson and Blaine Adkins behind bars.

I added a few links of recent news reports and pressed send.

It was a shot in the dark. I was just as likely to get hate mail as anything else, but it was worth a shot.

Then I went back and started looking at Blaine's credit card charges.

Blaine Adkins had definitely been researching Amanda's murder. Six weeks ago he'd ordered four criminal background checks for $350 a pop, and charged them to his card, although three days later the business had refunded $350 back onto the card.

Why the refund?

The obvious answer pointed to someone like Detective Knight. As a detective, any background check on him would have been flagged and Blaine would have been told that reporting personal information about an officer of the law was a Class B Misdemeanor. An honest business might have refunded Blaine his payment since they couldn't fulfill his request. Meanwhile, Internal Affairs at the SLPD would be made aware of the attempt, and from that moment on, Detective Tony Knight would have known that Blaine was looking into him.

It made me feel sick to think that one request might have been the thing that cost Blaine Adkins his life, but it was an explanation that made sense.

With nothing else to focus on, I stuck to analyzing where Blaine had been spending his money before he died. I singled out each charge, and identifying the recipients, the looking up the company online.

In addition to the nine background checks, Blaine had purchased two plane tickets on Southwest two weeks apart, paid for DNA tests from companies in three different states, and made several orders from Amazon.

Nothing I was seeing was concrete, but it supported the story Susan Adkins was screaming at the top of her lungs. In the last days of his life, Blaine had in no way been behaving like a man guilty of murder.

I glanced back up to the charges made to the private investigator firm Blaine had ordered the background checks from. They were local, and likely my best lead. I could find the names Blaine had been looking into, I might just have the names of the people who were related to Amanda Carson's murder. They almost certainly wouldn't be at work on a Sunday, but I could hunt the business owner down at home and explain my situation— P.I. to P.I.

It might be the break we needed to blow this open. Especially if Tony Knight's name was on that list.

I was just starting to hunt down the home address of the investigator when my inbox alerted me to a new email. I glanced at the clock on my screen. 3:01. Was it a news outlet in Europe?

I quickly switched over to Abby's email, noted that I didn't recognize the name and clicked on it.

Dear Abby (Never thought I'd type those two words together and mean it),

First off, my deepest condolences. As a true-crime writer I am flooded with emails from people who want me to do an expose on a crime in their area. These numerous stories are typically quite delusional, and I rarely have the time to read even half of them. I wouldn't have read your email either had your subject line not piqued my curiosity.

That said, it did pique my curiosity enough to search my inbox only to find that, yes, this man did email me about six weeks ago. I have included his message to me below and hope it helps with your investigation.

Please know that I will certainly be keeping my eye on this case from here on out. How can I not, knowing that maybe—just maybe—if I had taken the time to respond to an email a man might still be alive? If Blaine Adkins does turn out to be innocent, and if he did die trying to unmask a killer, I guess it is safe to say that I may be taking an extended trip to Utah in the near future. It only seems right.

Regardless, may justice be done,
Ann

Original email from Blaine:
Dear Ann,

Over the years you have chronicled how men have murdered their wives and nearly gotten away with it. What if I told you about a man who murdered his wife who stands to get away with it because a police detective helped him cover his tracks?

It is a murder case that has gone cold and there is only one "person of interest." That person is me. I knew Amanda, the victim, through work. It was there that I learned, quite accidentally, that my biological father raped her nineteen years ago. I didn't want to believe her when she first told me. But the fact is, her son is my half brother. Amanda said she never reported the attack officially, but she was fairly certain that her husband, Nathan, conspired with a local detective to have my father imprisoned for the past eighteen years for crimes my dad says he never committed. Maybe he did, maybe he didn't do what they said he did. I don't know. But I do believe my biological father is where he belongs. In prison.

I don't want to make this too long and have you lose interest, but I would love to tell you my story. And Amanda's story. She's was murdered by her husband—the same one that helped frame my dad. It sounds too weird, right? That the same man frame both me and my dad for crimes we didn't commit? Trust me, I get it. Everyone I talk to thinks I'm nuts. Sometimes I think I'm nuts, but that doesn't change the evidence. Besides, if it worked on my dad, why not do the same thing to me, right?

Point is, I need help. I'm in way over my head here. I'll always feel partly to blame for what happened to Amanda because if we hadn't traded secrets, I wouldn't have asked to meet my half-brother and Amanda would have never talked to her husband about telling Jeremy about his true paternity. I honestly don't know what happened that night between the two of them, but I know it ended in her getting shot.

I've gone as far as I can go alone. Now I need help. From you.

If you would do me the honor of writing me back it would be greatly appreciated. I will answer any questions you have and share the evidence I have gathered.

Talk to you soon!

Blaine

Holy. Crap. The sincerity in the email actually had me tearing up a bit. There was nothing wrong with Melanie Cunningham's guy-dar. Blaine Adkins had been a good man.

I read the email a second, then a third time just to make sure I was really seeing what I was seeing. It was a little mind-blowing to think that Blaine Adkins figured out as much as he had and not gotten a single person to listen to him. Given the suspicion around him, perhaps he was waiting until he had a slam-dunk case, but just what I'd seen so far was enough to blow the case open. True, he submitted no proof that what he was saying in the emails was true, but his words *felt* true to me. And I could see the charges to back up the claims that he'd done what he'd said he'd done.

So where was the proof?

I eyed the charges for the DNA tests again. The airline tickets that were definitely in line with round trip fare to Vegas from Salt Lake. Had Blaine taken those trips to get DNA sample from Jeremy, willingly or unwillingly?

Where were the results?

There were a billion questions that needed to be answered, but few of them could be answered at 3:30 in the morning, so I moved on to the next best thing I could do: Arm the media via a press release from Abby Straightway. Gloves off, no punches pulled. I was going to make life hard for Detective Tony Knight and anyone who had his back. That would be my payback for being arrested.

An hour later, I had my own version of a loaded gun.

Salt Lake Police Protect Their Own By Making False Arrest

Twenty-four hours ago, Utahns were relieved when Salt Lake Police announced their suspect in the recent murder of Blaine Adkins. Today citizens learn that this prime suspect is none other than a private investigator hired to look into the murder by a local news station.

Even more surprising? The lead investigator in the case, Detective Tony Knight, knew exactly who the investigator was and what she'd been hired to do when he issued the warrant for her arrest.

"I find this turn of events baffling," says local reporter, Kathryn McCoy. "I provided Detective Knight with the investigator's resume and contact information several days ago. She's worked with Salt Lake Police before, and always with success. To have Detective Knight respond by naming her his number one suspect is beyond me."

Motive for discrediting the investigator becomes more clear, however, when one learns what the investigator stands ready to reveal about Lead Detective Tony Knight.

- *Blaine Adkins has been posthumously convicted of killing Amanda Carson, wife of Detective Knight's best friend, Nathan Carson.*
- *The alibi used to clear Nathan Carson in the murder of his wife last December was a pre-scheduled flight itinerary, not the actual flight stub from the bumped-up flight he had actually taken three hours prior to his scheduled time.*
- *Blaine Adkins had three (3) DNA tests performed to prove that he and Amanda's son, Jeremy, share paternity—a claim police have disavowed in formal statements despite documented credit card charges and delivery of the tests to Blaine prior to his murder.*
- *Shortly before being murdered, Blaine claimed that Amanda shared the fact that Blaine and her son, Jeremy,*

shared paternity.

All this evidence is compounded by an additional fact:

- *The witness who discovered Blaine Adkins body the morning after his murder reported that Blaine's computer had been missing when she entered his apartment. Police claim, however, that the computer was present at the scene and taken into evidence.*

These facts, and more, have been uncovered by the "suspect" arrested by police Saturday evening, which forces the question of what previously undisclosed evidence the SLPD claims to have against their prime suspect, and if it could possibly be any more damning that what she has uncovered about one of their star detectives.

Kay would want to proof something like this before I pressed send. Unfortunately for her, I'd just been accused of murder that day and wasn't in the mood to take orders. I might regret sending it in the morning after I'd had a little sleep, but oh well. Live and learn. Given my day, I was feeling a little reckless. Besides, Kay would be too giddy fielding calls from New York and getting on a first-name basis with producers to have time to yell at me for pushing the envelope past her.

I finished up the press release by making Kay the only contact source, added her email address in the bcc: field and let the baby rip. I forwarded her the email from Ann as well, then sent Kay one more email including the names of the DNA testing facilities and the dates of Blaine's flights. She would need to have all that in her arsenal before she could be appropriately vague with her colleagues and confident in the face of pushback.

Check your inbox before you answer any calls, I texted, then went to my room and slept like a baby.

CHAPTER 28

An hour after I passed out on my bed my phone rang. Persistently. Seeing Kay's name, I picked up, not sure what I was going to get an earful of.

"It's Christmas!" she cheered. "Although I had to take a break between calls to check to see if you had an identity crisis overnight. You wrote that press release? *You?*"

"Guilty," I said, my voice scratchy.

"The queen of holding everything close to her chest being so wanton with information? I don't whether to clap or be scared."

"I'll accept both," I said, closing my eyes again. "It's early, even on the east coast. Who's biting?"

"Who *isn't*? And keep in mind that you sent your release to outlets like the Daily Mail and the Telegraph. It's noon there right now."

"Gotcha."

"AP's running with it. I just got off the phone with their reporter. Broadcast news is being a little more hesitant until we have a visual to hand them, although I'm fairly certain MSNBC and CNN will run with doing the story in front of one of the DNA testing locations. They all want facts, though. They want a smoking gun."

"So do I."

"But we have their full attention. Right now it's on their list as a developing story, but they love the crooked cop angle—which is why I'm sure you led with it."

"Yeah. I'm going to have a lot of cops really mad at me, though." Maybe even Dahl included. Hadn't thought of that. "They're going to think I'm collectively throwing them under the bus."

"They'll band together, that's for sure. But they'll also level some hard questions at Knight. One of the reporters already woke up an SLPD PR person and got a 'No comment' out of him."

"Poor guy," I muttered.

"Wrong place, wrong job," she said without sympathy. "The reporter forwarded the press release to him, which is something Abby needs to remember to do the next time around, and the PR guy hasn't answered his phone or an email since."

It was probably wrong for me to laugh at that, but I did. "I feel like a bad person somehow."

"Yeah? Well, I'm betting that Blaine Adkins and Amanda Carson are cheering on the other side, if that helps you get back to sleep."

"We'll see."

"My other line is beeping in with a 212 area code. Gotta go." Then she was gone.

And whether Kay's words did anything to soothe my conscience or not, I would never know. All I knew was that I went back to sleep within the next breath.

CHAPTER 29

I clocked another two hours of sleep before my internal clock and a series of anxiety dreams forced me out of bed again. My body sagged as I got up, even as my mind raced. Not a good combo, but I was going to have to make it work. The day was going to be a crazy, full day.

I found Ty right where I'd left him on the couch, only this time he was sitting up and the TV was on. He saw me emerge and gestured to the TV.

"What in the world happened while I was sleeping?"

I sent him a sleepy smile. "You tell me."

"Well, if anyone missed the news of your arrest last night, they will certainly hear your version of events this morning. Falsely arrested for being on the cusp of exposing a homicide detective who is guilty of homicide? How did this happen overnight?"

I wiggled my fingers in the air. "Magic?"

He shook his head, looking slightly shell shocked. "I really haven't seen you in action, have I?"

I shrugged, nervous at how he might be reacting until he added, "Remind me not to ever divorce you. Like, ever. I can only imagine what the payback might be then."

"Yes, remember this day," I said in a wise tone before heading to the kitchen. It was Sunday. No workout, and for once I was glad for it. Yesterday had drained me.

"You're going to be fielding some crazy questions today at church," he called out from the couch.

Seriously? Church? Now? Wasn't there some rule that said if you were falsely arrested for a crime and had all your worldly possessions yanked from you that you were excused for the week? I really didn't want to talk to anyone. Not even a little.

"Can't I play hookie just this once?" I asked, moving back to where we could see each other.

"Once turns to twice," he teased. "Then twice to thrice, and so on."

I hesitated, wondering if that would be such a bad thing. I'd just been accused of murder, for crying out loud. Falsely accused, but still, Mormons weren't used to sitting on a pew with people who had been accused at all.

"I'll just wonk up the vibe if I go," I said. "People can't feel the Spirit if they're wondering if the girl sitting two rows up is a hired assassin."

He shook his head. "No way they're thinking that if they're watching any of this."

"But a lot of Mormons don't turn on their TVs on Sundays. They're playing CDs of hymns right now, not tuning into the news."

I had a point and he knew it. "Fine. Obviously I won't force you," he said. "I'll just think you're a chicken."

If I'd had anything in my hands just then, I would have thrown it at him. I might have clocked him with a snarky retort instead, but then my doorbell rang. Both Ty and I froze.

"I assume you're not expecting anyone," he said.

I shook my head, walking toward the front window and pulling back on the curtains to make a crack large enough to see a news van. Of course. I should have expected them to hunt me down. The fact that I hadn't considered that only spoke to my state of mind the night before.

"Reporters?" Ty asked, coming up behind me.

I nodded. "Let me get ready and we'll see how sly the two of us can be at sneaking out the back and over to your place. Just stay away from windows in the meantime and I'll text Kay to have her tell them that I'm holed up in a hotel somewhere for my safety."

"Sounds like a plan," he said, and we both backed away from the window.

As we passed the TV again, I discreetly tried to turn it off when I noticed Kay on the screen with the Carson house in the background, and the CNN logo in the corner. Good to know someone was having a good morning.

"We just received word from local authorities," the anchor was saying, *"that Detective Knight has been placed on paid administrative leave, pending an investigation into the allegations*

against him. Any thoughts on this, Kathryn?"

"Well, it's exactly what they should do," Kay said into her mic as frost puffed out of her mouth. *"The SLPD is in the position of discovering that one of their best and brightest is actually a bad apple. A full investigation is required. The next obvious step is to re-open the Carson case. Because although the files are closed to the media at present, I'm betting that part of Nathan Carson's alibi for not killing his wife can be traced right back to Detective Knight, as well."*

"No word yet on—"

Ty turned the TV off for me. "We need to move before they find a way to peek in."

"Of course," I said, and headed back to my room with Ty close behind.

CHAPTER 30

We were Back Row Joes at church, but it was clear there were a number of people who were scouting to see if I would show my face. Ty was tense, too, and half way through the meeting I sent him a look. As in, *a* look.

"Let's get out of here."

He shook his head. "The bishop wants to talk to you after sacrament meeting. Then we can go."

People gave talks, but I didn't hear a word of it. All I could think about was Nathan Carson and how I knew absolutely nothing about him. I hadn't even met him face-to-face. And where was Jeremy in all this? He hadn't been to his classes in the past few days and he wasn't answering his phone, but I didn't know anything more than that.

I should know *way* more than that, just like I should have known what the speaker was talking about at the pulpit. There were a whole list of *shoulds* in my life that were currently left without checks next to them. The result was a hammering heart, a racing mind, and a sense of dizziness that could only be cured by getting to work.

Sabbath or not, I needed to get back to work.

I took a short, shallow breath and eyed the exit. I didn't need to talk to the bishop. I needed to get moving.

"Deep breath," Ty whispered into my ear.

"Won't help," I muttered back. "We should go. I'm distracted and I'm distracting everyone. It's lose-lose."

By the look on his face I could tell he didn't have a response.

"Why are you pushing this so hard, Ty?" I said, gathering my coat. "This isn't a time for me to take a break. I have national media and some very unhappy cops looking for me."

His hand gripped mine. "None of which are going to come into a church."

I studied him, realizing he was being protective of me.

"You don't have any resources, which means you're relying on Kay for information," he added. "She can text it to you here as easily as anywhere else."

His words were true, but they didn't help. "I can't just sit, Ty. I can't pretend I'm here to become a better person. Right now I just need to be me."

He let me exit the chapel, but did so one step behind me. Once we were in the lobby, he took my hand and led me over to the bishop's office, which was unlocked.

"I was stupid to try to play it past you," he said, shutting the door behind us and turning on the light. "But Dahl texted me this morning and said you need to stay off radar."

Of course he had. Dahl played things on the safe side. "Why didn't he text me?"

"Because you're stubborn," Ty said. "And I know that you and Dahl are like yin and yang when it comes to your working process, but I think he has a point this time. I think it's good if you're off radar."

I shook my head. "No, the safe place is the most uncomfortable place, Ty. Hiding in a church is natural. It's normal. It's what a coward does and it opens the door for someone less cowardly to change the game. They're not going to harass me again today."

"No," he agreed. "But they can do other things."

I leveled my eyes at Ty. "Right now there are two killers who, up until yesterday, thought they were going to get away with murder! And right now they are scrambling, Ty. They're twisting stories, calling in favors—doing *anything* they can to salvage the situation. And I'm hiding in a church."

"Safe," he added.

"Fine, safe, but does anyone know where Nathan Carson is? Jeremy Carson? Or even Tony Knight? He's on paid administrative leave, but are they tailing him? Is it just a PR thing, or is his department really considering him as a suspect? These are things I need to know, Ty. These are things I need to oversee. I need to know that Knight and Carson aren't squeezing out of everything somehow."

"I think Kay has your back there," he said. "I would not want to be either of those guys right now. That woman can spin a tale."

"Yes, she can," I agreed.

Then we just stood there for a moment.

"Let's look at the facts," Ty said diplomatically. "You don't have a car, you don't have any connections, and you don't have any legitimate reason for approaching these men. If you do, they can paint you as the bad guy and shift the focus back your direction."

"Agreed. But, Ty, I can't sit here. I can't hide. I can't pretend it's a normal Sunday."

"Yeah," he took a breath, looking lost for a moment. Then he straightened, clearly changing approaches. "So, you tell me. What's the next step here? What will you do if you leave here? You can't go home."

Man, he was right. I had nowhere to go and no way to get there.

But I couldn't stay.

"You have this crazy look in your eye right now," he said, bringing his hand up to my face. "Kind of frantic. Scattered. Like someone who's hopped up on something and thinks she needs to organize a drawer by alphabetizing everything inside it."

The description got a grin out of me for some reason. Then again, getting me to smile was kind of Ty's superpower. "Yeah? And you know what that looks like, how?"

"Diverse associates," he said. "But point being, you're running on like three hours of sleep, and I don't know how many hours you got the night before that. But knowing you, not that many."

His thumb stroked against my cheek, reducing my response to an elegant, "Yeah."

"And maybe not too many hours on any of the nights before that. So, how about this? How about we take this day of rest quite literally and let you take a nap?"

I opened my mouth to object and he countered by placing his hand over my lips.

"No, hear me out. Because the way I see it, it follows your rules. It's counter-intuitive, right? Who rattles the hornet's nest and then lays down and takes a nap while it's raging."

"Uh, no one," I said. Sleep? There was no way I could sleep at time like this. Sleeping was for *after* the case was done.

"And are you afraid to sleep? Does the thought of it make you panic?"

"Of course," I said. "Because everything is happening today!"

"And what if you just let it happen? What if all the time Tony Knight is walking around flexing his muscle and calling you out to war, you just go to sleep so you're not totally exhausted when you meet him on the battle field?"

"Ty—"

"It's the day of rest, Rhea," he said gently. "All I'm asking is what would happen if you actually rested? What if you didn't go out there and square off against Knight today? What if you saved it for tomorrow and followed your faith today?"

Oh, that was low. Making my decision a matter of faith rather than logic?

"You're exhausted, Rhea," he said gently. "I know that because I know you. And while I have every intent of supporting you as you finish this, I think it's important that one of us acknowledges that you don't run on willpower alone. Sometimes we all need to sleep and eat. It's how we're built. And I can pretty much guarantee you that no one in this building has worked harder and slept less than you this past week."

He was back to stroking my cheek again, and I realized too late that it was a tactic. My blinks were literally happening more slowly. With his simple, gentle touch I was beginning to doze off on my feet, while still trying to argue with him.

"It'll all still be here when you wake up, Rhea. Trust Kay on that. Trust her to stir the nest while you clock out for a few hours. You got things rolling while she slept last night. Now you get to switch shifts. She gets to stir the pot while you take a break."

"Where would I go?" I asked before realizing that the simple question also doubled as consent.

"Kay's?" he suggested. "You have a key and nobody will be looking there. She's still in Pleasant Grove."

"Someone might break in," I said, fighting a yawn. How had Ty done it? How had he gotten me to feel so tired, so fast? Sure, I'd been tired all along, but I'd been handling it.

"Then we'll be there to protect her place," he said, drawing me in to rest against his chest. I didn't fight it. "I'll stay there and keep updated, then I can fill you in when you wake up. We'll tag team it."

Was he pulling a *Tag, you're it?* That was my and Kay's thing. Was it time to make room for someone new in that little club?

"Trust me on this, Rhea," he said, wrapping his arms around me. "Trust that I know you, and that I've made it a hobby to know what you need."

I didn't argue, but I didn't say I trusted him either.

"How many times have I asked you to take a nap?" he said.

Never. Or at least not that I could remember. So either this was the first time he was asking me, or I was too tired to remember the last time. Either way, I got his point.

"Okay," I said against his chest. "But if this blows up while I'm taking a nap, you still have to marry me."

"Copy that," he said. "Now let's get you to Kay's."

CHAPTER 31

When I woke up, it was dark. I blinked my eyes, not believing what I saw the first couple of times. Then I panicked. Had I done one of those power sleeps where I missed a full twenty-four hours when I blacked out?

No, Ty wouldn't have let me sleep that long. Heck, Kay wouldn't have let me sleep that long—especially not in her bed.

So why was it dark? Was the time a.m. or p.m.?

My brain wasn't fully back into the waking world and I bobbled a few of the turns on the way to the living room where Ty sat with the TV on. He had his phone pressed to his ear.

"She's just emerging right now," he was saying. "You want to talk to her?"

I glanced at the clock. 6:55 p.m. I'd been asleep for nearly nine hours. Apparently Ty had been right. I'd been a little tired. I still was, if my current state of dizziness was any indicator. But no way I was going back to sleep. It was time to re-engage.

"Here she is," Ty said, handing me the phone.

"Glad you could join us," Kay said when I pressed the phone to my ear. "Have Ty fill you in, and be ready in forty minutes. Nick and I are coming to pick you up for our after-hours adventure. Your presence is required if we're going to get anything out of it. Bring a few of your toys."

"Sounds good. Pick me up at my place." I said, and we hung up. I looked at Ty expectantly, and he gestured to Kay's coffee table.

"I wrote everything down as the day went, so I wouldn't forget anything. I wrote Trevor's texts, just in case he deleted them, and took a few notes on his calls. There's a separate page for updates from Kay, and then another page for news updates, which aren't very many even though the story basically ran all day on several channels."

I walked over to the pages, looking over them in disbelief.

He'd done it. He'd gotten me to take a nap in the middle of a crisis and not regret it… yet.

The man was my own personal miracle.

"I love you," I blurted.

"You'd better," he said, coming up behind me and putting his hands on my shoulders. "Now what's next?"

CHAPTER 32

We took Ty's truck back to his place and found the street dark. No news vans, no new cars. I was small potatoes now, thanks to Kay's overtime.

"Guess we don't have to sneak through LeAnna's yard this time," Ty said, parking in his driveway.

I would have quipped back, but I was too busy looking at my dark porch. "I guess it's time to go see if my keys still work."

Ty's hand slid over mine. "It's going to be okay."

I took a slow breath and squeezed his hand. "Yeah. It will be."

Then we got out without another word and walked to my place. We kept the lights off, just in case someone was watching for movement, and I quickly changed into dark clothes, slip-resistant boots, and coat that could keep me warm if I had to sit around for a while.

With five minutes left until Kay's ETA, I headed out to the back shed.

"It's been a while since you came in here," Ty said, as I turned on the light.

"Yeah." I looked around, taking stock of my little war room. I would likely never see it again. Guns I'd never chosen to fire, gadgets used once, and others that were constant companions.

Tonight I was going for a bit of the tried and the true.

Accessory number one, my wrist band. Nine out of ten outings it came in handy, and the two of us had a lot of history. From now on, it was staying on my wrist until The Fours physically took it off of me.

I went to put on some gloves that would both keep my hands warm plus keep me from leaving prints, before realizing they wouldn't fit over the giant rock on my finger. Ty's engagement ring. One of those few things I actually got to keep through all this.

I sent him a look. "I know I just put it back on, but are you going to freak out if I take your ring off for this?"

He shook his head and held out his hand. "I'll hold it for you."

"Thanks," I said, sliding it off and handing it over to him. It really was gorgeous. He'd picked without me, and he'd picked well.

I slid the gloves on while Ty looked around and moved toward my trackers. "I forgot how much stuff you have in here."

"Me, too. And don't touch," I said when he reached out for a bulletproof vest. "Everything in here is wiped down. No prints." I wiggled my gloved fingers. "I only touch them after I'm wearing these."

He sent a one-sided grin my way. "That's my paranoid girl." He glanced at the gun wall. "You taking any of those?"

I shook my head. "Never have, never will."

"And yet you have them."

There was a question in there, but it wasn't the right time to answer it. Instead I said, "I think it's important to understand the weight and power of each. Besides, I have a lot of things in here that I never use."

His eyes went back to the vest. "Ever used one of these?"

I grabbed a few wi-fi cams and stuck them in my pocket. "Not for years, thank goodness."

His eyebrows shot up. "What did you have to wear them for?"

Yet another question to answer some other time. "For my training, mostly. It had its militant moments."

"But you never wore one while actually working?"

I shook my head. "No need." It was hard to know what to bring since I didn't know where we were going and what Kay was planning to pull off. But going in this blind, there was really only one acceptable option: surveillance. So I stuck to that and grabbed a pack.

Night vision binoculars, rope, carabiners, a pick pad, and a camera embedded into a cap that could capture things as I went along. Things like that were rarely useful, but sometimes it caught something on tape that you didn't see at the time. And with the news van technology we could go with a live feed, if we needed to.

"You should wear it tonight," Ty said from my right.

I glanced up from my pack. "Wear what?"

He indicated the vest again. "I don't know what's up, but

something just feels off to me. Ever since Kay called, I kind of feel sick—like you going isn't the best idea ever."

Not this again. "Ty—"

"I know, I know. I said I would let you go if you took a nap, but I'm telling you, something is off. Don't you feel it?"

I paused, trying to tune in to any sense of nervousness, but the only thing that came to mind were the tactical weaknesses of following Kay's lead without knowing her plan. But that was just ego. I had to have faith in other people sometimes, not always just in myself.

"I have concerns, but I don't feel weird," I said.

Ty didn't move for a moment, and when he let out an exhale it came out in a frozen puff. "Wear it? For me?"

Holy cow. Those eyes. If our kids could whip out looks like Ty, then I was in trouble.

"I don't need it, Ty. Everything is going to be fine." And in the mean time the clock was ticking. Kay and Nick would be arriving any second. I needed to concentrate.

He shook his head. "All I see when I close my eyes are these guys looking at you down a barrel of a gun and the cold look in their eyes as they pull the trigger. Because, if you're right, these guys have killed before—maybe twice. And call me superstitious, but things do come in threes." His hands rested on my shoulders. "I don't want you to be number three."

It wasn't as if the possibility hadn't occurred to me, but I had my own way of dealing with things. "Ty, I get what you're saying, I do. But I'm kind of superstitious when it comes to gearing up for battle. Every time I've done it, things have gone wrong. People are less likely to shoot if you're unarmed, and I make fewer mistakes when I'm unprotected."

"Yeah? Well, facing off against these guys unarmed didn't work too well for Amanda or Blaine. No one hesitated when shooting them."

He had a point. I glanced at my watch, noting that Kay and Nick were already a little late. "If I wear it, you'll feel better and you won't worry?"

"Definitely," he said without hesitation.

"And you'll let me go without any complaint?"

He thought for a moment and nodded. "This guy aims for the

heart, not the head, so yeah, if you wear a vest I'll keep my mouth shut about wanting you to pack a gun as well."

"Done," I said, unzipping my coat and grabbing the vest from the hooks on the wall. It was custom and less bulky than most brands on the market, which meant no one would see it under my coat.

"Thank you."

I sent him a smile over my shoulder. "Compromises, right?"

"Something like that," he said, watching me tighten the Velcro. "The way I see it, it's just common sense. I may be confident on a high bar, but I still have a mat beneath me when I do a routine, just in case I miss the bar. That mat pays for itself the first time I hit it instead of a cement floor."

I nodded. "Yes, but people also take different risks when they know they're protected than they do when they don't."

Patiently, Ty held out my coat for me to slide into. "All the same. My mom and sister died in a car accident where a set of guard rails on the road and possibly even air bags in the car could have saved them." He looked at me, eyes unblinking. "I'm done losing people for negligent reasons. And that means if my fiancée insists on facing off against bad guys who like to shoot people, she's going to at least go in wearing a vest that could save her life. Not just today, but any day. Got it?"

Well, when he put it like that. "Yes, dear," I said, turning and going up on my toes to kiss him.

"You'll thank me for it one day. Maybe not today, but someday," Ty said, turning me back to face him, and slowly zipping me up. Not going to lie, it was pretty hot. If I got treatment like this every time I wore a bulletproof vest, I might just have to wear one more often.

I kissed him again, this time taking a little more time with it. "I've missed you, you know that? I'm kind of a mess without you."

"And I watch entirely too much reality TV when I'm not with you," he countered.

I faked a grimace. "That doesn't sound pretty."

"Trust me, it's not. Add a lot of comfort eating to chain TV watching, and eventually one loses the desire to even take a shower. It's a pretty dark place." He patted the shoulders of the vest through my coat.

"Well, I'll try to make sure you take a lot of showers in the future, okay?"

He gave me a slow, sexy grin just as my phone rang.

"It's Kay" I said before giving him a quick peck. "Meet you back at her place?"

"Meet you at her place," he echoed. "I'll lock up."

"Thanks," I said, then brought my phone up to my ear. "I'm on my way to the front. Turn your phone off as soon as you hang up with me. They can track phones."

"That's a pain," Kay said. "We're idling on the curb."

"Great," I said, and slung my pack over my shoulder before pulling up Trevor's phone on my screen one last time. His phone had been offline ever since I'd woken up, and I wanted to know where he was. Ty said he had been home when his phone went offline, which meant Trevor had known exactly where he was going when he left and was being very careful about it.

Wherever he was, I hoped his phone popped back online before I turned my phone back on. It would make me feel much more in control, even if I wasn't. I was powering down my phone just as I slid into the backseat.

"Evening, overachievers," I said, shutting the door behind me. The SUV was way toasty. "I see you've been dominating the national media outlets today."

Kay nodded. "With more to come. Knight is rallying his troops. We know where, and we obviously know why. We just don't know who. That's why we need you."

"How do you know where they are?" I asked.

"Tip," she said, as if it was the most normal thing in the world.

I grew still. "A tip? Someone *tipped* you off as to where Detective Knight would be tonight."

"Don't worry. It's a good source."

If Ty would have asked me if I had a sense of foreboding in that moment, I would have definitely said yes. "Kay—"

"It was Jeremy, all right?" she interrupted. "Amanda's son. He hates the guy. He wants him to go down, so he told me where they were meeting tonight. It's a mechanic shop out in South Salt Lake. In Murray, I think. It actually belongs to that Mitchell Davis guy you told me to look up, so it's solid. And if it's not, then we waste an hour. No biggie."

"Or we walk right into a trap," I countered. She had met Jeremy? And I hadn't. How was I supposed to know what steps to take next when I hadn't even met the players and gotten a read on them. Everything felt wrong.

Kay shook her head. "You didn't look into this kid's eyes, Rhea. He wasn't lying."

Exactly. I *hadn't* looked into the kid's eyes, so I had no idea if he had been lying. I looked over at Nick. "What do you think?"

He hesitated, then nodded. "We'll find them there. I'd bet on it."

I watched the way his hands gripped the steering wheel, flexing then releasing lightly. There was something else on his mind. "And what else would you bet on?"

He glanced at me in the rearview mirror. "What do you mean?"

"She means, where do you disagree with me," Kay said.

Nick's lips pressed together and he looked back at the road. "Not sure what you mean by that."

"I mean, why are you nervous?" I said.

His hand milked the steering wheel again. "Meeting up when they know they're being watched is a huge risk. It's not smart, and these guys are smart."

I had to say that I was on Nick's side with this one—especially with how excited Kay seemed. Emotions during an investigation were never good. They led to impulsiveness, and when you were impulsive you frequently forgot to cover your blind side.

"So you think this could be a trap," I said, and he nodded.

Kay let out a huff. "It's not a trap."

"But it's a possibility."

Nick's hand relaxed on the wheel. "It's a possibility."

"And knowing that, what's the game plan?" I asked.

"We're getting there way after them," Kay said as we pulled onto the onramp to the freeway. "That means no tailing, which means they're not going to see us coming. We even switched rides back at the station in case the other truck was being tracked for some reason."

Smart of her. "Okay. So what's the plan when we get there?"

"We'll take video them as they come out and see who is in

their crew."

"With the three of us sitting in a news van?"

"We'll be out of sight," Kay said. "We go by, grab some plate numbers, and place some cameras where we can get a shot of some faces, and we wait until they all leave before we clean up and go. That easy."

Easy to say? Yes. Easy to do? That remained to be seen.

"There's no reason for them to believe that Jeremy ratted out their location. They've been extremely covert and seem very confident in themselves, so the chances of this being a trap are next to none. Certainly the mechanic wouldn't volunteer his business as the stage for something that could permanently ruin his reputation.

Okay, that I could agree with. "So we're there to find out who's on Team Knight while staying out of sight?"

"Yep."

This should be interesting. "All right. Let's do it then."

CHAPTER 33

We'd split up. Nick was on one side of Main Street, walking it from the south, Kay was on the other side, walking it from the north. I had West Temple. We each had one goal: make note of every license plate and make/model of car. That was the plan for now, but I had no doubt that Kay would come up with a follow-up plan somewhere on her little walk. Something hasty. I knew how her brain worked. She was going to want a money shot out of all this—something she could parade around the next day.

As it was, it looked like she was going to be disappointed. If Main Street was anything like West Temple, then she was looking at a ghost town. There were no cars, not even parked behind the barbed wire fences, unless you counted industrial trucks. The entire area looked abandoned. The next step would be to scout places to put cameras so we had eyes on the shop.

At least if I had been in charge. But I had slept all day, so I was decidedly not in charge. It said a lot about my personality, I guess, that I would have preferred being exhausted and in charge over being fully rested and following a leader who made emotional decisions.

"Where are the cars?" Kay huffed when I reached the rendezvous point between State and Main. Kay and Nick were already there.

"Maybe some of them park on State Street," Nick offered. "It's a lot less conspicuous and easier to blend in. It's what we did."

Nick's idea was logical, but it also presented a logistical challenge. There were way too many cars on State for us to take an inventory.

"Is there more than one entrance? Could they be coming in the other direction in a way that's totally off radar?" Kay asked.

"That would be some pretty intense organization on their part," Nick said, skepticism heavy.

I sent Nick an assessing look. He'd changed over his past few months with Kay—grown into his shoes a little bit. A few months back he would have kowtowed to anything Kay said. Now he was pushing back at strategic times—strategic meaning when she was almost certainly wrong. I liked it, even if it had Kay frowning.

For the moment, I tried for middle ground. "State Street is an option, but so is West Temple. It's all chain link, so we can look for an access point in the fence, or a way to drop over the fence. These guys have already proven that they like ninja tactics."

Kay eyed the over-tall fences with their rows of barbed wire and let out a sigh that had the frosty air streaming from her mouth like a smoker. None of us needed the reminder of how cold it was getting. She shifted her weight side-to-side as Nick and I waited for her response.

"Maybe they're already gone. Who knows?"

I did. Trevor's phone had been off less than ninety minutes. It would have taken at least thirty of those minutes to get to this location and thirty to get back. If Knight really was rounding up the troops, that meeting was going to last more than a few minutes. The man was fighting for his career and his freedom.

Chats like that didn't end quickly. Our best move was to set up cameras on Main and West Temple and see what and who we caught.

"Rhea?" Kay said, pulling me away from my thoughts.

Had I missed a cue? Was it my turn to talk? "Yeah?"

"I said *who knows,* and you're the person who typically does, so spill."

"Even though you won't like it?"

She frowned. "Go check the plates and set up cameras to see where they go?"

I nodded, shoving my hands deeper into my pockets as the chill of standing still started setting in. Couldn't we walk and talk?

"That gives us nothing," she complained. "I need a smoking gun—or at least the silhouette of a gun on the horizon, and I don't see where else I can get it after tonight. For all we know they're in there saying that they're going dark for a few months to help things blow over."

"They could be," I agreed.

"You know I'm a gut person, Rhea. And my gut says that if we don't get this in the bag tonight, we aren't going to get a second chance, so I need a solution that does not involve coming back to fight another day. Because in my brain, there won't be one."

"If the cop is crooked, he'll mess up again," Nick said. "And he'll do it while his own department is investigating him."

"Will he?" she said with a sniff. "The guy's reputation is virtually above reproach. People don't get where he is by messing up. Quite the opposite—this guy has perfected the art of *not* messing up while simultaneously bagging some serious bad guys. A lot of the local channels are countering my story by playing his highlight reel. We threw some hard pitches at him today, but it's not a sealed deal that he's for sure going down yet. This guy *knows* how not to screw up, just like he apparently knows how to get away with murder."

"He is a homicide detective," Nick said, not-so helpfully. "It would follow that he knew how to get away with murder."

"Ya' think?" Kay muttered.

I let them banter, trying to figure out how to get Kay something she could use. But it wasn't looking good. The mechanic shop looked empty. No lights. No cars. All was quiet, as it should be on a Sunday night.

Kay was putting a lot of stock in Jeremy Carson's tip.

"What's he like?" I asked, interrupting something Kay was saying.

"What?" she said. "Who?"

"Jeremy. He's been off radar until today, and suddenly he pops up and gives you—of all reporters—a tip? Something about him as a person must have sold you on all that being a logical sequence of events. What's he like?"

"He's confused, that's what he is," Kay snapped. "His mom is dead, and he doesn't know if his father killed her or not. He's still trying to believe that somehow someone else did it, but you can see the wheels turning, you know? He's thinking."

"He just got his mission call, too," Nick added. "He's headed to Portugal in June."

Poor kid. All this would be a lot to go through while planning to go on a mission. I didn't envy him one bit. "Where was his dad? Why weren't they together?"

Kay and Nick eyed each other.

"Why would he lead us here for a trap?" Kay blurted. "He was honestly nervous, Rhea. When he told us about this place, he was seriously stressing it."

"Because he felt like he was betraying his father, or because he's a kid going on a mission who knew he was sending a woman into danger?" I countered.

She shook her head. "I know how it sounds, Rhea, but I'm telling you that those guys are here."

"I think it was the mug shot of Blaine's dad that got to him," Nick said, almost as if talking to himself. "Jeremy has the same nose, same jaw line. I don't think Jeremy saw a picture of his supposed father until today, and he sees the resemblance. I think it has him a little freaked—a little confused."

Now that would make total sense.

"They're here," Kay insisted again.

"So we set up cameras," I said. "We find trees or areas on public property that give us a view of the exits. Then we wait to see who moves past them. There's no power play here, Kay. Not unless we want to risk exposing ourselves. And given how much you've cornered them throughout the day, I can say with certainty that we have no interest in going face-to-face with them tonight."

"Fine," Kay muttered, giving Nick a signal. "But I'm staying until I either see some action or until I'm sure the tip's a bust."

Nick started away, and I must have looked confused because Kay said, "He's bringing the truck closer so we can pick up feeds."

"Good," I said, patting my pocket. "Then I'll get started placing these."

Kay frowned, eyeing the street. "Where? All the trees are behind fences."

"We'll find overhanging branches."

"*Or* we could just anchor them to the fences," she offered. "The footage doesn't need to be evidence in a court of law, Rhea. We can fudge the rules here."

I shook my head. "Not if you want to use it legally. It either has to be taken from public property, or you need the permission of the property owner."

She didn't respond, which told me she still wasn't a fan of bad camera angles.

"Kay? Are we on the same page?"

She hesitated. "Maybe the best solution here is that you put your cameras where you want them, and Nick and I will choose where to put ours."

Well, that answered that. "Sounds good. I'll get started so we're not a pod of people on the street."

"Knock yourself out."

I started down the street knowing that Kay was fuming, but choosing not to let it bother me. She'd had a long day and she'd been running low on sleep as well. And while I had slept the day away, she was coming up on working twelve hours on her day off. Moody was allowed.

I had three cameras and was thinking of putting one in each direction of the Main Street exit, then the third camera on West Temple, which would technically only be an exit area for people playing ninja. It would be good to have a better idea of exactly how many of the people in the clan were video game characters incarnate.

I found a solid branch about two properties down from the mechanic shop and made quick work of attaching my camera. After all, it was likely I was on some other business owner's security camera and I didn't want to look too suspicious.

When my pocket monitor showed me that I had a good shot of the street, I kept moving down to the other side of the block. As before, the mechanic shop was dark, but this time I noticed that only the office windows faced the street. No windows from the garage area were visible. There could be a whole crew in there working on cars, and I wouldn't see a thing. Kay was right. They definitely could be in there.

The second camera was even easier because one of the businesses had a mailbox on the curb. I tagged it, checked the angle on my monitor, then kept on walking. One more to go.

I jogged the couple of blocks to the end of the street and then headed over to West Temple. Placing the camera there would be much easier, because I was just looking to get a body count at the exit vicinity, so I could do what Kay suggested and ignore the law. In the end, I used a fence across the street before jogging back to our original rendezvous point.

No Nick. No Kay. They were still setting up. The SUV had been moved to where I stood, so I opened the back and started setting up my feeds. They looked good—well, good enough. They were the right angle and level to get license plates if anyone pulled out of that parking garage. If not, then we should catch faces as they walked. There was no action for now, which wasn't a surprise. But since there wasn't anything better to do, I got the cameras on a rotation and studied what I was seeing. A few minutes later Nick popped in.

"Hey," he said, closing the door behind him and blowing some heat into his bare hands. "You all set up with yours?"

I moved to the side. "Yeah. Now we just need to add yours to the mix."

"We have four," he said, moving to the monitor. "I put two between State and Main on either side of the block and Kathryn took the other two. She said she was setting up with you. Did you two not find each other?"

Not even close, and I was betting that wasn't an accident. "Nope. But I'm guessing if you pull up her feeds then we'll know exactly where she is."

He nodded, getting to work doing what he did best. As the feeds from his cameras popped up, I saw that he used street signs to get his camera's eye level. If anyone walked up that street, we would see them. Then he brought up Kay's and neither of us said a word.

All we saw was black.

"Did she turn them on?" Nick muttered.

"I think so," I said, pointing near the top of the screen. The darkness is uneven. I think we're looking at shadows here."

He let out a longsuffering sigh. "There's a reason reporters are on one side of the camera and not the other."

I leaned in. "What does she think she's filming? I can't even tell where she's aiming."

"Maybe the shop," Nick offered. "There are no lights on. Maybe she's thinking that once there are headlights or something that we'll be able to see."

"Or something," I muttered, still trying to figure it out.

"She'll tell us when she gets back and we can act impressed." He sent me a smirk. "Better start practicing."

I laughed. "You're a lot more fun now that you talk sometimes."

"It took a while to figure out I wouldn't lose my head for having an opinion. And you were right," he said, stopping on Kay's other feed and squinting at the screen. "Life may be crazy working with Kathryn, but I feel like I've gotten six years of experience in six months. Wouldn't want to work with anyone else."

"I'm sure she feels the same—just don't tell her I told you so."

"Secret's safe," he said, crossing a finger over his heart and looking back at her feed. "You're right. I'm seeing shadows now. If I up the contrast we'll be able to get a better picture of where these babies are."

I glanced at the door. Where was she?

Nick was probably wondering the same thing because we both grew silent and we studied her camera shots with various brightness and contrast.

"She should be back by now," Nick said after a couple of minutes.

"Yeah. She should," I agreed.

Neither of us moved. I wasn't sure what the right move was. I couldn't exactly run down the street calling out.

"There!" Nick cried out, stabbing a finger at the screen. "That's the outline of her hair. She's standing right in front of the freaking camera!"

I didn't have time to see what he was seeing before light illuminated her face. Nick quickly adjust the resolution so we could see her.

"Where's that light coming from?" Nick asked.

"Her phone." She had turned on her phone. *Why* had she turned on her phone? They could track that.

"She's typing something," Nick said right before Kay held the screen of her phone toward the camera lens so we could see the text she'd typed for us. *I'm stuck. South side of the building. I got in but I can't get out.*

She *WHAT?* I nearly stood before realizing I would hit my head on the van's ceiling if I did.

"She's on the property?" Nick said, his face looking drawn. "That's bad."

"You stay here," I said. "If things get crazy and you have to leave, then leave. We'll meet up after. If not, wait here and hold down the fort."

"I—"

I didn't wait for an argument. Before he could respond I was out the door and sprinting down the street.

I was coming from the south, which meant she was somewhere within two blocks of me and on my side of Mitchell's shop. That was all I knew. I imagined the area surrounding that part of the property and tried to figure out how she had gotten over eight-foot chain link topped off with two feet of barbed wire. It had to be the fence of the neighboring property, which were more like jail bars.

I didn't think about it too much. All that mattered was that I could get in, and then quickly get her out again—without killing her first. If Ty had been with me, he would have made the entire debacle fun somehow. But since it was just me, I got to do things my way and be furious.

That fury had me leveraging a foot hold to vault me to the top of cement pillar adjoining Mitchell's property. From there, I latched on to the chain link fence on Mitchell's side and swung down.

I was officially trespassing. If the police wanted to arrest me now, it would actually stick.

I fought the urge to call out for Kay as I slinked through the shadows. The property went deeper than I'd initially thought and the area I was currently in seemed to be a storage area for retired tires.

"Kay," I hissed, then heard a bump a few feet ahead and quickly moved to the sound, finding her.

"I'm so sorry," she hissed, stepping out of shadow. "I wanted to get the garages, and I was sure I could get back out. I didn't see that—"

"Later," I hissed, noting she was only wearing a light jacket, but still had her purse of all things. "For now, we just need to get out. Where's your coat?"

She pointed toward the front of the building. "I tried to throw it over the barbed wire as cover and ended up throwing it entirely over. All those spikes and not one of them snagged. What are the chances?"

"Apparently good enough," I muttered, scoping our surroundings. At this point it made more sense to exit at the rear of the property since it was much closer and speed was our friend.

"I hope you're right," Kay said. "For the first time, I'm *really* hoping this was a bogus lead and there's no meeting here tonight."

"This way," I said, leading us both to the back of the property. I hadn't planned on it, but there was no barbed wire on the rear portion of the fence. That was a good thing.

"Well, now I feel stupid," she muttered. "All I had to do was go to the back?"

I didn't answer, noting that there were actually two exits since there was break in the fence leading to the neighboring lot as well. But since climbing vertical bars wasn't something that Kay had really trained for, I stuck with option number one.

"Go," I said, cupping my hands to give her a boost. "No talking. Just moving."

"Yes, sergeant."

"Call me what you want, just get over that fence!" To make my point, I took her purse and set it down next to me. "You're going to need both hands."

She didn't hesitate this time, and climbed the fence like a pro. I picked up her purse, waiting until she had both feet on the ground before holding it up.

"Ready?"

"Toss away," she said, and I did, not waiting for her to catch it before reaching out to climb the fence myself. I hadn't even raised my foot to climb when flood lights flashed on behind me. Kay squatted down in reflex, but I could tell it would be useless for me to do the same. The light was hitting me full on—as if aimed at me. The only good news was that Kay stood directly in the shadow I cast when the light came on and dropped out of sight an instant later. They hadn't seen her. I was sure of it, and that made things easier.

"Well, look who we have here," a voice called out. Knight's voice.

I could still go for it. I was fast enough...by myself. But I wasn't sure if I could beat these guys with Kay in tow. Not if people like Trevor were on my back at that moment. Kay and I together wouldn't have a shot.

"Hands up where I can see them," Knight said, sounding like the cop he was. "And fyi, you have a gun aimed at your back, and I don't miss."

I released the fence and kept my hands up, fingers spread.

"This is an interesting development," he mused, and by his tone I knew that he had some friends with him. He sounded overly cocky, but there was no underlying nervousness to his voice. If he really was aiming a gun at me, he had no anxiety about it. "Ms. Jensen, I presume?"

In lieu of answering, I turned to face him. My hope was to see who I was dealing with, or at least how many people I was dealing with, but instead all I saw was a whole lot of blinding light from a professional-grade search light. Whoever was standing behind it was a mystery to me and I was sure that was quite intentional.

"And there you are. I certainly wasn't expecting to have you gift wrapped and left on my door like this."

I said nothing. If this was the beginning of a cathartic monologue for him, then I was more than happy to listen to it while I tried to figure a way out of this mess.

"I think the obvious first step is to call the police and let them know that there's an intruder on the property," he mused.

Which he wouldn't do until all the men inside that building got out. No way he'd want all his friends listed as witnesses when the police arrived.

They hadn't called police yet.

"No need," I said calmly. "My people are watching us right now, and I'm sure they're already making the call. You can save yourself the effort."

Detective Knight laughed. "Cute attempt, but no, Ms. Jensen. I know you work alone. We've been watching you for days now, and you always fly solo when you want to get things done, then huddle up when you have something to share. No one is coming to save you. You're alone here, and we both know it."

He didn't know about Kay or Nick. That was good.

"And while we're waiting for the police *I'm* calling to arrive, why don't you tell us what brings you here this fine evening, Ms. Jensen."

So he didn't want a monologue so much as a dialogue. I needed to step carefully. "I was going to ask you the same question. What's with the powwow?"

I couldn't see his response, but the pause before he replied spoke volumes.

"Your arrogance will not serve you in this situation, Ms. Jensen. You'd be best served to stick to answering questions and not asking them."

"Oh? Are we supposed to pretend now that since you have a gun that you have this entire situation under control? And that because I'm trespassing I'm the bad guy here?"

I heard a bullet move into the chamber of a gun. "I don't think you understand the seriousness of your situation, Ms Jensen."

Ms. Jensen, Ms. Jensen, Ms. Jensen. I knew why he kept saying my name, but that didn't mean it wasn't obnoxious. "What? That you're going to shoot me down while I'm unarmed, in front of witnesses, and then have to explain yourself to a detective when he shows up and starts asking questions as to why you shot an unarmed woman? I don't think so."

I could hear the laugh in his voice. "Oh, we both know that's not an accurate description of you, don't we Ms. Jensen? You are, after all, an expert markswoman with a history of receiving large paychecks from influential people. It makes a person wonder what people are *really* paying you to do. Six figures for a day's work last March? That doesn't sound like a private investigator's paycheck to me. I doubt it will to a jury, either."

Ah, so that was his angle in all this. I was highly trained and highly paid, which was apparently enough to make me a suspect.

"Hate to break it to you, Detective Knight, but if you're hanging your freedom on that angle, you've got nowhere to go but down."

"Why? Because you know rich people?" he mocked. "Well then you also know that there's nothing the rich hate more than a scandal. Especially ones including death."

"What I *know* is that you're betting everything on the wrong horse here, Tony. No matter how you play this against me, you lose."

I heard someone guffaw, but I wasn't sure it came from Tony or someone standing near him. My eyes weren't adjusting to the blinding light, so I just kept them closed as I tried to think of a move they wouldn't see from a mile away.

"Really?" Knight scoffed. "Even after everyone learns about the nine guns you have registered in your name and your marksman certifications? And about the military camps you attended while in college, and the black belts you have in not one, but *three* different martial arts? Does that sound like a P.I. to you, or maybe more like someone who hires out as a specialist?"

He'd done a little homework, it seemed. He'd peeked into my financials, accessed my college transcripts, and gotten the rest from my resume. There was nothing secret there, and I was assuming that The Fours wouldn't allow him to dig any further.

"Having Ms. McCoy drop you in my lap was a gift I'll be glad to thank her for in the near future."

Vague threats. Those were always fun. But I ignored it and stuck with the subject at hand. "You can try to paint my past black all you like, but it doesn't change the facts, Tony. I'm not an assassin, and I've never killed anyone."

He chuckled. "Good luck getting anyone to believe that. I certainly don't."

My arms were getting tired. How long did he expect me to just stand there answering questions? "Trust me. I'll do fine."

"Such arrogance," he chided. "You know, the more you talk, the more clear it becomes that you have no idea what you're up against here, Ms. Jensen. You're in way over your head."

I smiled before I could stop myself. Then before I knew it the smile had bloomed to soft laughter.

The laughter was not appreciated.

"I'm sorry, Ms. Jensen, but do you find that funny?"

Funny? I'd just had everything I'd earned since I was eighteen years old swept out from under me by men who could kill me anytime, anywhere they chose. And now Knight was acting like he was the biggest, baddest guy I'd ever met?

Maybe I found it just a little funny.

I tried to straighten my face to match the gravity of the situation. Knight was a cop, after all, and he most definitely had a gun. But just when I gained my composure and opened my mouth to speak, his words echoed in my mind again, *You have no idea what you're up against here, Ms. Jensen.*

"No. Clearly this is very serious," I said, squinting into the light. "I can tell you have a friend or two with you now, and I'm sure there's more where they came from." Guys like Sonic and Yoda. Surely there were more video game characters just on the other side of the door to the shop.

For some reason my mind went literal with the imagery of video game characters that might be waiting to descend upon me. Maybe it was the nerves. Maybe it was the melodrama of it all, but something tipped the scales and got me laughing again. This whole situation was bad for both of us—so, so bad all around—and my sudden case of the giggles wasn't helping the situation any. I might find it relaxing, but I could tell Knight was not appreciating it one bit. I needed to put on cap on it, and quick.

"Sorry," I said, fighting for a neutral facial expression. "Truly. I don't know what's wrong with me." A lie, but the situation merited it.

"I don't think you understand your situation here, Ms. Jensen."

"I'm sure I don't. Why don't you fill me in?"

"Well, since you've already done your laughing, I guess don't mind giving you the punch line. Knock, knock."

"Uh, who's there?"

"Knight."

This was weird. "Knight, who?"

"Nighty-night, because an alive you is much harder to deal with than a missing you."

I didn't see the flash of his muzzle, but I definitely felt the impact of the shot on the left side of my chest. It didn't knock me down, but I let myself collapse just as I heard another shot fire. That one missed me, thank goodness, as did the one after that, and suddenly the world went dark. The flood light was gone and there was a whole bunch of yelling coming from Knight's direction.

Breathe. I needed to breathe, but all the air seemed to stop before it reached my throat and my ribs felt shattered. I needed to calm down and breathe slowly, but I couldn't.

"She shot him!" I thought I heard someone yell, which made no sense, but I had more important things to worry about. Like air and getting out of there... although that latter one was very unlikely at the moment.

"Lights!" someone was screaming. "We need lights out here!"

The door to the shop burst open. "What happened? Was that gunfire?"

Right then two hands scooped under my shoulders. "Are you okay?"

I couldn't believe my ears. "Ty?"

"Can you move?"

It was Ty. Either that, or I was delusional. "If you get me up I can try—right side, not left."

A split second later my right arm was wrapped around his neck and he was lifting me to my feet. I had to bite my lip not to cry out. There was no way I would be climbing a fence any time soon.

"There's a hole in the fence—"

"I know," Ty said. "We're going to it. Just push for as long as you can, okay? The truck isn't far."

Those were the last words we said before disappearing through the fence.

CHAPTER 34

Within a few minutes of being shot, I was in the cab of a very familiar truck. When Ty hopped in next to me and stabbed his key into the ignition, I found it in me to speak again.

"You followed me?"

He checked his blind spot for traffic, then pressed the gas.

What he had done was obvious, but the real question was how? How had he followed me while staying completely off my radar?

Then it hit me. "You tracked me? With my own equipment?"

When had he planted the tracker? While holding my coat when I put the vest on?

He sent me a glance, his expression unreadable. "Would you have done any differently if our roles were reversed?"

Touché. "What about trusting me to do my job?"

This time his look was incredulous. "You know I trust you, but I also know you're not a one-woman army. So if I sense you need some backup, then I'm going to show up, whether you order me to or not. Get used to it. In the meantime, feel free to say thank you."

The authority in his tone... the anger. The fact that he had sensed I was uneasy even when I told him things were business as usual, and the fact he had followed me without me having any idea.

Was it wrong that I found that all incredibly hot? Not that he was a total stalker, but the fact that he knew exactly when and how to stalk when necessary. Like me. It made me feel like a little bit less of a freak.

But for the moment I needed to focus on breathing, which was difficult to do without feeling like a hot poker was being stabbed into my ribs. Unzipping my coat, I reached for the straps of Velcro and undid them so the vest hung from my shoulders.

"Can you pull over somewhere there are no traffic cameras and help me get this thing off?" It might be only five pounds, but that was five pounds of weight I didn't need at the moment.

It seemed like forever before we reached a dark pocket in the business district and Ty pulled over.

"What do you need?" he asked, turning to me.

I turned my back to him. "Hold the collar of the coat so I can slide out of it."

He did as instructed, also grabbing my sleeves to help me slip out of the coat. Once it was off, I tapped the vest he'd made me put on just an hour earlier.

"Now just lift this off my shoulders and we're clear."

Seconds later the weight was gone, and with it some of the pressure off my ribs. I pressed my hand to the spot where the bullet had impacted, trying to feel if anything was broken and was surprised to hear Ty chuckle. Confused, I looked up.

He sent me a crooked smile. "I've imagined helping you out of your clothes for the first time a lot, but I can say that I never imagined it like this."

"Don't make me laugh," I said with a smile before both of us sobered.

"Are you going to let me take you to a hospital?" he asked.

For a moment we just looked at each other.

"Or are you going to say that Knight's a detective and he's going to be looking for hospital admissions and that means you can't go—at least not tonight?"

In response, I leaned across the space between us and pressed a kiss to his mouth. When I pulled away, he wasn't smiling.

"Rhea, this is all new turf to me, but not so new that anyone has to tell me that I broke the law back there, and we could both be in serious trouble."

I nodded. "Hence me telling you to wait at Kay's."

He put the truck back in drive. "If I had done that, you wouldn't be putting on a white dress this Saturday. You'd be going to jail, or worse."

There was that.

"What do we do next? I mean, Knight knew it was you there. He's going to come after you, right? What's our next move?"

Man, this was a mess. Bless Kay's heart, but I wasn't going to let her take the lead again for a *long* time. "We won't know that until we know how Knight spins what happened tonight. We need to talk to Kay and Nick. I'm sure Kay is ready to go to war on this, so I'd say we should all check in before making a move."

"Sure. Okay," Ty said, and I could tell by his eyes that his thoughts were still fueled by adrenaline. He hadn't come back to earth yet. It would be interesting to see how he reacted once he did.

For a moment the truck was silent.

"I can't believe he *shot* you!" Ty suddenly roared, his hand pounding the steering wheel. "He knew who you were. He *spoke* to you! Then he didn't even blink before pulling the trigger. What is going on here, Rhea? Who is this guy?"

"A guy who is trying to cover his butt."

"Who pulls a trigger that easily?"

"Someone who's pulled a trigger before," I said softly, only now truly believing it to my core.

It was a lot to process, even though I understood the slippery slope between being an agent of the law and thinking you were the law.

On the next inhale I noted that the pain over my heart was becoming more blunt, and not the sharp pain that usually accompanied a broken rib. That was good.

I looked over at Ty and studied him. He had saved my life twice that night. *Twice.*

First, he had insisted I wear the vest. Without it, I would be bleeding out on asphalt at that very moment. Second, he had dragged me from the scene as if we'd practiced for this exact scenario. No hesitation, no missteps, no unnecessary conversation.

He'd been perfect. He *was* perfect—for me at least. Although I still had grave concerns about me being perfect for him.

Still, I scooted over in the seat and leaned against him, letting my head rest against his excellent deltoid.

"You're too good to be true, you know that?" I said.

"And you, my love, are a hot mess."

His hand came off the steering wheel and slid into mine. Ty didn't have to be the tallest guy on the planet to have hands that dwarfed mine. Whenever I wanted to feel a little bit girly, all I had to do was press our palms together to see that my fingertips barely made it past the second knuckles of his fingers. My hands, which could sometimes look a bit tough on their own, looked like fairy hands next to his. Like the rest him, they were built for strength and were calloused from his years in gymnastics. Yet they felt soft to me. Gentle.

"Mister Too Good To Be True and Miss Hot Mess," I mused, sliding my fingers against his to try to distract from the pain in my chest with something pleasant. "Are we doomed for failure, or destined to balance each other out?"

His hand tightened its grip on mine. "I don't care if it's the pain endorphins talking right now or not, but I'm going to remind you about this moment the next time you try to pretend I could love someone else. Because you can bet that you're the only girl I'll ever commit felonies for. Got it?"

I nodded, pressing closer and breathing in his light cologne. "Got it."

CHAPTER 35

The second we got up to Kay's condo I powered up my phone and turned on the TV. If we were lucky, one of the network stations would catch wind of Knight's shooting and consider it "breaking news". So far there seemed to be nothing, and there hadn't been anything on the radio on the drive over either.

"Channels four and five are most-likely to pre-empt. Let's switch back and forth between those two."

Ty nodded, looking at my shoulder. "How's the pain?"

Debilitating. That was my first thought, but I stuck with saying, "I'll live."

"You really need x-rays," he said, coming closer.

I finished typing *Tag. You're it* into a text for Kay, then pressed send before shaking my head at Ty. "Not until we know what Knight is saying about tonight. If he's honest and says he shot me, then I'll totally go. But if he lies and we can keep this off radar, that would be better."

Ty frowned. "Better how?"

I sent him the best coy smile I could under the circumstances. "Better, as in I won't be out on parole and forbidden from leaving the state for our wedding if this isn't reported. We'd have to call it off, postpone, or do the wedding here and cancel the honeymoon, most likely."

"Well, when you put it like that..."

I leaned against him. "This is a gunshot wound. Even with the vest, a medical professional will look at the injury and know what it is. And they'll report it. If that happens, things get messy for us."

He didn't like it. I could tell, but he didn't argue with me anymore. "So if Knight fesses up and says he shot you, we're going to the hospital, but if not you're just toughing it out?"

"Yep."

He pulled his phone out of his pocket. "My buddy broke his

finger a few weeks back. Maybe he still has some decent painkillers he can pass off."

I didn't argue this time. Painkillers would be good. I wouldn't say no to prescription meds, even though they tended to give me insomnia. Insomnia might be a good thing that night. I definitely had some work ahead of me.

I was switching from channel four to five when my phone buzzed with a text. *Headed to my place. See you there?*

Affirmative.

So Kay and Nick had made it out okay. That was good. I almost didn't even care how. With all those shots flying, it was a miracle I was the only one who was hit. Well, besides Knight, I guess. I closed my eyes, reliving the moment the first bullet hit me. The second shot fired after that had been immediate. It should have hit me, too. Had his gun backfired? And after it backfired he dropped the light for everything to go dark?

Everything was still a bit jumbled in my head, but for some reason that explanation didn't fit. It wasn't until I played the scene through a few times in my head that I realized why it felt wrong: there had have been two guns. Knight's, which had been high caliber and with a heavy percussion of sound, and a second gun that had been lower caliber with much less percussion. It was tempting to rationalize that the first shot had just been such a jolt that the others faded in the aftermath, but that didn't fit.

I glanced at Ty, who was busy texting. "Did you see where the other gun came from?"

The way he froze momentarily told me that he had.

"Who had the second gun? How did it miss me?"

Ty put his phone in his pocket and faced me. "I figured I'd let Kay fill us both in on what—"

"Kay?" I interrupted, stunned. "She was the second shooter?"

He nodded solemnly. "She didn't see me, but I saw her angling and setting up on the other side of the fence. I was on the property behind you, trying to hide from the flood light, but when I sneaked a peek to see what was happening she was directly to your left and Knight's right. The three of you made a triangle and she had a clear view of Knight and the two guys with him—"

"Two?" I echoed. "Are you sure?"

"Yeah. Two guys. One looked to be in his thirties, the other in his forties. The older one was holding the light that Kay shot out right after she shot the gun out of Knight's hand. I didn't see where she hit Knight, but he dropped the gun like it had just shocked him. That woman is crazy good."

That changed things in a major way. "No hospital. No matter what."

He didn't like that. "Even if Knight calls you out?"

Man, this was a mess. I had no idea what to do. We were in uncharted territory. "Ty, no one can know what Kay did. That gets out and she never works as a reporter anywhere ever again. She'll be fired immediately. No questions, no severance, no nothing. Just done, forever. If Knight calls me out, I'll get myself some adrenaline to block the pain and do a press conference where I say that he must have shot someone else, because I'm ay-okay."

"You'd lie?" Ty asked, not looking too scandalized by the idea, but more like he was trying to figure out how all the pieces fit together.

I nodded. "I'd lie."

An unsettling silence fell between us as I continued to stalk the TV for an update and Ty continued to text his friends for something stronger than an aspirin.

When nothing came on the other networks before nine, I switched over to Fox for their full news broadcast and breathed a sigh of relief when I saw their leading story.

Hate Crime Against Embattled Officer? I turned up the volume.

"... who is reporting live outside the Intermountain Medical Center in Murray. What can you tell us, Shauna?"

The blonde, fledgling reporter had her serious face on. *"Well, we're still getting all the facts, but what we do know is that at about 8:30 this evening Detective Tony Knight, the former lead investigator in the Blaine Adkins murder, stumbled into the ER with a gunshot wound to his arm. The only facts we currently know is that he was fixing a flat tire when a blue Cadillac Deville pulled up alongside him and opened fire."*

Ty and I looked at each other, speechless.

"According to reports, only one shot connected before the detective was able to take cover and return fire. But once the car escaped, Detective Knight was left to fend for himself more than a

mile away from the nearest hospital."

"However did he survive, I wonder?" I mused, and although my sarcasm was evident, Ty didn't smile. He just kept watching as the news anchor helped Shauna push the story forward.

"Murray isn't known for its gang activity or its shootings, Shauna," he was saying. *"Do we have any word on whether or not this was a targeted shooting, or if it was random?"*

"I'm sure they'll be exploring both angles in regards to this shooting. The timing does seem suspicious, but in the mean time we have one more act of gun violence to add to an already too-long list of gun-related violence in recent months."

I put the TV on mute. There was no reason to listen anymore. "Knight knew they'd find their way to the gun-control issue," I grumbled. "He wanted them to. It makes him a victim and synonymizes him with people who are actually innocent gun-violence victims. Smart."

Ty looked like he wanted to punch the screen. "Seriously? That was all straight up fiction. We're going to let him get away with that?"

"He won't. Not for long. The evidence against him is too strong. And now that another detective gets to look at everything without Knight filtering the information for him, he'll go down." I reached out and squeezed Ty's hand. "Trust me on that. There are times to freelance, and times to trust the system. The latter fits in this case. Knight's days are numbered and he's just the last one to get the memo. At this point, I just want to make sure the two guys standing next to him when it happened go down, too. I'm not sure the system will get that right, so that's where I'm looking."

"I could try to describe them," Ty offered.

"That would help."

Just then we heard noise coming from the hallway. It was Dahl's raised voice making its way down the hall. He'd gotten the news, apparently. Had Kay told him, or had someone at the precinct spread the word after the shooting had been called in?

Ty and I shared a look as Kay's key slid into the lock on the door. I don't know what my expression said, but his clearly said, *We'll get through this.* I blinked, processing that even as a light tingle ran down my spine as the door opened and Kay yanked Dahl in, slamming the door behind him.

"I do have neighbors, you know," she hissed. "Neighbors with ears."

"What? Like they're not going to find out?" he said, voice still a few decibels above normal.

"Dahl," Ty said, stepping forward and motioning down with his hand. "Seriously step it down a bit. You're yelling."

Dahl's eyes focused in on Ty like a new target. "And *you*? What were *you* thinking?"

"Dude, you need to take a run around the block or something?" Ty said. "We don't want the neighbors to call the cops. It would just be funny if you were the only one who got arrested tonight."

The corner of Kay's mouth quirked as Dahl processed that. When he spoke again, his voice was much, much softer. "I don't think any of you know how serious your actions were tonight. A detective with the Salt Lake police department is in the emergency room as we speak."

"A *crooked* cop who shot Rhea first," Kay said, crossing over to me. "Where did he get you? Why are you here? You should be at a hospital!"

"What?" Dahl said, stepping toward me. "Where? Was it a graze?"

"Ty made me wear a vest," I said, patting my chest. I should probably get an icepack on it. "It was a shot straight at the heart."

Dahl's eyes narrowed in disbelief but also concern. "Let me see that."

Ty stepped forward. "It's kind of in a personal place."

I waved that off. "Not so much. At least not all of it." Plus, I wasn't worried about things getting awkward. Dahl had that military look in his eye that said he was all business. Two buttons later, everyone had a view of the top part of a black bruise spreading across my chest.

Dahl reached out and lightly pressed in. "Are any ribs broken?"

"Don't think so," I said, trying not to flinch. "I don't have much in the way of padding in my chest, but I think what I do have helped me out a little bit."

His hand moved across the injured area with precision. "I think you're right. I don't feel a break." Then he looked me in the eye. "That's a kill shot."

I nodded, and Kay jumped in.

"A shot Detective Knight took while she was unarmed, with her hands raised in the air, and knowing full well who she was. *That's* why I shot him, Ken. I couldn't give him a second chance. We got the whole thing on film."

We had? Had the camera in my cap picked it all up? Or a camera Kay set? Or both? I wanted to see it. "Where is Nick? I thought he'd come up."

"He's dealing with the footage," Kay said. "He'll call me when he has it all pieced together. We need to be ready to go when Knight claims you attacked him."

I gestured toward the muted TV. "For now he's claiming it was someone in a blue Cadillac Deville."

She frowned. "How did you know that before me?"

Dahl stepped between us. "Wai-wai-wait! Back up. So when I watch that footage, I'm going to see Detective Knight shooting an unarmed person with their hands raised in the air?"

"If, by 'unarmed person', you mean Rhea, then yes," Kay said.

"No sudden movements? Nothing that could be mistaken for a weapon in your hands?"

I shook my head. "He's way crooked, Dahl. He was trying to cover his butt by using me as a decoy."

Dahl started pacing. "And because of this we're all just supposed to stay calm about the fact that Kate shot a cop tonight and that Rhea isn't reporting that Detective Knight shot her, so this can all be investigated properly?"

Kay groaned in frustration. "See *this* is why we don't invite you to the party sometimes. We report this, and he twists it around to make our lives hell and ties our hands in the process. Sometimes, playing by the rules leads to an innocent guy being framed for a woman's murder, and a second person being framed for killing him, Ken. And sometimes breaking the rules means taking down a guy who's put himself above the law without anyone around him knowing it. We need to do this our way. Just this once, can you not defer to authority?"

There was an awkward beat of silence as Dahl and Kay faced off. It was broken when Dahl broke eye contact and looked at Ty.

"This is new to me, too," Ty said, without being prompted. "But the way I see it, they've gotten things this far. Rhea's right.

Detective Knight will be arrested in a matter of days. There's no reason for us to let him take our women down with him."

Dahl shook his head, but didn't respond to Ty. Instead he turned to Kay. "If your station even gets a sniff that it was you, you'll be fired and blackballed from the reporting world for as long as you live. No one will hire a reporter who lost objectivity and inserted herself into the narrative of her own story. Your career will be *done.*"

She nodded. "I know. I'm trying to work that part out. Trust me."

"I shouldn't be listening to this conversation," Dahl said, turning away from us and walking toward the window. "I could care less about journalistic ethics, but it's best if I don't know how many laws you've broken. Those I care about."

"Well, you're the one who came here," Kay pointed out. "No one called you—out of respect for your sensibilities, might I add—so don't blame us because you felt compelled to come over and yell at me."

He turned to face her. "That's not why I came over."

"No?"

He hesitated. "Okay, maybe partially. But I really couldn't believe what I'd heard. Add that to the fact that all of you were incommunicado, and I came here to prove to myself you two *hadn't* shot a cop. Not the other way around."

Kay's eyes turned icy. "You need to hear from my own lips that I shot one of your brother's in blue? Yes, Ken, I did. Although in retrospect I'm a little bit mad at myself for choosing such a thoughtful place to aim." She touched a finger to her forearm. "I got him right here—right between the radius and the ulna, because I wanted to make sure he wasn't physically capable of squeezing the trigger again. Good news for him is that it will heal right up, no problem. But if I had a second shot? I'd make sure that man never had a chance to reproduce for as long as he lives. That's what I think of him at this point."

Dahl shook his head solemnly, his face gaunt as he shoved his hands in his pockets. Not a good sign for us. "You shot a cop, Kate."

"A *crooked* cop who shot my friend," she retorted. "You seriously need to work on your allegiances here, Ken."

That got a bit of a flush out of him, but he kept his mouth shut.

"I think we're all in new territory here," Ty said diplomatically as he stepped toward Dahl. "I'm pretty sure Kay's never shot a cop before, and that Rhea's never had a cop shoot her. I've certainly never watched my fiancée get shot nor have I dragged anyone from a crime scene before. I think we're all still processing it, man."

That got a nod of acknowledgment from Dahl.

"You know how it is in the heat of the moment," Ty added. "The first priority is to get out alive. Once you're clear, then you deal with the aftermath. That's where we're standing right now. All this is going to play out. We know that. But if we're going to go down, then we're taking Knight and the two men who had his back tonight with us. I think that's the game plan now."

Kay sent me a rebellious look that told me she had no intention of going down. Neither did I, but this was not the time to make that declaration. Not when Ty was doing such a superb job talking Dahl down from turning whistle blower on us.

Dahl considered that. "So what if Knight changes his story to match the truth? What will you do then?"

"He won't," Kay said without hesitation. "That would involve him confessing that he shot an unarmed trespasser after telling her a knock-knock joke with a punch line that she dies. No way he'll do that."

She had him there, although I could tell Dahl wasn't exactly buying the knock-knock part. Neither was I, really, and I had been there. I clearly remembered it, but it was still too bizarre.

"And what if the shot he took is worse than you say?" Dahl challenged. "What if he doesn't make it?"

She rolled her eyes. "It's through and through. Hunters have survived worse hits in the middle of the woods. He'll be fine. Promise. If anything, we would be better off if he weren't in a position to rebound so quickly."

"We need to figure out their next move," I said, trying to get us back on track.

"Well, there were thirteen people at that meeting tonight, according to my camera," Kay said. "No cars. No faces. Just bodies. But Nick and I looked over it several times and agreed on thirteen. Things got a little crazy after they saw their fearless leader spring a leak in his arm. We have Mitchell loading Tony up in a car and the rest of them pretty much scattering on cue—all on foot."

"They must be spooked," Ty said.

"Or maybe not," I countered. "Depends on if they're used to things like this."

We all considered that. Even Dahl.

"Regardless," Kay said. "Anything they do from this point on is going to be totally covert, I think. Ty's right to point out that they'll be spooked out on that front. They won't want to meet again any

time soon."

"But they have things together enough to turn tonight's mess into some type of opportunity." I looked at Dahl. "I don't know who owns a blue Cadillac Deville, but I'm guessing it's someone else on Knight's hit list. Someone from another case that Knight thinks beat the system, maybe?"

His face stayed impassive. "Maybe."

"And he had the sense of mind to put that story together in the time it took to be driven to the hospital. He's thinking on his feet. That means he's also thinking about how to take me and Kay down at the end of this. He knows we're teamed up, which means that even though he's throwing some heat at this blue Deville, we're still his targets. He still has us in his sites. We just don't know his angle or what he's shooting."

Dahl's hand slowly went up. "Um, maybe that's where I come in?"

We all looked at him, confused.

"I'm the boy scout ex-cop, right? That's my rep. I'm by the books, and Detective Knight knows we know each other. And tonight I get a call from a buddy that says just enough to send me over here? Could that be a tactical play on their part?"

Yes. Definitely. Holy cow. Dahl was supposed to find me and report me, because that's what boy scouts did when they found felons. And if Knight was organized, he would be tracking Dahl throughout the entire process.

Hopefully, being in the hospital and all, had made Knight a little less organized.

"Turn your phone off," I said, pointing to his pocket. "They might be tracking you."

He shook his head. "He's suspended. He doesn't have access to that equipment anymore."

"And yet he got you here," I countered, then waited until he humored me and powered down before continuing. "Knight has all his men turn off their phones during their meetings, so I'm going to assume that he knows how to turn a phone into a microphone. And if he purposefully sent you over here to confront us? Well, it's not unthinkable that he's found a way to listen in or track you, or that he won't try to in the future. From here on out, no phones on when we talk about him, and no phone calls or texts with updates. All updates happen in person with phones turned off."

Dahl rolled his eyes. "It's illegal to clone phones, Rhea."

Ty sent me a nervous look, which I ignored.

"And shooting an unarmed civilian isn't?" Kay retorted. "I'm pretty sure this guy isn't the type to let something as silly as a law stand between him and what he wants."

"Not to interrupt," Ty said, moving forward. "But it seems to me like one advantage you might have is Knight's impression that you know more than you actually know, right? Why else would he shoot, unless he thought there was no other alternative? Killing someone seems pretty last resort-ish."

He had a point.

"I like it," Kay said, taking a seat on the couch across from me. "If he thinks he's backed into a corner, he's going to get aggressive. Aggressive people always make mistakes—which he did tonight. From what I can tell, Knight's MO is to be cold and calculated, which means we have him off his game. He was definitely a hothead tonight."

"Which means what?" Ty asked. "What do we do?"

Kay leveled her gaze at Dahl. "Well, I guess it depends on whether we can count on our friend here not to run to Big Brother with a tell all."

Dahl's face was military blank. "I want to see that footage."

"Because you don't believe us?" Kay snapped.

"No. Because you're asking me to break the law and ignore a whole lot of training. I could lose my job over this. You shot a cop, Kate!"

"And for the *last* time, that cop shot my unarmed friend *first*," she snapped back. "Can you not get it through your head that your beloved detective is a criminal with a badge and doesn't deserve your loyalty? Man, what in the world do they brainwash you with in the Academy? The same stuff they serve you at church?"

Uh-oh. It was definitely not the time for this conversation.

"Loyalty to the law is *not* brainwashing," Dahl shot back.

"No, it's a badge of honor, right?" she sneered. "The person who is the most obedient to the laws laid out for him is the 'best,' right? The most admirable? The most *righteous*. And the people who aren't so good at doing what they're told? Well, they should be imprisoned! Or at least be pariahs, right? Isn't that basically how it goes?"

Dahl square off against Kay. "No. That's not how it goes. Look, all I'm asking for here is to see the tapes."

"So you can believe us," Kay said with a prim nod. "Because that's how friends roll. They only believe each other if there's video proof, right?"

"It's not that," he said, stepping forward. "This is serious stuff here, Kate. You're laying some serious allegations—"

"Stop. Just stop!" Kay said over him. Then, in a move I'm sure surprised us all, she walked to the front door and opened it. "Get out."

"Kate—"

"I'm serious," she said. "Out. Do whatever you have to do, but I'm not going to show you a damn video tape to prove to you that Rhea, Ty, and I aren't lying to you. If you can't believe us just on our say-so—and if you can stand in this room with us and be loyal to a man you've barely met, then get out of my house."

This was bad. Way bad. Now was not the time to be challenging Dahl's built-in impulse to do the "right" thing. At this point that would involve all of us in a cell next to Knight.

"Wait. Let's talk this out," Dahl said, moving toward her.

"We just did," she said.

"Really? Because from what I recall, you were the one doing all the talking. Don't I get a say?"

"Not tonight. Tonight you get out."

Dahl sent Ty and me a desperate look. "Talk some sense into her?"

I shrugged, not knowing a thing I could say when Kay was like this. Dahl was on his own.

"Actually, it might be good for all of us to do some processing before we try to talk about this," Ty said, once again being Switzerland. "I say we all sleep on this before we make any big decisions. Especially those of us who had close encounters with bullets tonight."

After a few beats of hesitation Dahl took the bait, even though the look in his eyes told me sleep was not in his near future. He would be heading somewhere when he left the condo, but it wasn't home.

"Makes sense," he said.

"Yeah? Then why are you still here?" Kay said, motioning to the hall. "I said out."

He moved to the door, pausing when he was within arm's reach. "We're not done here."

"I am."

He shook his head. "We'll talk tomorrow."

Rather than answer, she pushed him out of the door and he didn't put up a fight. Once he cleared the threshold, Kay had the door closed and locked. Visibly angry, she stalked across the living room and joined me on the loveseat.

"Can you believe that guy?"

"It takes guys longer to process things," Ty said, sending her a smile as if he was slightly embarrassed by his sex at the moment. "And the process is even slower when they hear something rather than see it. He's on your side. His brain just hasn't caught up with what exactly that means yet."

Yep, I was going to marry that man. Every time he opened his mouth, I just wanted to kiss him for it. Not many women could claim that of their men.

"Well, whatever conclusion he comes to, I'm through dancing that lame dance of his. I'm done with that mess of a man."

Ty and I shared a look. Kay and Dahl not together? For real this time?

Nah. The gravitational pull between the two of them was just too strong.

"In the meantime, let's just hope he doesn't go Judas on us," I said, hoping Kay would miss the fact that I wasn't actually responding to what she said.

She shook her head. "No, he'll want to talk to me again before he betrays me. He won't tattle tonight. Maybe tomorrow, but not tonight."

I had to trust her judgment on that one. "What did you tell Nick to do with the footage?"

She took a slow breath and I saw her brain switch gears. "He's making that highlight reel I mentioned, then backing up all footage in a few different areas. We'll meet at work tomorrow."

"Good. Just remember to keep calls with him casual and normal. Don't say anything that lets them know he knows anything. They don't know who was there tonight or that there's any footage at all. Let's keep it that way."

She nodded. "Got it."

"Good. Now, do you have any ice packs?"

"I'm sorry," she blurted. "You got shot tonight because of me. I totally ignored what you said, and you paid the price for it."

"We got away. That's what matters," I said.

"Still, I'm sorry," she said, moving toward her freezer and pulling out a blue pack.

"I know," I said, sending her a smile she didn't return as she crossed the room and handed me the pack. "Now get some rest. Tomorrow's going to be a ride, I'm sure, and we can't have you sleep deprived and wired like you were tonight."

She nodded, stepping away. "Seriously. I don't know what got into me. I'm so sorry. Beyond sorry."

Ty gave my shoulder a squeeze. "I should probably get—"

"No way," Kay said, standing. "You stay until she passes out. Get her anything she needs so she doesn't walk around until she passes out somewhere in the vicinity of a sharp corner."

"I think I can do that," he said.

"Good," she said, heading over to her room. "We'll talk in the morning. A big, long talk. For now, I'm crashing."

"Night," I said before we both watched her disappear down the hall. Once she was gone, we looked at each other.

Man, there was a lot to talk about. I didn't even know where to start. But Ty, being a guy, began with the basics.

"So, have you had dinner yet?"

Yeah. That was a good place to start.

CHAPTER 36

Monday morning. It dawned quietly as I hashed over the plan again and again in my mind. I hadn't slept, but thanks to my extended nap the day before, I wasn't feeling it.

I stepped away from the chess board I had scrounged up to watch the sun creep over the mountain peaks. Kay's high rise condo offered me a bird's eye view of the city below. In a few hours it would be business as usual on the streets of Salt Lake, but for the moment the streets were all but bare in the light of dawn.

It was supposed to be a sunny day. And while that didn't mean it would be warm, it did mean that roads would be clear which never hurt. At this point I would take even the smallest things as a good omen. Sunshine counted. And by the time it set, several fates would be decided in a game of chess.

Literally.

The whole concept had come to me after taking the painkillers Ty found for me the night before. Clearly I had been a little high, because the shininess of my plan was fading under the light of day. But last night it had just made sense—a game of chess where Tony Knight was a knight and I was on a quest to corner his king?

Totally logical. As were the players on my side of the board.

Kay got to be the king because she ruled the air waves and was the face of Knight's media assault. I got to be the queen because I was mobile, obnoxious, and could come at him from any angle. Getting rid of me did damage, but it wasn't check mate.

Of course, Knight already thought he had done just that, so at the moment I was more of a cloaked queen. He wouldn't know where my starting point was until I made my first move, which meant I needed to stay off the board and out of sight until I was ready to reveal that I wasn't lying in a hospital bed somewhere.

For the knights on our team we had Ty, my personal knight in shining armor. And Dahl... well, the bishop was a pretty intuitive choice for him. But since Dahl would not knowingly be part of the game, he would double as a pawn.

Last, but not least, were the rooks. Those symbolized the station and Kay's bosses, which were tied to King Kay. Kay was the only one who could move the rook, and if she did, it wasn't a good thing.

Those were the players on our side of the board—the side I would be making moves for while Kay acted as my eyes and ears, showing me what Knight was doing by playing his side of the board.

It was a crazy idea. I knew that, now that I wasn't under the influence of Percocet. There was every reason for something to go wrong and yet it was the only idea I had, and Kay had already agreed to it when I explained it to her at four in the morning before letting her go back to sleep.

Sink or swim, we were locked in.

The sun had made it half way over the horizon when I heard the fridge open behind me, and I turned.

"Morning," I said.

"Apparently," Kay replied. "I swear it comes earlier every day."

I nodded. "Sorry for waking you up last night. Did you get back to sleep?"

"With a little chemical help. It's still rubbing off. Might be pulling out the triple shot at the espresso bar today."

I pointed to her counter. "I made a case for your phone to use as needed today. Ty and I have covers too. There's an extra there for Nick."

She picked it one, examining it. "Is this lined with tin foil?"

"It blocks the cell signal. No one will be able to track your GPS or pirate your phone if it's in there. It cuts off the second you put it inside, and you have your phone back online the second you take it out."

She turned it over in her hand. "Seriously? Tin foil does that?"

I nodded. "And it's pretty foolproof. You're covered even if a separate device is planted on your phone with an independent power source."

"Got it," she said, tucking them both into her purse. "What about you? Are you sure you're up for this? How are your ribs doing?"

"They're making themselves known, for sure."

She frowned. "I'll say it again. Sorry."

"And I'll say it again. It was my choice."

"Still," she mused, then seemed to get over it. "I got the cheat sheet you left on my bathroom counter and I've downloaded the chess game app."

"I saw. I'll wait for your cue."

She pulled out the paper where I had listed the potential moves. "It's going to be freaky not touching base like we usually do, but using a game app to communicate is pretty brilliant."

That remained to be seen. "They're unlikely to hack it. And if they do, they'll have no idea what the moves mean without the key, so just keep your hands on that paper and we're good."

"Done," she said, tucking it into her bra. "And might I say, I'm pretty flattered to be the king in all this."

I leaned against the window sill. "From their perspective, you are. If they can blindside you, it's check mate."

"And we're not using Dahl?"

I studied her, trying to tell if she was happy or unhappy about that fact. Her voice was carefully neutral. "You made that declaration last night when you kicked him out, so it seemed a little iffy to include him directly. He works better as a bishop who's actually a straw man."

"Yeah," she agreed. "He's really lucky I'm distracted by this disaster and your wedding plans, or I'd be ripping him a new one right now. Can you believe how long I let him string me along?" She pulled a yogurt out of her fridge. "I'll handle it. Don't worry. And as soon as we wrap this story tonight I'm putting that fool's face on a bull's eye and playing darts. You're coming."

If the night ended with me anywhere but in a jail cell, I'd go wherever she wanted to go. "Sure."

CHAPTER 37

In the game of chess—as in the game of life—the number of moves is nearly infinite. But unlike life, the victor in a game of chess is decided by who captures the other's king.

The all-nighter I'd pulled came with its fair share of revelations, one of which was the conclusion that Detective Knight was not the king in his organization. Kings did not expose themselves. They didn't pull triggers, and they certainly didn't lead the ground game. Generals did that. Second-in-commands did that while the king remained protected in a pocket of pawns.

That said, the goal of the day was not to take down whatever little organization Knight had affiliated him with. I didn't have half the information I needed to do that. The goal was to put the killer—or killers—of Amanda and Blaine behind bars, which meant giving whoever might be backing Tony Knight the opportunity to wash their hands of him by convincing them that Tony Knight's fall was inevitable.

And since any organization's first priority is to protect its king regardless of the cost to other personnel, I was 99% sure Knight's group—whoever they were—would cut ties and leave Tony, Nathan, and anyone else who helped the two of them to deal with the consequences of their actions.

Tony's side would keep their king while losing replaceable positions, and everyone would take their board and go home. Game over.

Definitely not how things would play out in a true game of chess, but in life it was something I could live with when the alternative was them wiping the floor with us. I already had one big showdown with a large organization planned. I didn't want to make it a double date.

Tactically, the main thing we had on our side was that Knight's team didn't know who the players were on my side of the board, so I could make moves without them seeing while moving decoys at the same time. In the meantime, Team Knight would assume Dahl was one of Kay's heavy hitters and hopefully assign a few strong assets to watch him as well as assigning other assets to hunt me down. Where was I? Was I injured? Was I dead? Where was I hiding out? Who shot Knight? Who had spirited me away?

A detective couldn't live with unanswered questions like these. Knight would be looking to find answers ASAP. The good news was that it was well within Kay's job duties to look into the shooting of a cop and see whether he was still in the hospital being treated while I stayed off radar and waited for Kay to show me her first move.

CHAPTER 38

I'd been staring at the same view for forty-five minutes, waiting for an update. The "brilliance" of my chess game idea was officially becoming my least-favorite idea ever. I had no visibility. None. Everything was just pieces on a chess board, without me being able to see any of the nuances.

Bird's eye view. Broad strokes. That's all I saw, and it left me with the symptoms of a panic attack.

I hadn't played chess since I was a kid—and even then I'd found it frustrating. My dad had loved it, though, and chess was one of his simple pleasures. I'd played now and again just for an excuse to spend time with him. Back then I'd thought thirty seconds between moves was enough to call the whole game off. But forty-five minutes?

Correction. Forty-seven minutes.

I needed to listen to music. I needed to do something besides obsess. I needed to play chess moves in my mind to make sure I really was accounting for all the plausible outcomes. Happily, I'd brought a chessboard just for the occasion. I could play myself all day by the looks of things.

Setting up the pieces made me think of my dad. Placing the pieces on a chessboard was a bit of a ceremony for him. Pawns first, then the king and the queen, then the rest of the pieces two-by-two from the inside of the board out. It was strange to have such a fond memory of a game I'd never really enjoyed. Maybe I would have liked it more if my dad let me win once and a while, but he'd always said that chess—like life—was a place to learn from your mistakes and try not to make the same one twice. As I child I'd kind of rolled my eyes when he said that. Now that I was older, I kind of got it.

Both in chess and in life, the only way to learn whether you were walking into a trap was to just walk into situations you didn't understand and see how they played out. If it ended up being a trap, then you not only knew how that particular trap worked and how to avoid it, but also how to set the trap yourself when you needed it. All you needed to do was find the trap your opponent didn't see—or better yet, a trap where your opponent did most of the heavy lifting for you.

Detective Knight was trained to be cautious, but I had two things in my favor. One, this wasn't just any case for him. This was personal, and he was very focused on covering his back. Second, he'd been shot within the past twelve hours.

He wouldn't be thinking straight. No one would. There was no doubt I was on his list to find and arrest—at least if I were still alive. Finding me would almost certainly be his top priority for the day. He'd use as many resources as he could to lay traps of his own for me to stumble into. He'd go back to last night's scene and look for blood spatter from me.

The temptation to pull in and watch his process somehow was overwhelming, but I didn't have the resources. Besides, tactically it wasn't necessary. Tactically, all that mattered was that Knight was more focused on finding me than he was on anything else.

Someone had shot him last night. And if I was alive, I knew who that someone was. And Knight really wanted that name. No doubt he was already contriving elaborate vigilante justice schemes to punish us for our crimes.

I closed my eyes and took a slow breath.

Focus. I needed to focus on what was, not on mental field trips... which was really hard to do when all I had to look at was a chessboard. I had no control. Everyone was making my moves for me while it was my task not to appear on the radar until I was tactically necessary. That could be five minutes, or it could be five hours.

Probably closer to five hours considering Kay and I had only made one move each. Kay had opened with her king's pawn E-4 to signal that she gotten out the office to work on the story.

I had responded by mirroring her move on my side.

King's pawn to E-5: my signal that I had Nick's car and was tucked away in a parking terrace downtown. We were both in position, as planned, and ready to roll.

I gave the steering wheel a light pat, reminding myself to take care of Nick's baby. It might be a ten-year-old Honda, but given the state of my bank accounts, I couldn't really afford to replace it if anything happened. The guy was totally going above and beyond by handing over the keys. I didn't plan to do anything crazy with it, but then again, you never planned for crazy.

Just then my app chimed with an update. Kay had made her next move. I quickly brought the screen up to see the move I'd been hoping for.

King's knight to F-3. Detective Knight was officially out of the hospital.

"Thank you," I said to whomever might be listening as I keyed in my response. Knight had moved from the hospital, which meant he was healthy enough to explain the events surrounding his shooting on more detail.

He wouldn't do that, of course. But he would have to look Kay in the face while she pelted him with questions without flinching or breaking. If Kay did her job, he would do anything in his power to pull her to the side at the end and ask some forceful questions of his own about last night.

But first things first. I had to make my move.

Queen's knight to C-6. If Kay's next move mirrored mine with her queen's knight from to C-3, that meant she'd baited Knight in and lit the fire under his fears while simultaneously denying that she knew anything about last night. She would lie to his face, and he would know it.

It would drive him crazy.

This time I only had to wait fifteen minutes before I got exactly what I wanted.

Queen's knight C-3. Kay had laid the bait and Knight had taken it. We were on a good track.

It kind of made me nervous to believe everything was unfolding how I wanted it to without me there to micromanage, but I couldn't let myself second guess the results. They were what they were, and based on the almighty chessboard, that meant my gambit was starting to take shape. If Kay had done her job right—and I had no doubt she had—Detective Knight should be out for blood, and an inch away from handcuffing Kay for no legal reason whatsoever.

Now I needed to give Knight a pawn. A small victory. Something that made him feel like he was both a step ahead and a step closer. Something that would blind him to the trap I was setting.

I played through my preferred options, sticking to the ones I had written out on the key I made for Kay. After a minute, I finally decided there was only one move that would get the job done.

"Sorry, Dahl," I muttered before moving my king's bishop to C-5.

It was a gamble, but I needed to assume that if Knight spent time in close proximity with Kay he had cloned her phone or bugged her in some fashion. He was a desperate guy, and desperate men pulled out all the stops. At least I hoped so, because otherwise my next move to have Kay send Dahl an ambiguous and ominous text wouldn't amount to much.

Introducing Dahl on Knight's radar accomplished several things. The two men had similar backgrounds, which meant that Detective Knight would see Dahl as a legitimate threat. And legitimate threats warranted a certain amount of thought and resources.

It also opened the door to Knight wondering if it was Dahl who had shot him last night. He would reject this notion when he thought about it logically, but the thought would itch at him. He would think of who could use a handgun to make a shot like that on a cold, dark night from a minimum of thirty yards away. And the more he thought about it, the more my connection to Dahl would gnaw at him.

I needed that itch in his brain, because I needed Knight to consider a straw man his greatest threat. It would divide his forces and send him on a wild goose chase as Dahl sent out false signals left and right.

Theoretically.

From my vantage point in the parking garage, however, there was no way to see if this tactic would play out as planned. All I could do was trust.

And wait.

Once again my phone chimed. Another move? So soon? Kay

was going to spoil me at this rate.

King's bishop to C-4. She'd mirrored my move yet again, which meant that it had played out as planned. Kay had officially been bugged in some fashion. That meant Dahl was officially on their radar and they would be tracking both of their steps in an effort to find me.

I didn't want to smile, but I gave in and let it out as I studied the real chessboard on the seat next to me. In his mind, Knight had just earned himself a small victory by locking in on Kay. Now he needed a reward for that. After one too-easy victory, he wouldn't question another easy break. He would feel like he had just earned it.

It was time to drop a bread crumb—a believable and tempting one. Something like my queen's knight—aka Ty—to D-4.

I switched from the chess app to the texting app, chose Ty's number, then typed *Yes* and pressed send. My real phone had been off all morning, but now it was time for it to bounce off some towers.

Ty's response time was admirable. I saw the GPS of my phone pop up on my temporary phone a few seconds before I got Ty's response of, *Cool.*

I'd just gone from being a needle in a haystack to being a sparkler in a haystack as far as Detective Knight was concerned. He would take the bait, no question. The only question was, how *far* would he take the bait?

My self-appointed dragon slayer was about to find out.

Ty Kimball. I took a deep breath and didn't fight the smile this time. How in the world had I ever broken up with that man? It still blew my mind when I thought about it. He'd dragged me away from a crime scene the night before, and now he was letting me send a half-rabid cop to his place of work.

Ty's part would be easy: text Dahl a vague text that read, *Need supervision to go up to 4:30,* and let Dahl text back whatever he would. Then he had to turn off my phone the second Knight got there, and refuse to cooperate with his almost certain demand to search for me. Ty wasn't to open any doors. He would demand a search warrant and encourage his coworkers to do the same. There was no way Knight would have a warrant to search for me, and when he saw my signal drop off the radar he would think he just missed me and sic some men on tracking me down.

In other words, Ty was going to help me scatter and frustrate Knight's resources. He was going to push the man's buttons, but not so hard that Knight looked into his eyes and figured out that Ty had been there the night before—that he'd been the one to save me. Knight could start suspecting it, sure. Another itch in his brain worked out perfectly for me, but I didn't want Knight to be absolutely confident. That might be dangerous for Ty.

But he was safe as long as he was at work. I had to remember that. And the fact that a news van would be visible nearby would also hold Knight in check... so to speak.

And speaking of a news van, I needed to update Kay that I'd set that particular play in motion.

I pulled out the app, moving my queen's knight to D-4 on the screen to match the chess board next to me. Now I could only wait. Kay would be my eyes and ears as to what Knight's next move was after things played out at Ty's work. That would be thirty minutes at best, but more likely closer to an hour.

Deciding it was a perfect time to stretch my legs, I got up and took a walk around the parking garage.

CHAPTER 39

Trevor's phone came to life minutes after my phone pinged at Ty's work. A number I didn't recognize demanded Trevor leave work immediately to rendezvous at Ty's work. Trevor tried to bow out at first, texting that he would lose his job if he left.

The next text he'd received had been very direct. *Then I guess you'll lose your job.*

En route, he'd texted back and seconds later his phone had gone on the move.

I fought the urge to get nervous for Ty. How many people were heading his way? I knew Knight would want to go personally, maybe flanked by one or two others, but it looked like he was calling in the foot soldiers.

Trevor had only been on the road a minute when he called Link. I put the call on speaker phone.

"They call you in, too?" he asked when his friend picked up.

"Yeah," Link replied. "Roark and Brian, too. We're headed over."

Trevor let out a slow exhale. "This is getting out of control, man. I don't have any more strikes at work."

"Hey, at least you're not Brian. He had to go all bulimic at the airport to fake the stomach flu. But this one's slippery. We need a crew, or she'll slide away again."

"With a bullet in her?" Trevor scoffed. "I don't think so, man. Wherever she's holed up, she's not moving very well."

"And yet we lost her last night," Link reminded him.

"Only because we were inside when it all went down. But still, man, none of this makes sense. We're supposed to believe that she was waiting to snipe all of us? We've both tailed her enough to know that story doesn't fit."

"But it's what happened," Link said loyally. "She got two shots off before Jedi tagged her."

Which made me the worst sniper *ever*, apparently.

"Maybe. I'm just saying this whole situation is coming unhinged. I mean, why aren't the actual police in on this? Why is it just us and all hush-hush?"

Link muttered something on his side of the line, then spoke again. "Roark just got here. We're en route."

"Okay."

"And Trev?"

"Yeah?"

"Stop thinking, okay? At least for now. Let's just get this done and we can have a Q&A after."

Trevor sighed. "Yeah. I'm three minutes out. See you when I see you."

"Out."

The lines went dead.

So a minimum of four men would be watching the outside of Ty's gym while Knight went in. The guys had referred to someone named Jedi, but it didn't take rocket science to figure out who that was. Gosh. Who would go by the name Jedi Knight?

That was a stumper.

The real enlightening part of the call was learning that the footmen didn't know about Tony and Nathan. But how was that possible if they were at the emergency meeting the night before? If the group hadn't been discussing the murder case, what *had* they been talking about?

I'd find out later. Right now I just had to fight the urge to text Ty and let him know he was about to be surrounded. It was an unnecessary move on my part and would probably just psych him out. There were times it was best not to know that you were surrounded and outnumbered—times when a false sense of security actually kept you safer. This was one of those times.

The good news was that Knight was taking the bait and following his training to investigate every lead. Some himself, some by proxy, but he was all in. His career, and possibly his future freedom, all hinged on getting to me before I opened my mouth to someone who mattered.

The option was on the table to do just that, of course. It was pretty much a last resort, though, since telling the truth would mess up more than just Knight's life. Kay and Ty would become collateral damage as well. But if worse came to worst and we all needed an eject button, walking into the police precinct and laying the whole story out was an option on the table.

Knight didn't know that, though. In his mind I was likely gathering all the evidence I could so I could report to his superior officers, and throw him under the bus. That was an assumption I was very happy to reinforce.

But for now, all I could do was wait. Again.

CHAPTER 40

I could have guessed Kay's next move based on Trevor's GPS. He had spent about twenty minutes at Ty's work before slowly venturing away. He was on foot, likely searching for me in surrounding areas while trying to come up with an excuse for leaving work that wouldn't lead to him getting fired.

Searching on foot was futile. Knight knew that, which meant he would move to more promising pastures. He'd barely missed me, which had him angry. And being angry made him bold.

King's Knight takes king's pawn. Translation: The knight was moving on our pawn.

"Sorry, Dahl," I muttered again.

Dahl would forgive me in retrospect, even if he might be a bit frustrated with me today. As much as it would tweak his pride to be kept out of the plan, he would eventually acknowledge that it couldn't have really been any other way given that we couldn't trust him not to approach Knight for a heart-to-heart.

I didn't blame Dahl for wanting to believe that Detective Knight was everything Dahl aspired to be. I couldn't judge the fact that he wanted to give a fellow officer the benefit of the doubt.

And that meant I couldn't trust him not to do any of the above. Quite the opposite. I had to assume he would. And if he did, it was pivotal that Knight not trust him at all.

No, being a pawn wasn't fun. But neither was sitting in a parking garage playing chess by yourself, and trying to talk yourself out of taking pain pills to take the edge off what felt like a broken boob.

I studied the board, not knowing what to do next. I knew what I wanted to do—get out of the stupid parking garage and get into the game. But was it too soon? Was jumping now a smart move, or was I just being restless?

After a moment I decided the move was more than restlessness. It was also strategic. A substantial amount of Knight's resources were looking for me on the south side of the city. When better to emerge from the city center and begin my hunt for the king?

I made the move on the real chessboard first, making sure it felt good.

It did. It totally did.

Game on.

Picking up the phone, I entered the move so Kay could see it: queen to G-5. The black queen was now in play and hunting for the white king.

The gambit was officially set and, one way or another, the day was going to end in check mate for somebody.

CHAPTER 41

Now that I was on the board, my next move needed to be one that caught the opposing king's attention—whoever that was.

King's knight to F-7. That was the next move Kay made on behalf of Knight, which meant he hadn't taken note that the queen was even on the board in any official capacity yet and was still focusing on Dahl in an effort to undermine and discredit Kay before she could beat him to the punch. That was ideal, because I wanted Knight to find out I was in play by way of some very pissed off bosses.

That meant I needed to take a pawn of my own.

Sure, I had Knight in a spot where I could face off again with him if I wanted to, but last time I'd tried that approach he'd shot me. No thanks. It would be much better to go after someone he considered secondary, if not disposable, and do so in a way that everyone in his group saw my move before he did. And the more I thought about how to get the done, the more all paths seemed to lead to Trevor.

Based on the conversation I'd overheard, he was the pawn I needed. Even better, I knew exactly where he was. Maybe it was time for a little chat—figuratively speaking. I would be the one doing all the talking. Then I would watch to see if he was doing any listening.

Trevor's 4Runner was still parked at Ty's work, which made things easy enough. The surrounding area would be an absolute pain to search. There was a high school across the street, a strip mall adjoining the gym, and tall trees and homes in every other direction. If ever there was an exercise in futility, Trevor Baxter was currently participating in it.

I spotted his 4Runner parked on the outskirts of the parking lot, near an exit. A pretty decent tactical parking job if he needed to get out in a hurry. It also made his vehicle quite an island, since the nearest car was about fifteen spots away. If he was watching his car, he would absolutely see me approach it.

Rather than park for a quick exit, I waited patiently for a spot to appear in the middle of the sea of cars. I needed the camouflage and a place to write Trevor a little note. Once parked, I pulled out a pad of paper and a pen.

What to write?

Hey Trev,

Sorry for all the drama. The good news? It'll be over in a few hours.

The bad news? Well, that depends on the answer to one question: Do you really not know that Jedi killed Blaine Adkins?

If you do know, and are covering for him, your day is about to get a whole lot worse than simply losing your job. If not, then we need to have a little chat.

On a helpful note, don't try to lie to me. I'll see through it. Promise.

I can see you right now. If you believe Detective Knight was right to shoot me last night and I'm a stone-cold assassin, call Link, Sonic, and Cloud in and concentrate your search back here. I'll give you a sporting chance of finding me. If you believe me when I say I'm a private investigator from Los Angeles with proof that Jedi killed Blaine to protect Nathan Carson, then let's go for a ride. Sit on the hood of your car, hands in plain sight, and I'll come pick you up.

If you call or talk to anyone after reading this, I'll assume that you're calling in reinforcements and you and all your friends will be implicated with Jedi.

It's a simple choice. Make it quickly. And remember that I'm licensed law enforcement. I won't abduct you, hold you for ransom, or anything crazy like that. I'll just tell you what I know and let you decide what should happen next.

Hope to talk to you soon.

Rhea

Short and to the point. Throwing the code names in there didn't hurt. It made me seem like I knew a whole more about their organization than I did.

Bundling up in my coat, I stuck a hat on top of my head and walked into Ty's gym. No eyes watched the front door when I entered, and no one looked out of place. I was in the clear for the moment.

"Oh my gosh, Rhea? Did you hear?" Brandi called out from the front desk. "Did Ty call you?"

I shook my head truthfully, and she motioned me toward her. "This place was, like, crazy an hour ago. All these undercover cops were here looking for a convict. They thought he was hiding out here—or she, I guess. They kept saying *she*."

"Crazy," I said, glad that Brandi apparently didn't watch the news or know anything about the weekend's events. I'd take small favors like that. "Everyone okay?"

"For sure. But Ty was totally in the middle of it. He asked for a description so we could find the person discreetly, but the cops totally wouldn't cooperate. They wanted to search the place, locker rooms and all, and Ty was like, 'No way.' And Michelle was kind of freaking because she didn't know what the exact policy was about the place being searched and stuff, but Ty made the point that we couldn't have men searching the women's locker room and showers. Then the lead cop was like, 'It's not like we're going to get off on it. We're looking for a criminal.' Then Ty was like, 'Then you can catch her on the way out or give us a description and we'll send a female employee in to see if anyone matches that description.' And when the cop wouldn't agree with that, Michelle sided with Ty and said that without a warrant they couldn't have them going through the whole building." Brandi took a deep breath, and I wondered if it was her first since she started talking. "You should have been here, Rhea. It was cra-zay!"

"Wow," I said. "Did they find her?"

She shook her head. "Not that I know of, but the guys are still around. Not the main guy, but I've seen the other ones around, still looking."

"Sounds insane," I said, wondering if Knight had really identified the men that were with him as cops, or if Brandi had simply assumed that part. "Is Ty okay? Is he here?"

She nodded, pointing to the free weights. "He's with a client. Need me to page him?"

"Yeah. It will only take a moment."

Brandi waved that off. "Take the time you need. He's always happier after he sees you."

I didn't get a chance to answer before she picked up the phone and hit the intercom button. "Ty, please come to the front desk. Ty to the front."

"Thanks," I said.

She smiled. "I'm just glad you two are back together. That was just crazy when you two broke up."

"Yeah, not one of my smarter moves," I conceded.

"Totally not," she said just as Ty jogged up.

"Hey," he said, his expression somewhere between confused, concerned, and glad. "Wasn't expecting to see you here."

"Couldn't stay away," I said, hooking my finger in his shirt and pulling him down to a kiss. He didn't need much coercion.

For a moment, I let the press of his lips against mine, the pressure of his hands on my hips, be the only thing that mattered. When we pulled apart I pressed my forehead to his. "You're kind of making a habit out of being my hero, you know that?"

He grinned. "It was kind of fun. Totally crazy, but kind of a payback for last night. It felt good."

I smiled back. "Yeah, defying authority can have that kind of an effect on a person."

"I'll bet." His eyes glanced at the entrance, and his voice dropped in volume. "What are you doing here? There are still several guys hanging around."

"I know," I said. "I need to get a note to one of them. Got thirty seconds to run an errand for me?"

"Thirty seconds? Sure. What do you need?"

I handed him the note. "Parked on the edge of the parking lot is a 4Runner you'll recognize from the other night. I need this under the windshield wiper. Then before you go, just lift the driver's side door handle. It'll set off his car alarm and maybe speed up the delivery time. Hopefully he'll be the only one who comes by to check out the alarm."

Ty nodded, gripping the note. "And you'll stay out of sight?"

I nodded. "Yeah. I just can't risk that they're watching the cars. It'll kind of ruin things if they know where I am."

"No problem," he said, dropping another quick kiss. "Thirty seconds. Time me."

He jogged out the door wearing only shorts, t-shirt, and shoes. My blood definitely wasn't thick enough for that.

Brandi watched him leave with concern. "Where's he headed?"

"He's just grabbing something from his truck. Then I'll be out of your hair."

"Oh. Okay," she said before a client approached her desk.

I didn't time Ty. I didn't need to. I just used the moment of distraction to exit myself and start back to Nick's car. By the time I got half way there, Ty was making his return run. When our eyes caught I gave a quick shake of my head and kept walking. He took the hint and ran right past me and back to the gym. His entrance coincided with me reaching the car, which meant I'd made about as clean of an exit as I could have. If anyone was watching the parking lot, they would have been looking at the guy running to the cars and back, not the girl exiting the gym to the beat up Honda.

Now it was time to wait again. Hopefully not long. Trevor's GPS put him about a quarter of a mile to the north of me. A guy like him could cover that distance in less than two minutes, so I had at least that long to wait.

"Please come alone," I whispered, just in case it might help. Then I started the car and pulled out of my spot. I drove to the opposite exit than Trevor was parked at, allowing me a clear view of his SUV while keeping to the area he was least likely to focus on.

His response time wasn't record breaking, but it could have been worse. Three minutes and thirty seconds after I settled in to wait for Trevor, he appeared. When he first came into sight he was at a full sprint, but once he saw his 4Runner right where it should be, his steps slowed a little and he started glancing around the parking lot. Smart kid. He would make a good investigator if he wanted to. Just a little bit of training, and he could be quite formidable.

By the time he reached his 4Runner, Trevor was at a light jog. He immediately spotted the note. I could see that by his body language, but he didn't reach for it right away. He stopped instead, turning a full 360 as he searched the parking lot for something... for me. He looked my direction twice, but didn't spot me. Only then did he reach toward his windshield wiper and pull out the paper.

I wished I could see his expression as he read the note. I would have known all I needed to know if I could just see his face as I call Knight a killer, but sadly I didn't have that luxury. All I could do was wait as he read, then watch as he fisted the note, paced, and started reading it again.

He was agitated. That much was clear. But from 150 yards, I couldn't tell if it was the agitation of a man who was caught, or that of a man who was considering the idea that his trust had been betrayed. It didn't become any clearer when he threw the crumpled note with all he had, only to have it catch on a breeze and drop a few feet away from him. He paced again, running his hands through his hair before picking up the note again and staring at it. A minute later he shoved it in his pocket. And thirty seconds later he sat on the hood of his car, hands in plain view.

I had my cue. I grabbed my phone, opening the chess app.

Black queen takes pawn at G-2. Kay now knew that I was

moving in on Knight's inner circle, which meant I needed her to keep him distracted downtown. Her leash was off, so to speak. Whatever she needed to do to keep Knight from looking my way, she was totally free to do at this point.

Tucking the phone in my bag, I cleared from the side to the back seat, and put the car into drive. It was time to set up check mate.

CHAPTER 42

As soon as Trevor took a seat in the car, I took his phone and slipped it into one of my tin foil cases. His jaw was clenched as if he were a breath away from changing his mind, but apparently he wasn't questioning his choice enough to step out of a moving car.

"Seat belt," I said, then pulled out onto the main road.

It took five minutes to get to the freeway. In that time neither Trevor nor I said a word. It wasn't until we hit the freeway onramp that I glanced at him.

"Gutsy move," I said, and sent him a smile. "Also the right move."

His expression wasn't quite so happy. "Are you really law enforcement?"

I nodded, reaching into my bag behind his chair and sliding my ID card out of my wallet. He looked like he expected a gun to appear when I brought my hand back up to the front.

"I'm not going to shoot you," I said, handing him the card.

"You shot Tony," he accused, not taking the card yet.

I shook my head. "Actually, no I didn't. I don't carry a gun, but someone with me does. When they saw Tony shoot me, they took it upon themselves to disarm him."

He gave me an appraising glance. "You don't look hurt."

I laughed lightly. "Trust me, this coat is covering up a lot." I offered my ID again. "You want to take a look at this, or no?"

He took it, examined it, then swore. "This doesn't mean you're right about Tony. Or was that song and dance just a ploy to get me in your car?"

I studied him, deciding the question was honest. "Who do you think killed Blaine?"

He didn't even blink. "Well, word on the street is that you did."

"Yeah? And what was my motive?"

"Money. Maybe that's really what you do. Because, let's face it, we both know you're not a typical private investigator."

"True enough," I agreed.

"So what are you?" he snapped. "Who hired you to look into this?"

"No one," I replied calmly, moving to the middle lane of traffic. "Looking into this is purely pro bono on my side." When he didn't respond, I sent him an assessing look. "You believe me?"

He kept his eyes on the road. "Yeah. I heard you talking to your reporter friend about it. She was saying something about wanting you to teach her how to investigate."

I nodded.

He fidgeted in his seat. "She's not very good."

"No?"

He shook his head, eyes still trained on the road, although this time I saw him glance at the sign pointing to the I-15 southbound exit. Without saying anything, I pulled into the lane. Looked like we'd be going south. Toward Pleasant Grove. I was thinking that wasn't an accident.

"Any pointers I can give her?"

For the first time he smiled. "Stick to her strengths. She's as subtle as a herd of elephants. She should stick to shock and awe, and leave the shadows to those of us who are capable of blending."

Valid point. I looked him over, imaging him saying those words to Kay's face and the resulting friction. It could be enough to make Dahl a little jealous—if this guy ended up being innocent, that was. "How tall are you?"

"What?" he asked, clearly confused.

"Six-two?" I guessed.

"Yeah, but what does that have to do with anything?"

"Maybe nothing. We should get back on topic."

"Which is?"

"Which is whether or not you're spending tonight in a jail cell," I said, looking him straight in the eyes as I moved onto the ramp to southbound I-15.

"Or whether *you* will," he shot back.

I nodded. "Sure. I'm guilty of criminal trespass and leaving the scene after being shot by an officer. I could get a fine and do some time for that, but you're looking at accessory to murder—maybe two."

"Two?" he asked, visibly confused. "And who else did Jedi allegedly kill?"

"Not Jedi, Nathan. Jedi just covered it up and used his weight to focus the investigation on a convenient suspect."

He was shaking his head, and meaning it. "Oh, please! Blaine totally killed Amanda. No question. All the evidence was there."

"All the *circumstantial* evidence was there," I corrected. "C'mon, Trevor, you're better than that. Something stinks in your organization right now, and you know it."

Trevor stayed stone faced, but I could see his mind racing behind those hazel eyes of his. He needed a push, a nudge, a reason. I was asking him to doubt people he respected—maybe even idolized. Even Dahl was slow to doubt Knight, why should Trevor be any quicker?

He needed information to help him see what he already knew.

"Did you know that Nate is incapable of having children?" I said casually. "He's infertile, always has been. Jeremy is not his biological son, and he knows it. I'm not sure if Jeremy does, but I think seeing the mug shot of the man his mother claims raped her kind of threw him for a loop. You should ask him. Because the man in that mug shot was also Blaine Adkins father, which would have made them half brothers and that's allegedly what started this entire tragedy. Amanda was ready to talk and Nathan wasn't. And their disagreement on what Jeremy should and should not know led to Amanda's death as well as the cover up."

He wasn't having it. "No way. I was *at* Amanda's funeral. I knew her. I know Nate. No way he killed her! Not a chance. He was absolutely devastated! Still is. He won't even date."

"Would you if you had just killed your wife?"

He didn't have an answer for that, so he chose a different angle. "So you're saying that she sprung that he wasn't the father and he flipped?"

"No. I think he knew all along," I said. "I think it was the idea of telling Jeremy the truth and informing him that he had a brother that was the problem for Nate, though. I also think Amanda found out that your group played some role in putting the rapist in prison. Maybe Knight told a story similar to the one about this alleged Blue Cadillac Deville that did the supposed drive-by shooting on him, only it was a different scene and he painted the target on a man who had gotten away with rape. Am I warm?"

Trevor said nothing for a moment. Then he looked at me. "How can you know something like that? That went down years ago. There are no records."

"There are always records," I said, not knowing if I was coaching him or convincing him. "Officer Knight was the one who arrested Blaine's father. You can look it up if you want."

He blinked, processing that. "But why kill Blaine then?" he said after several beats. "They had their out. No one was looking Nate's way anymore. Everyone thought Blaine did it."

"True," I said.

He looked at me, eyes full of true curiosity. "So why kill him?"

"You tell me," I said.

The following silence was heavy, but I could tell by the look in his eyes that Trevor was on the right path, and he didn't like what he was seeing. "Because Blaine would want Amanda's real killer caught. It's why he stayed close and didn't leave the state. A guilty person would have left to try for a clean slate, not stayed close where everyone knew who he was."

The kid was smart. I was starting to like him. "And a scapegoat who can prove his innocence also might be a scapegoat who has learned the truth somewhere along the way. So you tell me, how deep does the loyalty between Tony and Nate go?"

Trevor's only response was a curse before he leaned forward and rested his head in his hands. "You're not kidding, are you?" he muttered after a while. "Can you prove any of this?"

"I will. Bet on it," I said. "And if your people plan on protecting these guys I'll take you down right with them—which leads to your current abduction."

He nodded, as if that somehow made perfect sense to him.

"Last night two men in your group looked on as Tony shot me. They all knew who I was, and that I was unarmed. Now they're helping your Jedi cover it up. That doesn't speak well of your group."

He swore again, staring out the window and not letting me into his thoughts.

"Trevor? Talk to me."

"I'm just so mad that you're making sense!" he blurted. "I mean, nothing's made sense for the past week. Everything's weird, and all the protocols are being broken. Jedi said it was because we had to move fast on you because you're so dangerous, but you're right. The only thing tying you to Amanda's death is Tony's say-so."

"And never mind the fact that I lived in Los Angeles when Amanda was killed. I'm not your killer, Trevor. I think you know that without a doubt."

He nodded. He didn't even hesitate. Then his fist pounded the door. "How could he do this!"

It was a rhetorical question, and I let it be one as I glanced at the door to see if he left a mark. Luckily, no. Nick's car was still in original condition.

"He knows better! We all do. What in the world was he thinking?"

"Unfortunately, that doesn't matter at this point," I said. "What matters is what you do right now. Because I'm about to make you an offer. Coming into this today, I had no idea who I was dealing—what I was dealing with. Before taking what I have to the police, I need to know whether the people I'm reporting to are protecting Detective Knight. Are they going to flip on me? Frame me? Shoot me again? That's why I asked you into this car. I need to know who has Jedi's back."

Trevor nodded slowly. "You have to assume that he became detective so young because someone on the inside has his back—that there are other people in our group who are his superiors."

Okay, I officially liked this kid. "Exactly."

To my surprise, he grinned. "Well, I can tell you that Jedi's quick rise through the ranks isn't thanks to department favoritism. He got there with the help of people like me."

"Yeah. But I still don't know how he came to command a little army of urban ninjas."

He chuckled. "You wouldn't believe me if I told you."

"Which is why I'm going to insist you show me," I replied. "To be totally cliché, I need you to take me to your leader."

"I noticed," he said, looking at the freeway. "I'm sure it's no accident that we're driving her direction."

"No," I agreed, not letting him know that I'd simply followed his cue. "Your leader's a woman? That actually does surprise me."

"It won't when you meet her," he said, sounding tired. "Although everyone already knows that's where we're headed. I have a tracker in my phone."

"Not a problem," I said. "They have no idea where we are."

He shook his head. "I don't think you understand. It doesn't matter whether the phone is on or off, they can always track it."

"Not right now. Trust me."

He looked confused, but nodded. "If you say so."

"So are you going to take my deal? You take me to your boss, and if I believe she has no idea what Tony and Nate have done, I keep you and your group out of my report. If I sense she's in the know, you all fall down. Every single one of you."

"She has no idea," Trevor said firmly.

"You believe that enough to let me see for myself?"

He took a slow breath, then nodded. "You know what exit to take. I'll guide you from there.

CHAPTER 43

We parked in front of the Pleasant Grove library, of all places. Definitely wouldn't have been my first thought for where to find the mastermind leader of a mass group of urban ninjas in the Salt Lake area.

"Wait," I said when he reached for the door handle. I needed to check to see if Kay had made any moves during our thirty minute drive. If she had she was no doubt freaking out a little that she hadn't heard back from me yet.

Trevor watched as I pulled out my extra phone, but I didn't let him see the screen as I pulled up the app. Yep, Kay had made a move.

King's rook to F-1. Normally the rook was supposed to represent the station, but in this case she had moved the rook to block me from getting to Knight's king—the very person I was about to walk in and meet. And since it certainly wasn't the station standing between me and the king at this point, I had to assume that it was somebody else.

I touched Trevor's arm. "Slight change of plan."

He looked tense. "We're not going in?"

"Oh, we're going in," I said. "But I think someone is in there standing guard. You need to get your boss to me without them knowing—whoever they are. Assume that if they get a whiff that I'm here they will immediately report it to Tony. If that happens, our whole deal is off. Got it?"

He was beyond skeptical. "There's no way you could know that. *I* don't even know that. No one knows who Carol is. There's no reason to guard her."

"Other than the fact that you're off radar and no one knows where you are?" I offered. "You'll need a story for that, by the way. Tell the person you meet in there that you lost your phone in the snow and don't respond to any follow-up questions on the matter. Just find Carol right away. Got it?"

"I guess. But I'm telling you that no one is in there with her."

"Then you have nothing to worry about," I said. "What floor is she usually on?"

He pointed to the upper entrance. "She works in the children's section."

"Get to her and bring her to the bottom level. I'll be waiting for her by the ladies' room and we'll go into an available room from there. The guy guarding her *cannot* follow you two downstairs, got it? Tell him to keep an eye on the entrance—that you've got Carol covered and need to fill her in on a few things. Tell the other guy Jedi was right and I'm inbound and he needs to keep a close watch until you two get back."

He all but rolled his eyes. "It won't be a problem. Trust me."

I looked him in the eye. "I am. So don't let me down, okay?"

He held my gaze and nodded.

"Good," I said, moving the queen's pawn on my screen to D-6.

Knight needed a straight shot at a pawn if I was going to stop him from jumping into a car and headed straight for us. Dahl was about to be played again. How that happened was completely up to Kay. All that mattered on my end was that Knight stayed focused on a pawn. If Kay could make that happen, then brilliant. If not, I'd find a way to counter.

Tucking the phone in my pocket, I nodded. "Okay, we're on. I'll get out once you're through the front doors."

He nodded. "See you in a few."

I smiled and watched him go. I waited until he slammed the door behind him to say, "I certainly hope so."

He moved up the stairs quickly, and I waited until he was out of sight before exiting myself and heading for the lower entrance and finding the base level empty. That was both good and bad. I had my choice of rooms to meet Carol in, but I had no witnesses if things went bad. I was still trying to decide which room was best when my phone chimed. Kay had made a move. Crap. That almost certainly wasn't good.

I pulled out the phone. King's knight takes rook.

I stared at the knight sitting in H-8, and tried to figure out exactly what it meant. This time the rook almost certainly represented Kay's station. Detective Knight had done something to pull them into the picture—most likely something that would pressure them to drop the story.

Man, an actual text would really have come in handy right about then. Was Kay still on the Knight story? Was she still set to broadcast? I had to assume the answer to that was yes. Kay was wily beyond words. Whatever Knight was throwing at her, I had to assume she would hit it out of the park.

Just then I heard footsteps on the stairs. Two pairs, one slow and steady and the other a more stop-and-go staccato. Carol was on her way. I officially had the king cornered and let Kay know as much by moving my queen's bishop to G-4.

It wasn't check, but she couldn't move her King anywhere without moving into check. It also highly encouraged her to bring in her knight to protect the king and queen.

Translation: decoy time was over. It was time for Kay to let Knight know what was afoot, take the pressure off herself, and send the knight over to protect his king while she set up to broadcast live.

It all came down to now. It all came down to Carol.

I trained my eyes on the bottom of the stairs and felt my blood pressure rise when a grey-haired woman turned the corner.

Great. This was absolutely not what I needed. A senior citizen in the fray? I needed to get rid—just then Trevor stepped in behind her and I froze, looking back at the woman.

Carol? A grandma?

Trevor was totally right. This was absolutely not what I was expecting.

"Right here," I said, gesturing to the nearest door, then giving Trevor a pointed look. "Make sure no one comes in."

He nodded, face tense. "How did you know Chris was here? There's no *way* you could have known that!"

"Yeah, well, keep him out," I said simply. "Carol and I need to have a little chat."

He nodded, clearly wanting to say something else but swallowing it. "I can't promise you forever, but you've got a few minutes."

Carol's assessment of me seemed on par with what I thought of her. I was not what she had been expecting.

I opened the door to my right and motioned her in. "After you."

She gave me a long look, then walked in without a word. I followed and shut the door behind us. Then, for a moment we just looked at each other.

"So," I said. "You're the mastermind of this operation, huh?"

"And you're the girl who's outsmarting my Tony and out-parkouring my Trevor."

"I wouldn't say that," I said with a smile. "I still don't know how he crossed my yard without leaving tracks in the snow."

She nodded. "It's a neat trick."

"To say the least."

We watched each other again. Suddenly I didn't know where to start. She was a grandma—a grandma who worked in a library. How in the world was I supposed to process that?

I was still trying to figure out where to start when my phone chimed. I had to look. I needed to know if Kay had made the smart move and sent Knight my way and if I should be planning on some heat in the next few minutes.

"One sec," I said, pulling up the screen.

"You kids and technology," she said as only a grandma could. I smiled in response before looking at the screen.

Queen's knight to E-2. Detective Knight was officially aware of me and Carol and headed our way. No more stalling. I didn't have time for it.

"It's quite handy," I said, pocketing the phone again. "Your little group seems to be quite good with technology as well."

She nodded, slowly. "I still need help with my universal remote while they track each other using phones and gizmos. Things sure have changed in the past decade."

"Yes, but that's not what we're here to talk about."

"No," she agreed. "And let me just state the obvious when I say that I think both of us are a little surprised at who is standing across from us at the moment."

No joke. "Agreed. And I have to ask how you came to be a shot caller for guys like Tony Knight and Trevor. How did that all get started?"

Suddenly her eyes didn't look so grandmotherly. They were more like a mama bear's. "I wasn't always an old woman, my dear. And the men and women around me weren't always men and women. Once upon a time they were children who needed help, and I was a woman who couldn't stand by a system that wouldn't do anything to truly help them."

I nodded. Vague as it was, it was an answer that made sense. "You were a teacher?" I guessed.

"Of sorts. I did an after-school karate program for latchkey kids. You learn a lot about a kid by how they react when you fake punch them. Let's leave it at that."

"They were abused," I filled in for her.

Her laugh was short and angry. "That's putting it mildly. Unbelievable crap was going on, even back then. So unbelievable that law enforcement wouldn't believe that it was even possible in this sleepy little town. Not without irrefutable proof. So that's what we got them—irrefutable proof. That's how this little group got started back before you were even born, my dear. But all that's neither here nor there. Trevor is very adamant that I hear what you have to say, so here I am. Speak."

Speak? Fine. "Well, I'm here because Nate killed Amanda, Tony helped him cover it up, and a few days ago Tony went so far as to kill Blaine Adkins himself to keep the truth from coming out. Now Tony's using your merry band to cover his tracks, while convincing your people that I'm the killer. That's the long and the short of it. I'm here because Tony and Nate are about to go down. So are the two men who are helping them, and I need to know who else among you is committed to letting them get away with murder."

Carol said nothing, so I added to the pile.

"I'm guessing you know that Jeremy is not Nate's biological son—that he's the result of a rape that took place while Amanda was in college."

Carol nodded slowly. "Nate joined us for the very purpose of getting justice for his wife. There wasn't enough evidence to get Ted on Amanda's rape, so we caught him at something else. Tony oversaw it all. He wanted to make sure there were no screw ups. Not when it came to Nate. Those two have always shared a bond."

Well, well, well. Wasn't she being forthcoming? Why? It didn't make sense. There was so much love in her voice as she spoke of Nathan and Tony. Devotion. Carol wasn't quite the military leader I'd been expecting.

"A bond that ended up killing two people," I said before I got too sentimental.

To my surprise, she didn't contradict me. She simply sat,

folding her hands together. Then she looked at me, eyes near tears. "I've felt something was very wrong for a while now, but I was hoping it was just the paranoia of an old lady staying too long in the game. When you know men from the time they are boys, you're bound to see into their souls a bit. And you know when they're hiding. You know when they're lying. And while I want to call you a liar and be angry at Trevor for bringing you here, he did the right thing, didn't he? He made the right choice by bringing you here."

I nodded. "They did it, Carol. I think Amanda was an accident, but Blaine definitely wasn't. Tony all but confessed before he shot me." I pulled the neck of my shirt down, showing her the bruise. "There's zero question as to Tony's guilt. He's a killer, Carol. So is Nate. And at least two of your guys are helping them."

She rested forward on her elbows, aging a decade before my eyes. "What were they thinking? Honestly. All the lies they've told over the last year. I wanted to believe them. I tried to believe them, but I must have known all along, because I'm believing you right now. You haven't brought any evidence with you, and yet I believe you just for saying it out loud."

I didn't know what to say. She looked broken.

"How did they ever think they were going to get away with it?" The question wasn't really for me. It was more of a moment of soul searching.

So she believed me. No blind loyalty. No aiming her anger at me. Just sadness.

In a way, that was almost worse than wild accusations and threats.

She took a deep breath and sat up straight, pulling strength from some unseen place and pushing back her tears. "The funny thing is I knew something like this might happen. Almost expected it, I think." She glanced at me, eyes tired, then looked away at something I couldn't see. "This has all gotten quite a bit bigger than me, you see. I may have called the shots for the first few years, but as my kids have gotten older, they've also gotten more opinionated. Stronger. And when you run an operation like this, what are the chances that every person who joins you is going to toe the line? That they're going to play by the rules and not start making up their own?"

I didn't need to answer that one for her. She knew the answer as well as anyone with common sense. Change was inevitable.

"You love them," I heard myself say. "It's natural to try to think the best of those we love."

She nodded, a sad smile on her face. "It does make us selectively blind, doesn't it?"

I watched her, trying to figure out what to say next. "I'm here to tell you that I'm not looking to take your whole group down. But if you step in and try to help these guys, you'll go down with them. Everyone who's loyal to Tony needs to know the truth before they start making themselves human shields to protect him."

"Indeed," she said, then took a slow breath. "Truth is, in the scheme of the group these days I'm a bit like the Queen of England. A nice focal point when you need someone to wave at the crowds for morale, but mostly just a token relic from another time. Tony was the one taking his place as the new figure head. Everyone looks up to him. They're going to have a hard time believing any of this is true."

All said with a calmness that defied the tragicness of the situation. She had skipped right through the anger and denial and jumped straight to acceptance—maybe because, like she'd said, she saw this day coming long ago. Either way, she was doing exactly what a leader should be doing: dealing with the facts. It kind of left me without anything else to say.

I'd come to meet her expecting threats, denials, ultimatums, and maybe even guns only to find a well-meaning grandma who had made it her life's purpose to right a few of the wrongs in the world. In a weird way, I kind of wanted to give her a hug and tell her everything would be okay.

I settled for resting my hand on hers.

"I feel for you. I do. But that's not going to stop me from doing what I've got to do. Tony and Nate will be going to jail, but I can make sure nothing links back to you. As far as I'm concerned, they acted alone."

"Thank you. Not for me, necessarily," she added. "I don't know if I deserve the consideration you're offering, but my kids sure do. They're good kids. It would break my heart to see them arrested."

"At this point that's up to Tony and Nate," I said pulling out my phone.

"Indeed," she said as I opened the app. "Are you sending a signal now? Are they going to be arrested?"

I nodded then reached up to the screen and made my final move.

King's knight to F-3.

Check mate.

Carol blinked. "That's it? A swipe of your finger and it's done?"

"It will be," I said. "As soon as they're located they'll be arrested."

She regarded my phone skeptically. "That's a nice trick now, isn't it? You wonder how my boys run in the snow and you're able to get my boys arrested with a swipe of a finger?"

I sent her a wan smile. "Maybe we can trade secrets."

"Maybe," she mused just as my phone rang. I picked up.

"Are you serious?" Kay said loud enough for Carol to hear her.

"Yep. You're 100% clear to roll."

"With which version? The whole group or rogue?"

"Rogue." I started to elaborate, but Kay interrupted.

"And Ty and I both identified the same guys from last night. They're Mitchell Davis and a guy named Paul Adams. More later." Then she hung up. No doubt she would be interrupting regularly scheduled programming in the next thirty seconds, or so.

Paul Adams? It spoke to how shoddy my investigation was that I hadn't even heard the guy's name before. I was betting Carol had, though.

Either way, the Salt Lake Police Department was about to learn why they were going to arrest their own detective and his best friend for murder. And in true Kathryn McCoy style, they were about to learn all the details right along with the rest of the viewing public.

"Let's get you back to Trevor," I said, motioning to the door. "I have a feeling you're going to have a busy night ahead of you."

She only nodded, staying where she was until I opened the door. Trevor stood on the other side expectantly, and I assumed the angry-looking guy across from him was Chris.

"She could probably use a hug," I said softly, before exiting the building and taking Nick's car safely home to its owner.

CHAPTER 44

The celebration at Kay's place that night was Christmas, New Year's, and the Fourth of July all rolled up into one. She'd downloaded her "Breaking News" broadcast and was playing it on a loop as she took victory shots and recounted her day for us in a play-by-play.

Yeah, she was a little drunk, but having a blast with it. And Ty and I were more than happy to snuggle on the couch and watch the show.

"I'm glad you're safe," he whispered into my ear as Kay finished rehashing a little face-off she'd had with Mindy earlier. "I'm glad this time the big boss turned out to be Old Mother Hubbard and not some psycho, multi-national warlord."

"Small favors," I said, pressing my lips to his. "I'll deal with the multi-national warlord next month. Tonight, we celebrate Kay's unprecedented scoop."

"Yeah," he agreed, glancing her way. "She's really on one, isn't she? She usually doesn't drink like this. Ever. It's kind of weird."

I had to agree. I'd known Kay since college, and I'd never quite seen her like this but it was her home. If she passed out, it would be in her own bed. No harm, no foul until she woke up tomorrow.

She'd gotten to the part of the story where Carla had called Kay into office and informed her that Kay was being accused of interfering with an investigation.

"And I was like, 'On what evidence, Carla? How am I interfering? Tell me that!' And of course she had no answer, because I wasn't doing anything wrong, and Detective Knight was officially on administrative leave." Kay smiled smugly then, leaning against the arm of the loveseat. "Even Carla knew something was up, and when I told her to give me just a little more leash, she looked me in the eyes and said, 'Fine, but if this bombs, you're gone. Period.' Can you believe it? I'm on the verge of handing her the story of the year and she's talking about firing me. I swear, I should just tell them I was the one who shot Knight and get it all over with. All they want are stupid puppets that say whatever some stupid, official press release says they should say." She raised her glass in what I assumed to be a gesture of defiance. "I WILL NOT BECOME A PROPAGANDIST!" she announced to anyone within ear shot. "You hear me? I won't!"

Ty chuckled behind me while I stole a look at the clock. It was nearly midnight. "We heard you," I said.

"I won't," she muttered, scowling at the bottle she spotted across the room. Now she had to make the decision of whether or not she wanted another drink enough to stand up and go get it.

"I'm done with the bullshit," she said, then sent me a pointed look. "And yeah, call the Sesame Street police. I said shit. So shoot me. Kate has a potty mouth."

Kate? Only Dahl called her that, which begged the question of where the guy was. He certainly wasn't at work, and I had invited him over. I owed him both many thanks and many apologies. He deserved an explanation after the day he'd had.

"And the whole time I was talking to Carla, Ken kept texting, saying we needed to meet…needed to talk. But I was a good girl," she said, wagging her finger at me. "I waited until you said it was okay before inviting him to my cozy cubicle. I figured it was safe, you know? There was no way Knight could get eyes and ears inside the station. But then Ken comes in, telling me how I'm all off base, and that you and I are jumping the gun—actually threatening to tattle on me for pulling the trigger on Knight last night, and suddenly everything became so clear. Ken and I are never going to happen. We aren't… we just aren't."

Ty tensed behind me, and I'm sure he felt me do the same.

"Kay," I started, but she cut me off.

She waved her hand to cut me off. "No, don't deny it. We're different to the core. I love him—it's kind of crazy how much I love that idiot. It actually hurts, you know? Like a sickness, a hollowness whenever he's not around. And maybe he feels the same. Who knows, right? Because he'll never say, and he'll never do anything about it unless I go get dunked in your little font. *Then* he'd love me. *Then* he'd say the words, because if I was Mormon then it would all be okay. Our love would be 'approved.'" She threw her fingers up in uncoordinated air quotes. "All the men in suits that he respects so much would clap for him and he'd have it all. He'd have respect, admiration, love, sex. Everything a Ken Dahl could ever want: the perfect image. And all I have to do is fall in line. All I have to do is give him what I know he wants. Just like Carla wants to me read a press release like it's news and not a paid-for PR pitch. Just fall in line, Katie. That's all you have to do. Just give everyone what they want and life will get so easy. Just. Don't. Be. You."

This was full meltdown mode. Before I knew it I was sitting up and Ty rested his hand on my shoulder to get me to look at him. We both knew now why Dahl hadn't come over. The night had just taken a very unpredictable turn.

"I should find him," Ty whispered. "Make sure he's okay."

I nodded. "I'll be here."

He nodded in return and I moved so he could stand. He did, making his way over to Kay and pressing a light kiss to her forehead. "I'm going to leave you two here for some girl talk," he said lightly.

"Whatever," she scoffed. "You're going to find Ken."

Ty nodded. "I am. You okay with that?"

She started crying then, falling to her side on the loveseat. "Yeah. Maybe he's sad. He'd *better* be sad. But you should talk to him. You should find him. Let him know he's still invited to the wedding. I'm good if he comes, okay? He can come. I won't freak."

Her mind never failed to amaze me. She had just broken up with the first guy she'd ever truly loved, and she was worried about my wedding? The woman was crazy.

"I'll let him know," Ty said before giving her arm a squeeze and heading to the door. I watched him go, my heart hammering in my chest. Best. Guy. Ever.

I love you, he mouthed when he reached the door.

I want you, I mouthed back, earning a light blush and a smile before he disappeared. When the door shut, I crossed the room over to Kay, lifting her head so I could sit then resting it on my lap.

"Are you sure about this?" I asked, clearing the hair from her face. "It sounds for real this time."

She took a shaky breath. "I've known all along he'd never choose me. Maybe that's why I felt so safe with him, you know? He respects hierarchy. Maybe he'll never meet all the men on the rungs above him, but he wants their nods of approval way more than he wants to be with me." She stared off at nothing, blinking a few times before continuing. "He'll never choose me. I've known that from the beginning just like you knew you would end up with the Ty from the beginning. It's the same thing, only reversed with me."

I didn't know what to say. There was truth to her words. Dahl wanted to be married in the temple. And if that's what he wanted, Kay was not his girl.

She took a staccato breath then sniffed again. "He's ashamed of me, Rhea. No matter what I do, I embarrass him. I can't be with a guy who's embarrassed of me—a guy who will look me in the face and defend a guy he doesn't even know, just because of who he is, and not take my word on the matter. I want more. I *deserve* more."

"You're right," I heard myself say. "You do deserve more. You deserve the best."

"You've got that right," she huffed. "But in the pulling off this wedding of yours, I'm going to be the most psychotic wedding planner you've ever seen. So you'd better deal with it and shut up, because you *owe* me this! I freakin' shot a cop for you, you're welcome very much. So tag, you're it and I'm calling my favor in."

I couldn't help but laugh. "Kay, you're drunk. You're not thinking straight. And besides, it's all arranged. It's going to be simple. Perfect."

"Whatever," she pouted. "We both know I have higher standards for a wedding than you do, so you're going to let me add some embellishments. You *will* have a gorgeous wedding, and you won't tell me to calm down. If you do, I'll drink all your dad's liquor and make a big scene boohooing about how I was stupid enough to think that love was stronger than religious conviction. I'll make you and your dad have awkward conversations and ask him how long he's been sleeping with Meredith. Got it?"

I blinked. "Meredith? How do you know about that?"

She sent me the driest look I'd ever seen in my life. "Oh, please, Miss Greatest Detective Ever. Like it's not totally obvious."

I was ready to give Meredith and my dad my blessing, but that didn't mean I was ready for Kay to initiate awkward conversations.

"Threat received," I said. "You are officially my wedding planner. But those duties come second to making sure Tony Knight and his crew are all in jail on the day of the wedding. Don't lose focus on that."

"Hmmph," was her only reply before her breathing slowed and evened. Between one breath and the next, she had fallen to sleep. She definitely deserved it.

It had been a crazy day.

CHAPTER 45

Saturday afternoon. Clear skies, sunny, and a temperature of 74°F. I'd seen thousands of days just like it in my life. This one, in particular, just happened to be my wedding day.

It was fully surreal.

Back in Utah it was 36°F and Tony Knight and Nathan Carson were in jail, while Mitchell Davis and Paul Adams were officially "persons of interest". Without our video footage from the shop, Paul and Mitchell couldn't really be linked to any of the crimes, but I had faith that a connection would pop up eventually. If worse came to worse, yes, we could use the tape. But now that the police knew where to look, I had no doubt no stone would be left unturned. Knight and his co-conspirators would go down.

Meanwhile, everyone from my side of the chessboard was at my wedding, plus about fifty other guests. I watched from the window of my old bedroom as they all took their seats for the ceremony.

The yard was perfection, the fountain currently in its full glory, although it would be turned off for the ceremony. At the end of the walkway leading to the fountain, a canopied arch had been set up with several dozen chairs facing the arch. Most of the guests were friends of family of Ty's, all of which had flown in for the occasion and were being seated while a string quartet played *A Thousand Years*.

For the wedding. It was really happening.

"Breathe," Kay said coming up behind me, her hands gripping my arms and turning me to face her. She took in my simple silk gown. "Wow, you look gorgeous."

"Thanks," I managed, feeling a little light headed. I took few deep breaths. It couldn't hurt.

"The guests are accounted for and Ty's grandfather is ready. Everyone lines up in five and then that's your cue."

A wave of excitement washed over me, matched in equal parts with panic. Then the panic starting winning over everything else.

Kay took a moment to reposition a lock of my hair that had apparently strayed. "Do yourself a favor and try to smile. You look like you're ready to face a firing squad."

I nodded, my stomach too tight to smile. "Is my dad ready?"

She nodded. "Yeah. Of course." She hesitated a moment then added, "See you downstairs."

"See you downstairs."

Then I was alone in my room.

"Don't panic," I coached myself, trying to focus on how surreally beautiful my bouquet was. "If Ty can do this, you can do this."

It didn't help. And with every moment that passed, my heart pounded a little harder. And not in a good way.

Then five words brought me back to reality. "Rhea, darling, you look breathtaking."

My dad. He was here. He would tell me if I was making a mistake. He was always honest. But I didn't lead with my fears. "The yard is perfect, Dad. Thank you for that."

He crossed the room to stand next to me at the window. "We couldn't have custom ordered a better day for the first week of March."

I took an unsteady breath. "Yeah."

"Nervous?" he asked.

I sent him a sidelong look. "Is it that obvious?"

To my surprise, he smiled. "Well, no one ever said I didn't have a smart daughter."

It wasn't the response I'd been expecting, and my expression must have said as much.

"Getting married is exciting, yes," my dad added quickly. "I know you love Ty—and I know he loves you, too. The way you *deserve* to be loved, or he wouldn't be at this house right now. But you're smart enough to know that when you love someone that much, you're in for a bumpy ride."

Yes. Exactly. It was so good to hear someone else say it out loud.

"No one will ever love you like Ty, but no one will hurt you like him either," he said, giving my hand a squeeze. "And deep down, you know you're going to hurt him and love him right back. It's part of the deal."

"I know," I whispered, feeling tears sting my eyes.

"But you know what, daughter?"

"Hmmm," I said, not able to form an actual word around the lump in my throat.

He leaned in, laying his head against mine as he softly said, "It's worth it."

Tears nearly pushed past my eyes right then. I had to do a series of machine gun blinks to tamp them back and preserve my makeup.

"I can tell you that I've never felt pain as acute as what I felt the morning your mom died, but I can also tell you that she is still the center of my best memories. I'd marry her and do it all over again in a heartbeat, even knowing what was coming." He reached across me, grabbing my other hand and turning me to face him. "Getting married is for the naïve and the brave, Rhea. And since naïve isn't an option for you, you're stuck with the other option."

I laughed. I couldn't help it. "Just my luck."

My dad shook his head. "Nah, you were never one to lean on luck much. Very practical, my girl."

My arms were around him before I was fully aware that my brain had given the command to hug my dad. But how could I not? And how could I not close my eyes and enjoy the moment when he rocked me gently.

"If you think Ty isn't a good man and this marriage is a bad fit, say the word and we'll send everyone home," he said. "But if you're questioning all this because you're afraid you'll hurt him, let me just lay it out for you. You will. Repeatedly. And he'll hurt you—so badly you won't be able to breathe. But your mom taught me that's how the universe keeps things fair." He leaned away from me and looked me in the eyes. "The universe can't just dump bliss on some people, and heartache on others. There's no balance in that. We all get a little of both—or a lot of both—depending on how wide we open our hearts."

He reached over and grabbed a tissue from the dressing table for me just in time for me to catch a tear before it spilled over.

Best. Dad. Ever. It was the truth. In fact, if there was any tragedy to him being a dad, it was the fact that he'd only had one kid. He'd never remarried. Never given me a step-mom or step-siblings. Never even brought home a date. He had to have had relationships with other women at some point over all these years, but he'd kept it private and I hadn't snooped.

A man like him shouldn't be alone, though. He deserved to be loved. I wanted that for him. It was long past time I tell him as much, but he didn't let me. Not in that moment.

"So, kid, you ready for the ride of your life?" he asked. "Are you sure you've got the right partner for when things get a little crazy?"

I nodded without hesitation. "Oh, I definitely have that."

He looked me dead in the eye. "Do you trust him?"

"Completely."

"With money?"

"Yes."

"With your heart?"

The grin that filled my face was involuntary. "Definitely."

"With your reputation?"

"Yes."

This time he blinked back a tear. "With your children?"

The question hit me like a curve ball to the heart. I was still afraid to think that far ahead, but that didn't change my answer. "Yeah, I do, Dad. He'll be an awesome dad. Like you."

He smiled, and I saw his eyes mist up before he pulled me into one more hug. "You made it easy. You practically raised yourself. Never made me deal with so much as a speeding ticket or a car accident while all the other kids in the neighborhood were moving into rehab centers."

I gripped him a little tighter. "Like I said. I had a good dad."

For a moment we just stood there, locked in that hug. And then, it was time. Neither of us said anything, but we both stepped away at the same moment.

"You want to touch up your makeup before we go down?" he asked.

I nodded, moving to the mirror to inspect the cosmetic damage of our little heart to heart. By some small miracle, I only needed to make a few adjustments before turning to my dad and nodding.

He offered his arm. "Shall we?"

I slid my arm through his. "We shall."

Arm in arm, we moved down the hall where Kay stood waiting at the top of the stairs. When she saw the look on my face, I saw the anxiety melt from her expression. Her eyes moved over me in a swift once-over of the front before meeting us half way and circling to inspect the back.

"Looks perfect," she breathed, clearly wanting to say a whole lot more. "I'll go cue the orchestra. Count to thirty, then start down the stairs."

I nodded, gripping her hand as she walked away. "Kay?"

She paused, not fully turning around to face me. "Yeah?"

"Thank you. For all of this. You made today happen...on more levels than one."

She smiled over her shoulder at me and gave my hand a little squeeze. "Yeah. Well, you don't need help when it comes to many things, but I'm happy to help out in the areas where you're a complete invalid."

I laughed then, as did my dad. It was true. No point in denying it.

"I won't miss my cue," I assured her.

"Good," Kay said. "Because I can tell you that there's a very anxious guy in a tux standing not too far away who is praying he won't be stood up."

She moved down the stairs quickly then, and I felt my heart thump against my chest, pushing a pleasant heat throughout my body.

Ty. He was standing out there in the gardens, alone and waiting. And yeah, he had to be freaking out a little. How many times had I pressed the eject button on him right when it seemed like we were solid?

Well, after today that wasn't an option anymore. No more eject button. I had a copilot—a better one than I deserved, really. Someone I didn't have to be afraid to love. Someone I could trust. Someone who knew my weak spots and didn't exploit them. An anchor to hold on to when things got crazy.

Ty was it for me, plain and simple. That was the conclusion I came to as I counted to thirty.

Halfway down the stairs I heard the small orchestra cut to the end of their piece. By the time my dad and I were at the landing, they were striking their final chord.

"I love you, Rhea," my dad said just before we stepped into the doorway. "And I couldn't be happier with your taste in men, but know I'm always here for you, okay? You'll always be my little girl."

He was going to make me cry again, but this time I took those tears and turned them into a kiss on his cheek. "Love you, too, Dad. And thank you. I'll never outgrow needing you."

I was still looking at him as we stepped into the doorway leading out to the gardens. On any other day it was just a cobblestone patio, but a lavender runner now covered the distance between the house and the altar that had been set up where the patio met the gardens. And on that altar, a pair of blue eyes flooded with relief when they saw me.

Man, I'd landed me a hotty. God had put in a little extra care when He'd made Ty. Strong, chiseled body with a great face and a dangerous smile. And that hair. If we ever had a little girl, she would want that hair—copper without being actually red, and so soft it was impossible not to play with.

I was going to get to play with that hair the rest of my life. It seemed a bizarre thing to care about at the moment, but I went with it as I sent Ty a smile.

Everyone stood. I noticed only because their collective motion blocked my view of the only person I wanted to see. Luckily for me, Ty stepped forward so we could see each other. He was smiling. I could see that much—his eyes moving over my dress as he took a deep breath in and exhaled with an expression I couldn't describe.

You're beautiful, he mouthed knowing that I was the only one looking at him, and time stopped for the briefest moment as if taking a snapshot. A few minutes later Ty and I said our formal "I dos" and exchanged rings, but I would swear that the actual ceremony took place right then, right there. With my first step onto that lavender runner—when our eyes met and Ty and I both knew that neither of us would be walking away again. Ever.

He was a knight in shining armor who had fallen for a paper bag princess. Together we were going to try to slay a dragon and live happily ever after. And I kind of liked our chances.

SHERALYN PRATT graduated from the University of Utah with a BA in Communication. A gypsy at heart, she enjoys traveling and acquiring new skills. These days she can nearly always be found out and about with her dog, who has spend hundreds hours watching her type. Visit Sheralyn online at www.SheralynPratt.com.

Made in the USA
San Bernardino, CA
15 November 2013